"What will y[ou]

Will answered without hes[itation...]
bride."

"I see. Perhaps you should consider hiring a nanny, at least for now."

"No." He gave one decisive shake of his head. "I don't want my children getting used to someone who will eventually leave them like…" He let his words trail off.

"Won't you at least consider me for the position? It would be a great honor to—"

"No." His tone indicated the discussion was over. His children already adored Bridget. If she took a position in his home, then changed her mind, where would that leave Olivia and Caleb?

Although…

What if Will made a different offer? What if he supplied her with a more permanent position in his home?

"Bridget Murphy." He captured her hand in his and held on tight. "Would you consider becoming my wife?"

**IRISH BRIDES: Adventure—and love—
await these Irish sisters on the way to America….**

RENEE RYAN

grew up in a small Florida beach town. To entertain herself during countless hours of "lying out" she read all the classics. It wasn't until the summer between her sophomore and junior years at Florida State University that she read her first romance novel. Hooked from page one, she spent hours consuming one book after another while working on the best (and last!) tan of her life.

Two years later, armed with a degree in economics and religion, she explored various career opportunities, including stints at a Florida theme park, a modeling agency and a cosmetics conglomerate. She moved on to teach high school economics, American government and Latin while coaching award-winning cheerleading teams. Several years later, with an eclectic cast of characters swimming around in her head, she began seriously pursuing a writing career.

She lives an action-packed life in Georgia, with her supportive husband, lovely teenage daughter and two ornery cats who hate each other.

RENEE RYAN

Mistaken Bride

Love Inspired

Special thanks and acknowledgment to Renee Ryan for her contribution to the Irish Brides miniseries.

Recycling programs for this product may not exist in your area.

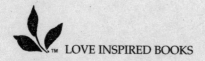

LOVE INSPIRED BOOKS

ISBN-13: 978-0-373-82915-6

MISTAKEN BRIDE

www.LoveInspiredBooks.com

Printed in U.S.A.

And now these three remain: faith, hope and love.
But the greatest of these is love.
—*1 Corinthians* 13:13

To Harlequin Love Inspired editors Emily Rodmell and Elizabeth Mazer. Thank you for your hard work and unceasing efforts in editing this book. I'm in your debt. Your suggestions made the story much stronger. It was a joy working with you both!

Chapter One

Boston Harbor, July 1850

To Bridget Murphy's way of thinking the voyage to America was more than a thrilling journey across the vast Atlantic Ocean. It was the beginning of a new life. For her and her two sisters. But especially for her.

From the moment she'd boarded the *Annie McGee,* Bridget was simply Bridget, the soft-spoken Irish lass earning her way to America as a stand-in nanny for the Atwater family.

No more humiliation hanging over her head. No more whispers trailing in her wake. The past had finally become *the past.*

And now the wait was over. Today she would begin her new life in earnest. Endless possibilities awaited her in her new country—her new home.

Bridget leaned over the ship's railing for her first glimpse of America, the ribbon streamers at her elbows billowed in the breeze. A gasp of delight flew past her lips, not only because she felt very smart in her new green sateen dress, but at the sight that met her gaze. Chaos, utter and complete chaos, met her gaze. The air vibrated with seagull shrieks, calls for carriages, laughter and commands.

Caught up in the madness, she took a moment and simply watched the activity below. Passengers disembarked the ship with hurried steps. Workmen staggered under the weight of their cargo. Carts full of wares were scattered everywhere. Children darted headlong past the lopsided piles.

Although she recognized many of the people already on the docks, none noticed her.

More the better.

A sudden movement in the distance caught her attention. She narrowed her eyes. A man, alone, worked his way through the crowd with methodical grace. His tall, lithe form stopped every few moments to speak with one of the passengers. There was something about him…

Something that tugged at her very core.

She couldn't tear her gaze away.

He moved with the kind of steps only a man confident in his own worth could pull off. Bridget placed her hand on her forehead to shade her eyes from the sun and continued watching him. He had broad shoulders, long legs and lean hips. Even though she couldn't see him clearly from this distance, she knew his eyes would be a vivid, piercing blue. The kind of color that turned silver in the light.

A little shocked at herself, at the fact that she was admiring a man when her heart was still so tender, she tried to pull back, to duck out of sight. But she found herself leaning forward ever so slightly.

As if sensing her eyes on him, he looked straight in her direction.

Her breath caught in her throat and she pulled back from the rail. Surely he hadn't seen her watching him. The distance was far too great.

Torn between embarrassment and a sudden wish to see the man up close, to discover if his eyes were truly the color of the sky, she hesitated a moment longer. She'd tarried long enough.

Joining the rest of her fellow passengers, she hurried across the ship's main deck. She'd told the Atwater siblings farewell earlier this morning. Pamela, the youngest, had been the saddest over their parting. Well, besides Bridget. Laurel and Hilary had been too busy arguing over a treasured bonnet to care overmuch that they'd never see their temporary nanny again.

Bridget sighed to herself. The journey hadn't been long enough to win over the older two girls. If only—

No. No more regrets. No more *if only*. Bridget was finished trying to fix the unfixable. Never again would she dwell on things she couldn't change.

Increasing her pace, her boot heels struck the weathered planks in perfect rhythm with the rapid beating of her heart.

She'd lost sight of her older sister, Nora. No matter. Nora, being Nora, had prepared for this very contingency and had set up a common meeting place near the gangplank.

Not wishing to hear yet another lecture on setting priorities and keeping to timetables, Bridget increased her pace. She resisted the urge to look over the railing at the wharf below. Was *he* still there? Winding his way through the thick knots of people and cargo, looking for someone in particular? Someone special?

Who? she wondered.

Without breaking stride, Bridget tossed a jaunty wave at the widow Mrs. Fitzwilliam, who had befriended the Murphy sisters on the journey. With her was her attendant Stillman and the three McCorkle brothers Mrs. Fitzwilliam had taken in as her wards. Good-hearted, gracious souls, getting to know them all had been a real blessing. Already running late, Bridget did not stop to speak to them.

Then again...

She'd already fallen behind. What would be the harm in saying one more goodbye to her new friend and those darling boys?

Just as she changed direction, a throng of passengers surged from behind, shoving her back on course at an even greater speed. She would have to catch up with Mrs. Fitzwilliam and the boys later.

Nearing her destination, Bridget wrenched free of the crowd and slid into another small, unoccupied spot along the ship's railing. At the precise location she'd been told.

Nora was nowhere in sight.

More relieved than annoyed, Bridget took a deep, steadying breath. And promptly wrinkled her nose in chagrin.

Throughout the month-long journey across the Atlantic, she had created vivid pictures of America in her mind. She had *not* accounted for the smell.

She raised a gloved hand to her mouth. One moment passed. Two. On the third she drew in another tentative gulp of air. Her eyes immediately filled with water. The stench was truly, truly awful. A mixture of rotting fish, animal sweat, burnt tar and something else entirely—garbage, perhaps?

Another jostle from behind and Nora wiggled in beside her.

"There you are," Nora said, familiar frustration in her tone. "You weren't here earlier."

Bridget ignored the gentle reprimand and smiled at her sister. She, too, wore her new dress, a gift from fellow passengers Ardeen Nolan and her aunt, Mrs. Kennedy. "Don't fuss, Nora. I only just arrived."

"Well, that explains it, then."

With her dark chestnut hair parted in the middle and contained in a tight bun, Nora should look severe. Instead, she positively glowed. Perhaps it was the vivid blue of her new gown. Or the paisley shawl. Or perhaps Nora glowed for an entirely different reason.

They had arrived safely in America and had added a new member to their small family.

Smiling, Bridget lowered her gaze to the squirming infant clutched possessively in her sister's arms. "I see no one has come forward to claim baby Grace."

Nora's pretty blue eyes narrowed to tiny slits. "Not a single person."

Bridget bit her lip to keep from stating the obvious—that Grace had likely been left behind for good. She'd suggested it before, but Nora refused to believe it. Sometimes Nora was the wisest person she knew, and sometimes surprisingly naive. Baby Grace had been abandoned days after her birth. Nora had found her shortly after the start of their journey, and had cared for her ever since.

"I suppose she'll have to make do with us for the time being." And Bridget wasn't completely sorry for it, either. The baby had become a part of both their lives, Nora's more than hers, even if only on a temporary basis. Grace wasn't really theirs, no matter how much they wished it to be so, but for now, they were all she had.

Nora looked out in the distance, her eyes taking on a troubled look. "I'm sure there's been a mistake." She lowered her gaze to the child in her arms. "Who could abandon such a precious little girl?"

Who, indeed?

In Bridget's estimation anyone who walked away from their own baby didn't know the first thing about love. Every child deserved to be loved. Even the difficult ones.

Familiar stirrings of regret filled her. She had so wanted to turn all three Atwater girls into friends, as much as charges. She'd almost succeeded. With a little more time...

She was doing it again. Trying to change the unchangeable.

"We'll have to report her situation to the American authorities as soon as possible," Nora said only halfheartedly.

It was, of course, the right thing to do.

Though Grace's mother had left her behind, there may well be other family with a claim.

"I suppose we must." Bridget reached out and touched the baby's flawless cheek. Large blue eyes stared back at her. "She's really quite beautiful, isn't she?"

"She's perfect."

Bridget couldn't argue with that bit of truth. All children were a gift straight from the Lord. One day Bridget wanted at least five tiny blessings for herself.

A space opened up along the gangplank and she started forward, then stopped and looked back at Nora. "Are we to meet Maeve here or on the docks below?"

"Below," she said. "Flynn had a few last-minute details he needed to address before he could leave the ship. Maeve chose to stay behind with him."

Of course she had. Bridget's younger sister adored her new husband, as did they all. The ship's doctor was now a part of their family. Best of all, Maeve's shipboard romance had restored Bridget's faith in the possibility of finding love again for herself.

Love. Romance. Marriage.

Were they still possible for her at the age of four and twenty? Had she missed her chance when Daniel had decided he didn't want to marry her?

She ignored the pang in her heart and reminded herself anything was possible with God. Despite the thirteen years between their ages, Flynn Gallagher was a perfect match for Maeve. Their union was a blessing and a testimony to the power of love.

Finished feeling sorry for herself, Bridget tossed her shoulders back and stepped away from the railing. "Right, then. Here we go."

Without looking back, she moved onto the gangplank. For once Nora allowed her to take the lead.

All the planning, prayer and gathering of meager funds had brought them to this glorious day. The moment Bridget's feet touched the wooden dock, her legs wobbled beneath her and her breath caught in her throat. "Oh, Nora, we're finally in America. Isn't it wonderful?"

"Breathtaking." Nora made a face. "As long as you cover your nose."

Bridget waved a dismissive hand. Nothing was going to ruin this moment for her. Not even the awful smells. Besides, Boston wasn't their final destination. Once they gathered their few belongings, Flynn would hire a carriage to take them to the small town of Faith Glen.

Faith Glen. The name had a nice Irish ring to it.

Heart slamming against her ribs, Bridget turned in a slow circle. She wavered a bit, not yet used to the feel of the docks beneath her. There were so many sights to take in, so much noise to filter through her mind. The shouts and laughter mingled together from every corner of the wharf.

A stiff breeze kicked up, tugging several tendrils free from their pins. Bridget shoved at her loose hair, which was quickly becoming an untidy mess. It seemed the wind always won the battle against her best efforts to tame her unruly curls.

She waved at her new friends, Ardeen and her aunt. They returned the gesture but didn't approach, too intent on finding their luggage. The two had been so kind to Bridget and her sisters. Ardeen wasn't particularly young, but was attractive and fashionable. Mrs. Kennedy was shorter and a little fuller figured. Both were single and appeared out of their depth amidst the chaos on the wharf. Bridget should help.

"Watch yourself," came a shout from behind her.

With only seconds to spare Bridget dashed out of the way of a cart careening by. Undaunted by the near-miss, she cut a glance to the other end of the wharf but couldn't find Ardeen and Mrs. Kennedy.

People of every age, size and station milled about. Caught up in the excitement, Bridget gravitated to a location out of the main thoroughfare. All she wanted to do was watch, listen and learn the many secrets of her new homeland.

"Stay focused, Bridget." Nora placed a light touch to her arm. "We still need to locate our luggage before we rendezvous with Maeve and Flynn." Her tone was pure Nora—brisk, efficient and more than a little impatient.

Nora was in her sensible mood. Best to move out of the way and let her take charge.

"Why don't you give Grace to me?" Bridget reached out her arms to the wiggling bundle. "I'll take her out of the hot sun while you search for our luggage."

Nora hesitated.

"If I stand over there—" Bridget cocked her head toward a spot directly behind her "—I'll be able to watch for Maeve and Flynn."

"That's not a bad plan." Slowly, with more than a little reluctance, Nora handed over the baby. "But stay put," she ordered, her warning gaze proving she knew there was a good chance Bridget might not do as commanded. "I won't be long."

Bridget had no doubt. "Run along, Nora. Grace will be quite fine with me."

That seemed to mollify her and she scurried off at a quick pace.

With the infant nestled safely against her, Bridget moved into the shadow cast by the ship's hull and continued watching the activity around her.

As though sensing all was well, the baby promptly fell asleep in her arms.

Equally content, Bridget sighed. The starkly handsome ship rocked in the brackish water behind her. Caged in the dark pool, the enormous structure swayed its lofty head in impatience. The groan of the rigging sounded like an angry mutter of protest against its current confinement.

Bridget had felt that same way back in Ireland. At least in the end. But she and her sisters would soon claim a home of their own, their first, the one deeded to their mother years ago. It was the discovery of that long-hidden deed that had spurred the sisters to set out for America. Now, she couldn't wait to see where their journey led.

So many possibilities lay ahead. Her mind wanted to wander. She let it.

Far too little time passed before Bridget caught sight of Maeve disembarking with her new husband. They hadn't seen Bridget yet. Arms linked, leaning into one another, the newlyweds moved as a single unit. Flynn's dark head bent over Maeve's lighter one. He whispered something in her ear. They both laughed, and the sound reached all the way to where Bridget stood with Grace.

Did they know how happy they appeared to outsiders?

Something hard knotted in Bridget's stomach and she looked away as a familiar sense of loss filled her.

No. She would not give Daniel McGrath such power. It had been a year since he'd left her heartbroken and humiliated. Nothing was going to ruin this day for her, especially not bad memories of the one man who'd disappointed her.

For I will turn their mourning into joy...

Letting the Scripture sink in, Bridget decided to wait a moment longer before she approached Maeve and her husband.

Just as she was ready to step out of the shadows, a movement caught her eye.

Something was coming toward her. No, some*one*—weaving through the thick crowd with purpose.

Bridget struggled to moderate her breathing, even as she craned her neck to see over the bobbing heads.

One blink, two and she saw him. The same man she'd watched from the ship's main deck.

The sound of her heartbeat echoed in her ears.

How could a stranger affect her so?

He was a full hundred feet away and Bridget still couldn't make out his features, yet she couldn't look away. She knew—*she knew*—he was different. Special. And just like earlier, she was inexplicably drawn to him, fascinated, perhaps even bewildered.

A shiver of anticipation skittered up her spine and she instinctively leaned forward. Toward him. Her eyes narrowed for a better look.

He wore a dark frock coat over lighter-colored trousers and carried what looked like a soft-crowned brown hat in his right hand. By his dress alone she knew he was no average dock worker. Or weary traveler.

He had to be a businessman. An American businessman?

In spite of the impeccable clothing and dark hair cut in a very modern style, a shocking air of raw masculinity resonated out of him.

He surveyed his surroundings with meticulous care, checking faces only. Occasionally he would stop and ask a question of someone, shake his head, then continue his search.

She still couldn't see the color of his eyes, but he seemed to be looking for someone in particular.

Grace? Was he here to claim Grace?

No, that couldn't be right. The baby had been born on

the journey over. This man had not been on the ship, she would have remembered him. He couldn't possibly know of the child's existence. Could he?

Her body reacted with an odd sensation and she tightened her hold on Grace. The baby wriggled in her sleep but didn't awaken.

Bridget lowered a soothing kiss to the child's forehead, even as she kept her gaze locked on the stranger.

Meeting such a person on her first day in America could be a dangerous prospect, especially if he was here to seize Grace.

If only Bridget could see his eyes, she would know more about the man's intentions and his character.

Look at me, she silently ordered.

As though hearing her call, his head turned in her direction. It was only then that Bridget realized several people were pointing at her.

Her? Or Grace?

Oh, Lord, please no. No...

Despite her desperation, or perhaps because of it, the moment her gaze met the stranger's Bridget lost her ability to breathe. She couldn't look away, didn't *want* to look away. The man's eyes were indeed blue, a liquid silver-blue, and filled with a fathomless pool of blank emotion, except for a flicker of...what? What was it she saw in that instant? Hurt? Loneliness?

For that brief instant, she felt an undeniable pull. She reached out her hand, as if she could soothe him from this distance.

He gave one hard blink and the moment passed.

Her throat clenched.

He was coming her way.

And looking very determined.

She almost considered melting deeper into the shadows,

but if Grace belonged to him, Bridget couldn't deny him his right. She had to trust he would be good to her.

She took a step forward. Toward him.

He took one slow deliberate step, as well.

Feeling a bit light-headed, Bridget sighed.

Grace gurgled.

The stranger took another step forward.

Bridget sighed again. Really, this odd reaction to a total stranger was beyond ridiculous. She didn't know this man. Or his intentions. She should slip back into the safety of the shadows.

She almost did just that, thinking it the wisest course of action. Except one of Bridget's flaws was that she never retreated from a dare. And, *oh, my,* the man's intense blue eyes held quite the dare.

Chapter Two

William Black stood in muted astonishment. *That hair*. Wild and glorious, the sight of those untamed curls refusing to obey their pins drew him yet another step forward.

Was this woman his future bride, the one he'd sent for all those months ago?

Surely not. Yet several people had pointed at her when he'd mentioned her name—Bridget—and then given her ordinary description of brown hair and dark eyes.

There had to be some mistake. There was nothing ordinary about the woman. She was a blend of the unexpected and the extraordinary, a beautiful female impossible to overlook. In short, everything he avoided in a woman.

As if to mock him, a beam of sunlight escaped like a finger through a crack in the clouds, landing directly on her, bathing her in golden brilliance. Under the bold light of midday she looked delicate, inviting, almost ethereal.

What if this was *his* Bridget?

He'd paid for her passage and promised to marry her, promised to make her a much-needed part of his family. He couldn't go back on his word, regardless of his current misgivings. Duty and honor were the principles that guided his life, all that a man had left when everything else was stripped away.

Will swallowed, remembering what had driven him to acquire an Irish mail-order bride in the first place. Irish women were supposed to be honest, hardworking and proper.

No proper woman had hair like that.

Whoever she was, the beauty staring back at him was perfectly unsuitable to become the mother of his three-year-old twins.

Not after the pain Fanny had put them through this past year and a half.

For a dangerous moment Will's mind fled back in time. To the day when he'd been fool enough to think he could make his marriage work. When he'd thought love was enough to conquer every obstacle thrown their way.

He knew better now. He would never marry for love again. His children deserved stability. And his poor mother deserved relief from the physical demands of caring for a pair of toddlers, no matter how well-behaved.

If this woman with her wild hair and commanding eyes was the one with which he'd corresponded, then Will would honor his promise. As he would any other business transaction. But what would become of his family then?

Mind made up, he continued forward, then stopped, frowned, dropped his gaze. The woman was holding a baby in her arms.

The letter hadn't mentioned a child. Had his intended lied to him? A burning throb knotted in his throat. Was she using him to—

He cut off the rest of his thoughts. He was jumping to conclusions before he'd even met her. The baby might not be hers. And there was still no proof this was indeed his bride.

Will owed it to his children to find out for sure, before he brought the woman into his home and his life. As much as he wanted stability for the twins he would not condemn them to living with a woman of loose morals. Not again. Not *ever* again.

Closing the distance, he forced a smile on his lips and put as much charm into his voice as possible. "Are you Bridget?"

"I...well, yes." Her lovely Irish lilt washed over him and brought an odd sensation of comfort. "Yes, I am Bridget."

An echo of a smile trembled on her lips and Will found himself responding in kind.

Despite his first impression, this woman with her radiant smile and soft expression looked the picture of innocence. A bolt of yearning struck him out of nowhere.

Will ruthlessly suppressed the unwelcome sensation. He didn't want, or need, a wife for his own sake.

"Hello, Bridget. I'm Will," he said without feeling. "Your future husband."

Her future...*what*? Her...her...husband?

The boldly spoken words echoed around in Bridget's mind, yet she couldn't make sense of them. She must have misunderstood the stranger—no, not a stranger anymore. Will, his name was Will.

Bridget shook her head free of her jumbled thoughts and tried to focus on the relevant matter at hand. He wasn't here to claim Grace.

Relief made her legs go weak. But then confusion took hold. Surely this man, this...his name was Will. Surely *Will* hadn't just referred to himself as her future husband.

It was really quite absurd to think that he had.

So Bridget waited for him to continue, or rather to explain himself in greater detail.

He remained completely, perfectly silent.

When the moment stretched into the uncomfortable, she

swallowed several times and then opened her mouth to respond.

To her horror, nothing came out.

She snapped her mouth closed.

And still, Will held to his silence, with only a hint of impatience in his stance.

All Bridget could do was blink up at him in return. He towered over her by at least six inches. The breadth of his shoulders and the powerful muscles beneath his finely cut jacket indicated a man familiar with physical labor.

Bridget should be afraid of him.

She was not.

She was, however, rendered speechless. Still.

"I...I..." The rest of what she'd meant to say sputtered out in a gurgle. She swallowed and tried again. "I'm sorry, I must have heard you incorrectly, you said you were my, my—"

"Future husband."

Oh, my. His deep, raspy voice skimmed over her. A warm, curious sense of inevitability pulled her a step closer to him. Foot poised in midair, she stopped herself before she took another. "That is quite impossible. You have mistaken me for someone else."

His gaze instantly dropped to the baby in her arms and his eyebrows slammed together. Bridget could practically hear the thoughts running through his mind. She braced for the unavoidable questions, trying to decide how best to answer them when they came. She was no stranger to uncomfortable questions.

Will surprised her by skirting the issue of baby Grace altogether. "You are Bridget, are you not?"

"I am, yes." She cleared her throat, comprehending his mistake if he did not. "But I am not *your* Bridget."

His frown deepened. Something dark and turbulent flashed in his eyes.

As she recognized the shift in his mood, it occurred to her once again that she should be afraid of the man.

Why am I not more frightened?

They were surrounded by hundreds of people, yes, any of whom would come to her rescue if she screamed for help. But that wasn't the reason for her lack of fear. It was Will himself. Or rather, his eyes. They were a deep, liquid blue so compelling and beautiful and yet so—very—bleak.

Bridget felt the familiar quickening of compassion in her heart. Something had made this man sad.

The realization brought an unexpected yearning. She'd never been able to turn away from a person in need. Daniel had considered her sympathy for the wounded and disadvantaged her greatest flaw. Bridget considered it her greatest strength. Their difference of opinion had been enough to cause a permanent rift, one that had ultimately torn them apart and brought her profound unhappiness over the past year.

Although she couldn't explain why, her desire to help this man, this stranger, was different than any other time before. Stronger.

Personal.

Had the Lord brought Will to her for a reason?

No. This entire meeting was a mistake. She didn't know him. And he didn't know her, regardless of what he seemed to think.

Baby Grace chose that moment to wiggle in her sleep and then cry out in frustration. Bridget had been holding on too tightly.

Loosening her grip, she took a step back. Away from Will. Away from whatever it was drawing her to him.

The shadows cast by the ship enveloped her, bringing instant relief from the heat of the day.

"I'm sorry," she said again, wishing she could be of more help but knowing it was best to walk away.

His face turned impassive, but she recognized the desperation that lay just below the surface. He wasn't going to walk away from her. Not yet. Not until he was certain she wasn't the woman he'd come searching for.

Oddly enough, Bridget wasn't surprised by his determination. Will was not a man who accepted defeat easily. She wasn't sure how she knew that about him. She just *knew*.

How was it she understood more about his stranger than she had Daniel, a man she'd known all her life and had been willing to marry?

"Perhaps this will spark your memory." Will reached inside his coat and retrieved what looked like a letter. He unfolded the worn parchment and thrust it toward her.

Rearranging the sleeping baby in her arms, Bridget took the letter. The handwriting with its soft, looping scroll clearly belonged to a female.

A female that was not her.

Nevertheless she read each word slowly, carefully, and soon realized she was holding an acceptance letter. The woman had agreed to become this man's bride. Not just any bride, his *mail-order* bride.

Bridget tried not to gasp aloud. She'd heard of such things. The potato famine had left many families destitute, eager to latch on to any lifeline, even if it meant marrying a stranger and moving far from home. But as she looked at Will from beneath her lowered lashes she decided he didn't seem the type who needed to pay a woman to marry him. He was too handsome, too inherently confident, too…masculine.

Women should be lining up to become his wife.

Yet he'd sent all the way to Ireland for a bride.

Hands shaking, Bridget turned over the letter and skimmed to the bottom. The signature read Bridget *Collins*.

He did, indeed, have the wrong woman. Sorrow settled inside her heart. The sensation made her feel as though she'd lost something important, life-changing.

She sighed.

Without meeting Will's gaze directly, Bridget returned the letter to him. "I was right. You have the wrong woman." Her voice wasn't quite steady, even to her own ears. "My name isn't Bridget Collins. It's Bridget Murphy."

For a long, tense moment he looked taken aback by her words. He swallowed once, twice and again, each time harder than the first.

"You did not write this letter?"

"I'm sorry, no." Why she felt the need to apologize, she couldn't say. But he seemed truly shocked by the news and she wanted to make everything better. If only she knew how.

"I see." He glanced down at the baby. Understanding dawned in his eyes. "You are already married."

"No. I am not. I—"

"Forgive me." He took a step back. A very large step, the gesture confirming her worst fears. He thought Grace was hers and she'd had the child out of wedlock.

"The baby isn't mine," she said in a halting voice.

"Of course not." He turned to go.

"No. Wait." She reached out a hand to his retreating back then quickly curled it around the baby once more. "Please."

He swung back around to face her, a question in his eyes.

Although she knew she would never see him again, she couldn't bear him thinking ill of her. "This is baby Grace," she said past the lump in her throat. "I'm holding her for my sister."

It was the truth, if not entirely accurate. The situation was far too complicated to explain in a few succinct sentences.

"I understand."

Did he? Oh, his words were kind enough, but in the next

instant he gave her a formal nod of his head. The gesture was cool, polite and an obvious dismissal. Yet he didn't leave right away. He just stood there staring at her.

"I'm sorry I couldn't be of more help." She meant every word.

"As am I."

Once again he turned to go. This time he stopped himself before he took the next step. "Might I ask you one last question?"

"Yes, of course."

"Do you know Bridget Collins?"

She searched her brain, reviewing all the women and girls she'd met on board the *Annie McGee* named Bridget. It was a common enough name, so much so she counted four off the top of her head. None of them had the last name Collins, though, not that she remembered. Then again, she hadn't known most of her fellow passengers' full names.

Collins. The name triggered a memory, one Bridget couldn't quite grasp. There was a Collins family back in Castleville and there were several daughters among the eight children. Had there been a Bridget among them?

Yes, that must be why the name sounded familiar. "I'm afraid I don't remember meeting your Bridget aboard ship."

"Pity."

It was, indeed.

"Thank you for your understanding, Bridget, I mean, Miss Murphy." He shoved his hat onto his head. "I apologize for disturbing you and the child."

A heartbeat later he was gone, disappearing into the crowd to continue the search for his bride.

Feeling oddly lost without his company, Bridget watched him weave through the maze of people and piles of luggage along the wharf. He moved with masculine elegance, the fluid motion proving he was a man used to controlling his body, confident in who he was and exceedingly comfortable in his own skin.

It was a very attractive, heady combination of traits. Just watching him made her feel very feminine.

In spite of the awkwardness of their meeting, Bridget had liked him. Even now as she watched him search for his bride, concentrating only on the faces of women near her same age, she felt a pull of—something. Something strong and lingering and very, very pleasant. Attraction?

Maybe.

Or perhaps the sensation was simple curiosity. Yes, that must be it. She couldn't possibly find this man attractive when she knew the potential for heartache. Her sisters claimed she was a romantic, but that did not make her naive. Giving in to *curiosity,* she wondered what possible scenario would induce a man like Will to seek out a mail-order bride, a man with undeniable breeding, wealth and good looks.

Before she could contemplate the matter further, Nora returned.

"I found our luggage," she said, a wee bit breathless, her eyes shining. "It's on the other side of the gangplank, about a hundred yards down."

When Bridget merely blinked at her, Nora indicated the spot with a jerk of her head.

Realizing she was expected to respond, Bridget nodded.

Eyebrows pulling together, Nora made an impatient sound deep in her throat. "What's wrong with you? You don't seem yourself."

"I… It's…nothing. I'm simply preoccupied." That was true enough. "There are so many new things to see and hear, to feel, to comprehend. My head is spinning."

"It's all very exciting." Nora reached out her arms. "I'll take Grace now."

Bridget handed over the baby without argument.

Hoping for one last glimpse of Will, she lifted onto her toes and caught sight of another familiar set of faces heading straight for them.

Head held high, marching along in all her regal glory, Mrs. Fitzwilliam led her new charges through the bustling wharf. The three McCorkle brothers following in her wake watched the activity around them with wide eyes. Although it had taken Bridget a while to warm up to the imperious widow, the boys had been a different matter. From the moment Bridget had met them, they'd inspired her sympathy *and* her faith. She was pleased to see them find a happy ending with Mrs. Fitzwilliam as their foster mother.

As was her custom, the older woman had chosen to wear a dress designed in the latest fashion. The pale blue silk, adorned with delicate lace and ribbon trim, was undeniably beautiful but couldn't possibly be comfortable in the midday heat.

The widow didn't seem to notice. She looked cool, elegant, her dark auburn hair contained in a beaded snood that would have been more fitting for a ballroom. Bridget wondered briefly where her attendant Stillman had gone. Perhaps to hire a carriage?

"Well, hello, my dear Murphy sisters." Mrs. Fitzwilliam drew to a stop, her nose in the air, eyes cast downward. "I see you still have that precious baby with you." She reached out and caressed Grace's cheek with a loving, gentle touch. "Such a beautiful child."

Nora accepted the compliment with genuine pride in her eyes, as though the baby was her own. "I couldn't agree more."

Nodding her approval, Mrs. Fitzwilliam continued studying Grace's sweet face. "My stepgranddaughter Mary had the same coloring."

At the mention of the girl, a sad, faraway look entered

Mrs. Fitzwilliam's eyes. The widow's quest to find her missing relative had led her to make this trip to America. The rebellious Mary had run off with her boyfriend, Thomas. The lack of any contact from the girl, not a single letter, had left Mrs. Fitzwilliam quite concerned, enough to seek the help of a professional.

"Will you be meeting with a detective soon?" Bridget asked, unable to hold her tongue in light of the distress she saw in the woman's gaze.

"As soon as possible. Oh, yes indeed. As *soon* as possible."

"You will keep us informed?" Nora asked.

Never taking her eyes off the baby, she gave one firm nod. "You may count on it."

After touching Grace's cheek one final time, Mrs. Fitzwilliam turned her attention back to Bridget. "Enough with all this gloom." She shook her head as if to wipe away the remains of any negative thoughts swirling around. "Now tell me, my dear girl, are you prepared to claim your new home today?"

"Oh, aye," Bridget answered, all but cradling her reticule against her waist as snugly as Nora held the infant. "You will come visit us once we're settled, yes?" She made eye contact with each of the McCorkle boys. "The invitation includes you three, as well."

"Thank you," Gavin, the oldest of the brothers, answered for all of them. "We would enjoy that very much, Miss Bridget."

"Then it's agreed." Bridget punctuated her statement with a smile.

Gavin smiled back. Tall and lanky, at just eighteen he was on the cusp of manhood and took his role as big brother seriously. Emmett and Sean were considerably younger than him, eight and ten years old respectively. Despite the age difference there was no mistaking the three belonged to one another. All had the same reddish blond hair, pleasing features and big blue eyes.

They were a little rough around the edges, but they were good boys with big hearts. Back in Ireland they'd nearly starved to death in a workhouse.

"...and once Stillman hires the carriage the five of us will head to my home here in Boston." Mrs. Fitzwilliam's voice broke into Bridget's thoughts. "After I meet with the detective and determine my next step concerning Mary, we will make the trip to Faith Glen." She spoke as if the four of them were already a family.

Who would have thought the haughty woman of weeks ago would turn out to be so—sweet. Bridget felt her smile widening. The widow was doing a wonderful thing, taking in the boys and raising them as if they were her own kin.

Although Gavin had done his best to provide for his younger brothers, he wasn't educated and had had no job prospects in America. The McCorkles had taken a large risk when they'd set out to stow away on the *Annie McGee*. The Lord had protected them when things hadn't worked out as planned. Their leap of faith had ultimately brought them a kind, if somewhat stern, benefactor in Mrs. Fitzwilliam.

God was good. And now the lonely widow had a family of her own.

Would Will's story end so happily?

Rising to her toes, Bridget caught his attention just as he left another group of women. At the questioning lift of her eyebrows he shook his head in the negative.

Bridget lowered back onto her heels and sighed.

"Bridget Murphy." Mrs. Fitzwilliam's tone held a considerable amount of reproach. "Were you flirting with that man?"

Flirting? "No, of course not."

"And yet, I wonder. I saw you speaking with him earlier, without the benefit of a chaperone in sight." The widow's eyes had turned a hard, dark blue, reminding Bridget of the imposing woman they'd first met on the ship weeks ago.

Refusing to be intimidated—after all, she'd done nothing wrong—Bridget raised her chin in the air. "Yes, I spoke with him earlier. But I assure you, Mrs. Fitzwilliam, nothing unseemly occurred between us." The words tumbled out of her mouth. "He mistook me for his bride."

She realized she'd spoken too plainly the moment Mrs. Fitzwilliam's eyes narrowed.

"That man thought you were his bride?"

Nora gasped at the implication. But before she could speak, Mrs. Fitzwilliam sniffed loudly, her disapproval evident in the unladylike sound. The gesture reminded Bridget that the woman had always adhered to a strict moral code of conduct.

A wave of heat rose in Bridget's face. She glanced at Nora, noted her widened gaze, then hastened to explain. "It wasn't unseemly, but rather a simple mistake. He thought I was his *mail-order* bride. Her name is Bridget, as well. And aside from sharing her name, apparently I fit the woman's description, too."

After a moment of consideration—a long, tense moment where Bridget fought the urge to continue defending herself—Mrs. Fitzwilliam conceded the fact with a short nod of her head. "I suppose that could happen."

She sounded as skeptical as she looked. But Bridget had other concerns besides earning Mrs. Fitzwilliam's approval on the matter. "He still hasn't found her," she said more to herself than the rest of the party.

As if to prove her point, Will approached another group of passengers disembarking from the *Annie McGee*. After a brief conversation, he walked away empty-handed. Again.

"Wait a minute." Nora swung into Bridget's line of vision,

her face full of concern. "Did you say the man's bride has similar features as you?"

"Yes."

"Don't you remember, Bridget?" Nora said. "The terrible accident when the girl fell from the forecastle onto the deck."

"I…" Bridget closed her eyes and thought back. A young girl with dark hair had fallen to her death. There was some confusion over her identity. In fact, Flynn had feared the dead girl was Bridget at first, and had gone to inform Maeve of the terrible accident. They'd all been happily surprised when Bridget had joined them in the middle of his story.

"Yes, oh, my stars, *yes*," Nora said with more conviction than before, her voice breaking into Bridget's thoughts. Nora gasped as though remembering the moment when they'd thought Bridget was dead. "It was all so horrible."

Bridget remembered now. The girl had died early in the voyage. Maeve, acting in the role of Flynn's medical assistant by then, had been upset over the entire matter, especially when they hadn't been able to identify her conclusively. Bridget wasn't even sure they knew her identity still, not without doubts, but she did remember hearing someone say that she was called Bridget.

"Oh, dear." Could this be the reason why Will hadn't located his bride yet? Because she was dead?

The crowds had thinned out and, still, he continued searching for his bride. To no avail.

Bridget couldn't bear to watch any longer. She had to tell him what she knew. Or at least what she *thought* she knew. She and Nora could be wrong. But if they were correct, if Will's bride had died during the sea voyage over, someone needed to tell him. And that someone should be her, not some stranger who wouldn't take care with their words.

Bridget bid a hasty farewell to Mrs. Fitzwilliam and the boys, then set out.

"Bridget," Nora called after her. "Where are you going?"

"I must tell him about the accident." She tossed the words over her shoulder, her mind made up, her feet moving quickly.

"Bridget, it's really none of your concern."

Oh, but it was. It had become her concern the moment Will had introduced himself to her.

Chapter Three

Will caught sight of Bridget Murphy hurrying toward him at an alarming speed. Still reeling from his earlier encounter with the young woman, he noted two things about her as she approached. She no longer held a baby in her arms and she had a very determined look on her face.

Oddly enough, the fierce expression made her more appealing, not less. For a brief moment he experienced a wave of regret that she wasn't *his* Bridget. She was truly beautiful, if he looked past the unruliness of her hair. She had a smooth, oval face, a gently bowed mouth and hazel eyes, more green than brown, a color so rich and intricate he could stare at them for hours and still come away fascinated.

But her hair gave him pause, that glorious, untamed hair that refused to obey its pins. The silky strands snapping in the wind gave her a spirited look that Will found dangerously appealing. He hadn't been this attracted to a woman in—never. He'd *never* met a woman that made his blood rush and his brain spin out of control. Not even Fanny.

It was a very good thing this particular Bridget was not his bride after all.

Swerving around a group of her fellow passengers, the woman skidded to a stop directly in front of him.

She was breathing hard and blinking rapidly.

Something had upset her greatly.

"I have news for you, sir, I…" She let her words trail off and her brows pulled together in a frown.

No woman should look that attractive while frowning.

"I just realized," she said in that soft Irish lilt that left him feeling warm and comforted, like the melted chocolate his mill workers turned into hard cakes. "I don't know your full name."

He blinked again. "It's William. William Black." He paused. "But, please, call me Will. Considering the circumstances of our first meeting anything else would seem too formal."

She digested his words a moment, watching him closely as she did, and then gave him one firm nod. "And you may call me Bridget."

He smiled his agreement.

After another moment passed, she took a deep, shuddering breath, opened her mouth to speak again but stopped herself just as quickly.

Will continued looking into her eyes, those beautiful, gut-wrenching eyes that were fully green in the sunlight with only a few flecks of gold woven throughout. There was no subterfuge in her gaze, no secretive games being played. Or rather, none that he could decipher.

Despite knowing he should keep up his guard, despite her beauty, he sensed this was a woman he could trust. An illusion he didn't dare give in to, for the sake of his children if not for himself. They needed stability and a mother. No matter what his personal feelings were on the matter the job was already filled. Will was firmly committed to following through with his promise.

He cleared his throat. "You said you have news for me?"

"Yes." She worried her bottom lip between her teeth. "I'm afraid it concerns your bride."

By her manner alone he knew he wasn't going to like what she had to say. "Go on."

"There was a young woman on board who bore my same description, one I had forgotten about until my sister reminded me. Her name was Bridget, and she had dark hair and eyes and…" Her words trailed off again. He could feel the misery rolling off her in waves.

Now he knew for certain he wasn't going to like what she had to say. Nevertheless he pressed her to continue. "And?"

"And…" She sighed. "The Bridget I'm speaking of died on the crossing over."

Dead? His future bride was dead?

His gut rolled at the news.

No. Not dead. Not possible. The words refused to register in his brain. And yet he found himself asking, "How did she die?"

"From what I remember, although I didn't see the accident myself, she lost her footing and fell from the forecastle to the deck." She touched his arm with tentative fingers then quickly pulled back when he lowered his gaze. "She did not survive the fall."

Will shook his head, the news sinking in slowly, painfully, but far too clearly. "When did this happen?"

She cocked her head at a curious angle, as though unsure why he'd asked the question. "It was a few days into the journey."

His worst fear confirmed. His bride had fallen to her death on board the ship, *after* she'd left the safety of her homeland.

All his careful planning, all the research he'd done to avoid making another mistake, and for what? Another woman was dead because of him.

* * *

Bridget watched a complicated array of emotions cross Will's face. He was no longer stoic, or unreadable. He was distressed. Visibly so.

That terrible look of despair, that awful pain in his eyes. She'd done that to him.

Her heart constricted with sympathy. It wasn't in her to watch such suffering. She desperately wanted to erase the worry from his eyes.

"I'm sorry, Will, I mean…Mr. Black," she corrected, knowing it was best to keep their relationship formal, at least at the moment. "I'm very sorry."

He blinked down at her, his eyes unfocused, as though he'd forgotten she was still standing beside him. In the next instant his troubled gaze darted up the gangplank, then across the wharf, then back to her again. "Are you certain the woman was Bridget Collins?"

"I… No." A moment of doubt whipped through her. "No, I'm not certain at all. From what I understand there was some initial confusion over her identity. She looked enough like me for the ship's doctor to believe it was me that had died." *Oh, please, Lord, please, let me be wrong. For this man's sake.*

"Then you will excuse me?" He looked over his shoulder, heaved a hard pull of air into his lungs. "I must check with the ship's officials to determine if this unfortunate news is, indeed, true."

Of course he would want to verify the information she'd just given him. "I think that's a very wise idea. I could very well be incorrect." *Oh, please, please.*

"Let us hope that you are." His words were abrupt, but not unkind. More distracted than anything else.

He gave her a brief, formal bow. "Good day, Bridget."

"Good day. And—" she placed her fingertips on his arm once again "—Godspeed in your search for your bride."

He stared at her hand for a breathless moment. Then, shrugging away from her, he left without another word.

Not at all offended by his abrupt departure—well, only a little—Bridget watched him work his way toward a small, official-looking building that was most likely the shipping office. Even in his distress, William Black paced through the wharf with those same fluid, masculine, ground-eating strides she'd noticed earlier.

Her heart heavy with the distress of bearing such devastating news, Bridget continued staring after him until he disappeared inside the building. She might have sighed a few times in the process.

What would Will do if his bride was the young woman who had died aboard ship? Why did it matter so much to her? Why did she sense there was more to his story, something tragic that made this news so much worse?

Caught up in her troubling thoughts, she didn't notice Nora's approach until a firm hand gripped her shoulder. She nearly jumped out of her boots. Spinning around, she glared at her sister. "Nora! You scared me half to death."

"So sorry." She didn't look remorseful in the least. "But I did call your name three times. You didn't answer."

"My mind was otherwise engaged."

"I figured as much." She hitched her chin in the direction of the building. "How did he take the news?"

"Not well." Bridget sighed. "Not well at all."

"I don't suppose anyone in his situation would."

"No." She lowered her gaze and noted that Nora's arms were empty. Completely empty. Terrible possibilities filled her mind. A wordless cry lodged in her throat. "Where's Grace?"

"Maeve has her. The two of them are sitting with our luggage while Flynn is over by the street hiring a carriage.

Come, Bridget." Nora tugged on her arm. "Our new home is waiting."

Their new home. She'd almost forgotten why she was here in America. And no wonder. Her excitement had been dampened by the unfortunate incident with William Black. Or rather, Will, as he'd first introduced himself and then later asked her to call him. Proper or not, she would forever think of him as *Will*.

Again she wondered why he had sent all the way to Ireland for a bride. What was the rest of his story?

And what will he do if his bride is dead?

Bridget wished there was more she could do to help the man, and perhaps there was. An idea began formulating in her brain, one that might not bring Will the good news he hoped for but at least would give him accurate information. As her dear mother used to say, it was always easier to plan once you had all the facts.

With that in mind, Bridget hurried ahead of Nora, eyeing the pile of luggage where her sister Maeve waited with baby Grace cradled in her arms.

Was someone out there missing the tiny infant? If that was so, why hadn't she, or perhaps even he, come forward to claim the child? What terrible event had occurred to warrant abandoning a newborn in the ship's galley?

They may never find a definitive answer.

And Bridget had another pressing matter to address, one she hoped would bring Will certainty if not relief.

As she stopped in front of her youngest sister, Bridget couldn't help but notice how good Maeve and Grace looked together, how natural.

Maeve had left her hair falling in loose curls down her back. Like Bridget and Nora, she wore her new dress, as well. Hers was a French plaid, the orange, yellow and green setting off her coloring. Her rich strawberry-blond hair had turned a soft ginger in the sunlight and she looked as pretty as a picture as she smiled down at the baby.

Maeve would make a wonderful mother, evidenced by the careful attention she showed Grace now. Bridget once again experienced a pang of regret. Had Daniel wanted to marry her, had he followed through with his promise, she could be holding her own baby right now.

Bridget didn't take the time to linger over the thought. "Maeve, where's your husband?" Impatience made her voice just short of shrill. "I need Flynn at once."

"What's the rush?" Maeve's eyes widened. "Has someone been hurt?"

"No, nothing like that." Bridget shook her head decisively. "But I need Flynn's help right now."

"Whatever for?" Maeve's eyes narrowed in confusion.

Holding on to the last thread of her patience, Bridget quickly explained Will's situation. Nora added what she thought she remembered about the girl who'd fallen from the forecastle. Between the two of them they laid out the sequence of events as best they could recall.

When they finished Maeve's gaze turned thoughtful, then sad. From that look alone, Bridget knew her sister remembered the day the girl in question had died. Maeve never forgot a patient, nor did Flynn for that matter, but this one's death was especially heartbreaking.

"Do you remember her?" Bridget asked, trying her best to keep her voice steady. "Did you ever discover her name? Was she Bridget? Bridget Collins?"

Maeve's eyes misted slightly, a small switch in mood, easily missed if Bridget hadn't been looking. "As the ship's doctor, and custodian of all the medical records on board, Flynn would be the one to ask."

Bridget wasn't fooled by her sister's evasive words. Maeve knew the answer, but wasn't saying anything more.

"Please, Maeve. It's important. Will has been searching for his bride all morning, wondering why he can't find her. Wouldn't it be best for him to know the truth, whatever it is, even if it's bad news?"

"You know I can't give you that information, Bridget." An apology settled in Maeve's eyes. "I was only an assistant in the infirmary. You'll have to ask Flynn."

"Ask me what?"

Bridget swung around at the sound of the familiar deep voice, her gaze landing squarely on Maeve's new husband, Dr. Flynn Gallagher. Or rather, her gaze landed on Dr. Flynn Gallagher's black cravat.

The man was taller than any of the Murphy sisters, even Nora. He was muscular and lean like William Black, just as handsome and so in love with his new wife that he reflexively looked to Maeve for the answer to his question as though she was the only one in their tiny group.

Maeve nodded to Bridget. "Go on," she urged. "Tell him what you just told me."

Practically shaking with impatience, Bridget went through the story again, faster this time and without waiting for Nora's input. Just as she drew to the end of the tale she caught sight of Will exiting the building he'd entered only a few moments before. Head down, jaw firm, he approached yet another group of passengers.

He must have been unsuccessful in the shipping office.

"There." She pointed to Will. "That's him, the man approaching that small cluster of people."

Her hand moved instinctively in his direction, aching to soothe away his worries. She started out.

"No, Bridget." Flynn stopped her with a gentle hand on her arm. "You've done your duty. Let me handle the rest."

"But—"

"I insist you stay here with your sisters." He shared a look with his wife, one that seemed to communicate a message only the two of them understood.

Maeve quickly stood, handed the baby to Nora and then drew alongside her husband. Side by side they made a dazzling pair.

"It'll be all right, Bridget." Maeve touched her arm and smiled. "Flynn will handle the matter with great care, like he always does."

Flynn dropped a tender kiss to Maeve's forehead. "I'll be back shortly."

He left them to stare after his retreating back.

Bridget had always considered herself an obedient woman, one who usually adhered to the Christian precepts of ideal female behavior. Her manners were impeccable, as well. Consequently she shocked even herself when she trotted after Flynn, all the while ignoring Maeve's cries to leave the matter alone, that it didn't concern her. The same words Nora had used earlier.

She knew it didn't concern her. And yet, somehow, after all that had happened, it did.

She picked up her pace.

With determination on her side, and the element of surprise, she bypassed Flynn at the last possible moment and approached Will first.

As though sensing her standing behind him, he turned to face her at the very same moment she spoke his name.

He seemed stunned to see her again. "Bridget?"

Breathless from her rapid trek across the docks, her words came out in a jumbled rush. "I have brought someone to help you find your bride, or at least give you more information."

The look in his blue, blue eyes plainly said: *What are you talking about?*

"The ship's doctor," she said in reply, her heart pounding with the force of her urgency. "I have come to introduce you."

She didn't have time to explain further before Flynn closed the distance between them.

Will lifted his gaze from her to Flynn then thrust out his hand. "William Black."

With his characteristic professional manner, Flynn took the offered hand. "Flynn Gallagher, the doctor in charge of the infirmary on the *Annie McGee*."

Will wasted no time getting to the point. "Do you know what happened to Bridget Collins on the voyage over?"

The ensuing silence pressed in on them all. Will looked so concerned, so in need of kindness. Bridget almost went to him and wrapped her arms around him.

"I believe I can enlighten you." Flynn's expression was that of a man about to give the most terrible news of all.

Will must have understood what was about to come because he asked, "Is she…dead?"

"I'm afraid that she—" Flynn cut off the rest of his words and looked down at Bridget. He frowned at her briefly then returned his attention to Will. "Perhaps we should continue this conversation aboard the *Annie McGee*. Just the two of us."

Bridget opened her mouth to object, but Flynn stopped her with a look. "My dear Bridget," he said, his voice filled with equal parts authority and understanding. "You must wait with your sisters while I escort Mr. Black to the infirmary."

And with that one sentence her *dear* brother-in-law had revealed his intentions. He had no plans of allowing her to accompany them any further. Perhaps, like Maeve and Nora, he didn't think the matter was any of her business.

Did Will agree? She glanced into his vivid expression and discovered her answer. He didn't want her in the infirmary with him, either.

Horrified to feel the sting of tears, she lowered her gaze

and concentrated blindly on the wooden dock below her feet. She knew the matter was none of her business, and yet…

And yet…

They were all correct. She had no right to insinuate herself into a stranger's private affairs. She should have realized that sooner. Her concern had made her act impulsively, perhaps even rudely. She'd meddled, something so unlike her that her cheeks began to flame.

Clenching her fingers into the material of her skirt, she forced a pleasant smile onto her lips. "I will tell Maeve where you are."

"No." Flynn's voice stopped her from leaving. "On second thought, please have my wife join Mr. Black and me in the infirmary."

Hard as she tried to remain calm, Bridget cast him a dark look. Why would Flynn allow his wife to accompany him on this errand and not her?

He answered her unspoken question aloud. "Your sister was my assistant, Bridget. As such, she was in charge of keeping the medical records in order. Maeve will know precisely where to look for the information Mr. Black needs."

How could Bridget possibly argue with that bit of logic? "Of course." She released her death grip on her skirt. "I will tell her to find you at once."

Before she turned to go, Will covered her hand with the reassuring pressure of his own. "Thank you, Bridget." He squeezed gently. "Thank you for your help and…*thank you.*"

For a moment she stared down at his fingers wrapped around her own, wondering why she experienced that mystifying feeling again, the one where puzzle pieces seemed to be fitting together perfectly. "Oh, Will, you are quite welcome."

He released her hand.

This time when she turned to go, neither man stopped her.

As she made her way back across the docks, for good this time, Bridget only looked back in Will's direction once. All right, twice. She only looked back twice.

Chapter Four

As it turned out, Flynn and Maeve did not accompany them to Faith Glen. The last Bridget saw of the pair were their retreating backs as they climbed the gangplank, with William Black following closely behind. Maeve had told Nora and Bridget to go on without them and Nora, efficient to a fault, had them on the road in no time at all.

If Bridget was truthful with herself she'd admit she wasn't completely sorry Maeve and Flynn weren't making the trip to the new town just yet. Since Flynn had a house in Boston, she knew they would be just fine on their own. Better than fine. Although Bridget would miss her sister dreadfully, the newlyweds needed time alone.

That left Bridget and Nora the task of claiming the house bequeathed to their mother. Her stomach rolled at the thought, at the possibility all may not turn out as they hoped. The rocking of the carriage added to her queasiness.

Swallowing back her nausea, she focused on the scenery passing by. The countryside was very green, the gently rolling hills much like the ones they'd left back in Ireland. The lingering sound and smell of the ocean was familiar, as well.

A sense of homecoming filled her.

She caught Nora's eye.

Her sister smiled. "I've directed the driver to stop at the Sheriff's Office before we head to the house."

"I suppose it's for the best." She tried not to sigh again. She'd done quite enough of that for one day. "I assume you plan to publicly announce Grace is in our care?"

"It's the right thing to do, Bridget. She's not ours."

"She feels like ours."

"Yes, she does." Nora's eyes filled with tears. She lowered her head and whispered, *"Grá mo chroí."* Sweetheart in Gaelic.

The baby's little eyelids fluttered open and she yawned. Nora was already rummaging in her bag. A few seconds later and Grace suckled a bottle of milk in noisy contentment.

Leaning her head against the cushions behind her, Nora breathed out deeply.

"Tired?" Bridget asked.

"A bit. But excited, too." She straightened. "We should probably show the deed to the sheriff while we're there. If nothing else, he'll be able to direct us to the house."

Or take it away from them. "Oh, Nora. What if the deed isn't legal?"

The horrible scenario was possible. Laird O'Malley, a former suitor of their mother's, had left for America years ago. He'd been heartbroken their mother hadn't wanted to marry him, but not enough that he'd lost hope she would one day change her mind.

He'd built her a house in Faith Glen and had put the deed of ownership in her name. The wording had made it possible for Colleen Murphy's daughters to inherit the property.

Or so they were all counting on.

But what if they were wrong? What if the property wasn't theirs for the taking? This entire trip to America had hinged on that promise.

As though sensing where her mind had gone, Nora nudged

Bridget's foot with the toe of her boot. "You leave the worrying to me, Bridget Murphy. I had the document verified in Ireland. Everything will work out fine."

"Who are you trying to convince? Me or you?"

Nora patently ignored the question. "We'll stop at the Sheriff's Office, report Grace's situation and then head to our new home."

Their new home. What a wonderful, exciting, terrifying prospect. But what if the deed wasn't legal, or if the house had been torn down?

Faith. All she needed was a little more faith.

Stiffening her spine, Bridget turned her attention back to the passing scenery. The road ran parallel to a small, fast-moving river. If she closed her eyes she could envision walking the high banks, dipping her toes in the fresh, cool water. There was a man by her side. A tall man with dark hair and blue eyes the color of the midday sky. The haunted look was gone from his expression and…

Bridget quickly snapped open her eyes. William Black was not the man of her dreams. He couldn't be. There was no man in her dreams—not after what Daniel had done. And even if, sometime in the future, she let herself trust a man enough to consider love and marriage—well, surely Will wouldn't be the man at her side. For all she knew he'd sorted out the situation with his missing bride and was at this very moment escorting the woman to his home in Boston.

She paused midthought, realizing it would do her no good to dwell on a man she would never see again.

Determined to put William Black out of her mind, her gaze landed on a sizable building, a mill of some sort. The large wheel churning in the river filled the moment with the happy, trickling sound of rushing water. The scent wafting in the air was nothing she'd ever smelled before, a heavy, almost sweet aroma.

Delighted, Bridget leaned out the carriage window. A few moments later they crested a hill and a small village came into view. The large green-and-white wooden sign in the shape of a rectangle identified the town as Faith Glen.

The main feature of the town was a tidy village square. A white clapboard church dominated all the other buildings. A general store sat on one side of the church and on the other was—Bridget squinted to read the sign hooked to the porch ceiling—Rose's Boardinghouse.

On the opposite side of the square was the Sheriff's Office. The bars on the windows gave it away, as did the fact that the structure had been built out of stone. Not brick or wood like the other buildings in town, but solid stone.

"We're nearly there," Bridget said.

Nora pulled the bottle from Grace's mouth and gently swung the child to her shoulder. When the carriage drew to a stop Bridget scrambled out of the carriage ahead of her sister.

The driver, an older man with thinning hair and a thick, handlebar mustache, had already released the ropes securing their trunks and was fast at work unloading their belongings.

Bridget rushed forward. "What are you doing? We haven't reached our final destination yet."

"This is as far as I go, miss." His gruff voice had a Scottish burr underneath the words. And a hint of meanness.

"But Dr. Gallagher paid you to take us to our new home."

"He paid me enough to get you to the town," he corrected. "Not a foot more."

That was a bold-faced lie. Bridget knew Flynn would never leave them stranded like this.

"It's all right, Bridget," Nora said, exiting the carriage with sure steps. "We'll ask the sheriff for assistance once our business is complete."

Bridget relented, a little, but only because the driver was already in his seat and spurring his horses forward.

"Well, now." A deep, masculine voice drifted over her. "What have we here?"

Heart lodged in her throat, Bridget swung around to face a tall man with kind eyes. Blond-haired, blue-eyed, the man looked to be of Nordic descent. The tin star pinned to his chest told her she was staring at the sheriff of Faith Glen.

He was very handsome, in a rugged, earthy sort of way, and Bridget immediately noticed how Nora stood frozen in place, eyes blinking rapidly as she stared at him.

Bridget's sentiments exactly. In the next few minutes they would either lose Grace or their new home, perhaps both, or—God willing—take the next step in claiming a new life for themselves in America.

When Bridget and Nora continued staring at him, neither making a move to speak, the man smiled warmly. "I'm Cameron Long. The sheriff of Faith Glen." His gaze lingered a moment longer on Nora than Bridget. "What brings you two lovely women to our fair town?"

When Nora remained surprisingly silent under the sheriff's scrutiny, Bridget stepped forward. "My name is Bridget Murphy and this is my sister Nora. We've just arrived from Ireland—"

Grace let out an earsplitting wail. Bridget smiled. "And *that* healthy-lunged child is Grace. One of the reasons we've come here today."

He glanced briefly at the bundle in Nora's arms, then proceeded to ignore Grace. "You've come to Faith Glen because of a baby?"

"No." Nora found her voice at last. "We came to *you* because of a baby."

His eyes widened ever-so-slightly. "Me?"

"You are the sheriff of Faith Glen?" Nora looked pointedly at his badge. "Are you not?"

Instead of being offended by the haughty tone, Cameron Long appeared amused. "I am, indeed."

His lips quirked at an attractive, lopsided angle, making him look even more handsome than before.

And if Bridget wasn't mistaken, she heard Nora's breath hitch in her throat. Interesting. But unsurprisingly, her sister recovered quickly and explained how they'd found the baby in the ship's galley. "When no one came to claim her, we realized the child had been abandoned. And we," Nora said as she smiled at Bridget, "plan to care for her until someone comes forward to claim her."

"Commendable, to be sure," he said, his eyes again holding Nora's a beat too long. "But that doesn't explain why you've brought the baby to me. Why not report her situation to the authorities in Boston?"

"Can you not do that for us?" Nora asked.

"Of course I can." He stuffed his hands in his pockets. "But that doesn't explain why you are *here,* in Faith Glen."

Nora turned to Bridget. "Show him the deed."

She dutifully reached inside her reticule and retrieved the precious document that had led them to America.

The sheriff accepted the deed and Bridget held her breath. After what seemed an endless eternity, he raised his head. "Who is Colleen Murphy?"

"Our mother," Nora answered. "She died ten years ago."

He considered her response a moment then redirected his gaze to the document once again.

"Is the deed legal or not?" Nora demanded, her patience evidently reaching its end.

"It would appear so."

"Well, then." She plucked the paper out of his hand, relief softening the tight lines around her mouth. "If you would be so kind as to direct us to our home we would be ever grateful."

"I'm afraid I can't do that."

Bridget gasped. "But you said the deed was legal."

"I said it *appears* to be legal." He ran a hand through his hair. "Unfortunately, there's no way of knowing for certain until we check your document against the official copy in the County Clerk's Office."

Bridget's heart sank. "But we were told the deed was all we needed to claim the property."

"That may be true in Ireland, but not in the state of Massachusetts. Every land deal requires two copies of the transaction." He spoke with genuine remorse, as though he understood how important this was to them.

"Two copies." Bridget pushed the words past a very tense jaw. No one had warned them of this possibility.

"The law originated back in the early colonial days," he explained. "When fraud was at a premium."

Nora rose to her full height. "We did not travel all this way to commit fraud."

"Didn't say that you had." He lifted his broad shoulders in a gesture surprisingly elegant for such a big man. "Nevertheless the law requires that the original deed be compared against the copy, the one that is kept in—"

"The County Clerk's Office," Nora finished for him. "And where is this…office?"

"In Dedham, about eight miles due north."

Bridget glanced at the afternoon sky in frustration. Even if they left now, there wouldn't be enough time to travel eight miles north and back again before the sun set.

"What are we going to do?" she whispered.

The question had been rhetorical, but the sheriff answered her anyway. "You will be able to verify the deed come Monday morning. I'll escort you there myself."

It was a gallant offer, but Monday was three days away.

"It's just a formality," he promised, his voice full of encouragement, his smile wide.

"Will you at least show us the house?" Bridget asked.

Not quite meeting her gaze, he shook his head no. "I would suggest you wait until we've verified ownership."

He wasn't telling them something, something important about the house. "But we only wish to see the property."

"Not today."

And with those concise words, spoken in the brief, decisive tone of a determined lawman, Bridget accepted the reality of the situation at last. She would have to put her dreams on hold for another three days. Three…more…days.

Early the next morning Will entered his private study with a heavy heart and a mind full of turmoil. Regret played with his composure as he lowered himself into the chair behind his desk and closed his hand in a tight fist. Bridget Collins had, indeed, fallen to her death. And now he was in possession of the girl's luggage, the undeniable proof of her identity.

Closing his eyes, he sucked in a harsh breath. He'd been responsible for the woman, having taken on the cost of her passage and ensuring the details of her trip were in order. Yet he'd failed her. And, in the process, his children, as well. His sad, motherless children.

Will swallowed back the hard ache rising in his throat. He was in no better position than before he'd decided to acquire a mail-order bride. Acquire. What a miserable way to put it, as though finding a wife was a matter of walking over to the general store and pointing to the woman he liked best. *There. That one, I want that one to be my wife.*

He should have known better.

Yet what other choice had there been? His aging mother

was doing her best with the children. But the physical demands were taking their toll.

Running a hand through his hair, Will looked out the bay of windows on his right. The sun was making its grand entrance for the day, spreading tentative, golden fingers through the hazy dawn. A kaleidoscope of moving shadows flickered across the floor at his feet, creating an eerie accompaniment to his somber mood.

Pulling out the ledger he'd brought home with him from the mill, Will went to work. Despite the early hour, the air already felt hot and sticky and promised to turn unbearable once the sun was fully in the sky. He'd made the right decision to close the mill for the next two days. Grinding cocoa beans and turning them into blocks of chocolate was hot work on any given day. Deadly during a heat wave like this one.

Will was proud of the fact that the Huntley-Black Mill had a reputation for treating its workers well. He employed most of the residents of Faith Glen, including many of the Irish immigrants unable to find work elsewhere.

An unexpected image materialized in his head of the pretty Irish lass he'd met yesterday on the docks in Boston. Bridget Murphy had been beautiful and compassionate. But not his. *His* Bridget was dead.

"Forgive me," he whispered, rubbing his forehead with his palm. The gesture did nothing to relieve the ache growing stronger behind his eyes.

He had to find someone to care for his children, a stable woman who wouldn't leave them when boredom struck and then show up again when the round of parties ceased to amuse her. In other words, a woman nothing like their mother. At least in death Fanny had finally offered her children the consistency she'd denied them in life.

But her loss had still come at a cost to both Olivia and Caleb. They were far too subdued for their age. Will had never wanted perfect children in his home. He wanted *happy* children.

A tentative knock sounded at the door. He set down the quill and called out, "It's open."

The door creaked on its hinges and soon a head full of white-silver hair poked through the tiny opening.

"Well," his mother said with a smile. "You're up early."

"No earlier than usual."

"I suppose not." She stepped deeper into the room, looking especially tired this morning with the dull light emphasizing the purple shadows under her eyes.

He'd intended to bring home his new bride last night, one who would take the burden off his mother and love his children as much as he did. A beautiful woman with wild, dark hair, mesmerizing green eyes, a soft Irish lilt and…

Wrong woman, Will. You're thinking about the wrong woman.

He slammed the ledger shut. No more work today. Not for him, *or* his mother.

Rising, he shoved the chair out of his way and then circled around his desk. Everything in him softened as he caught sight of two small heads peeking out from behind his mother's skirts.

He might have vowed never to love another woman after Fanny, but Olivia and Caleb were a different matter altogether. His love for his twins grew daily, his heart nearly bursting with emotion at times like this.

If only he could figure out a way to let them know they were allowed to be happy, playful. Even noisy and messy sometimes. He feared they followed too closely after his own sober, saddened behavior, and wished he knew how to bring some joy into their lives. And his own.

"I see we have more early risers." He bent low enough

to look into both children's eyes. "Good morning, Olivia, Caleb."

They each gave him a wobbly smile in return. Will hated these moments, when he couldn't read his own children's moods. Their three-year-old thoughts were impossible to decipher behind those solemn masks.

Nevertheless, he forged ahead. "Did you sleep well?"

"Yes, sir," they answered in unison, their words filled with that polite tone he dreaded most.

Hoping to alleviate their shyness, Will opened his arms in silent appeal and went for the direct approach. "Can I have a morning hug?"

Caleb toed the ornate rug at his feet, his eyes huge and luminous. Olivia's mouth slowly quirked into a sweet, tentative grin. A heartbeat later she rushed forward and flung her spindly arms around Will's neck.

His throat tightened.

With Olivia tucked in close, he reached out and ruffled Caleb's hair. The little boy lifted his chin, the look so full of adoration Will found himself struggling for his next breath. These two beautiful, perfect children were the best thing he'd done in his thirty years of life. He would not fail them.

Letting go of his shyness, Caleb launched himself into the air and landed on top of his sister, tumbling all three of them to the ground. Will shifted midair to soften the children's fall. In the next moment the sweetest sound of all filled the air. Laughter. His children were laughing.

Will levered himself onto an elbow. Peace filled him as he watched his smiling, happy children. But he knew the moment wouldn't last long. Far too soon they would grow somber again. His poor, innocent children had faced too much sorrow in their short lives, and here was the sad result. Even if they wanted to continue their moment of playfulness, they simply didn't know how.

He couldn't bear it. Not today. "What do you say we go on an outing, just the three of us?" Even Will was surprised at the words that had come out of his mouth. But then again, why *not* go on an outing? Maybe all three of them could use a lesson in having fun.

Both children froze, their mouths gaping open at him. Caleb was the first to speak. "Truly?"

Will confirmed it with a nod. "Truly."

"Where?" the little boy asked. "Where will we go?"

"Well…" For a moment his mind went blank. He hadn't thought that far ahead.

Olivia scrambled onto his lap. "Can we go to the store?" she asked with a hopeful smile.

The store? He'd had something a little more exciting in mind. Say, fishing. He hadn't gone fishing in years. Maybe even a decade, before his father had died. "I was thinking about taking you down to the river to try some fishing."

"Oh." Olivia clasped her hands together and her tiny shoulders heaved with the force of her disappointment.

Not the reaction he'd hoped for. "You don't want to go fishing, sweetheart?"

"I'll go with you, Papa." Caleb wiggled onto Will's lap.

"Well, I suppose I could, too, if…" Olivia turned her big blue eyes in his direction, "I can get a new dolly first."

Now her earlier suggestion to go to the store made sense. His daughter was mad about dolls.

"I think a new dolly is a definite possibility." He wrapped his arms around the children, pulling each of them close against his chest. "And perhaps a toy ship for Caleb."

Caleb gasped. "Truly?"

"Truly." Will squeezed both sets of shoulders. "Now go get dressed and then we'll leave."

They sped out of the room, Caleb leading the way. Will

smiled after them, pleased by their excitement. They so rarely showed enthusiasm since their mother left.

He clenched his jaw against a jolt of ugly emotion. He tried not to give in to his anger, anger he could just as easily turn inward. Fanny might have started this, with her selfish abandonment of her family, but Will hadn't done enough to rectify the situation.

That changed today.

Chapter Five

Two. More. Days. Bridget thought she might go mad from the wait. She didn't know what to do with herself. Rose of Rose's Boardinghouse was friendly enough. She'd offered Bridget and Nora a place to stay until they discovered if Laird's house was theirs free and clear. But sitting in someone else's front parlor and sharing tea with a roomful of strangers, many also from Ireland, wasn't how Bridget wanted to spend her first full day in America.

The decor didn't help matters. The room was too ornate, the wallpaper too bold, the furniture too fragile. Taking tea in here, where she was afraid she might spill and ruin the brocade upholstery was—well, not something she wished to endure.

She decided to take a walk instead. She needed to be alone. To think. To plan. And, God forgive her, to worry. With their money running low, she and Nora would have to find jobs soon. But how many prospects were available in a town this size? Surely not many.

With nothing but her depressing thoughts to keep her company, Bridget allowed herself a moment to wallow as she made her way down the boardinghouse stairs. Five steps out she'd remembered God's faithful promise: *Never will I leave you; never will I forsake you.*

It was a good reminder. So she handed her concerns to the Lord as best she could and made her way around the tidy square. Birds sang a happy tune, the smell of fresh grass and wildflowers wafted on the air, children laughed in the distance. A horse whinnied.

Her heart was already feeling lighter. Oh, the worry was still there, working into a hard knot in the pit of her stomach, but she was able to shove it aside momentarily and focus on her new home.

What treasures awaited her here? Bridget couldn't wait to find out. She quickened her steps, and stopped at the small building on the opposite side of the church.

The general store wasn't much to look at from the outside, but it beckoned her forward all the same. Once she pushed through the door, the pleasant smell of spices and lavender filled her nose. The aroma was followed by the scent of grain and oats and—she sniffed—licorice.

There were no other customers that she could tell, only astonishing amounts of merchandise. Bridget swept her gaze across barrels of dry goods, past the sacks of flour and shelves filled with kitchen utensils, canned goods and so much more. The store seemed to have every item imaginable for sale. She noted a counter that not only had jars filled with colorful candy but all sorts of children's toys. One whole row was dedicated to an array of dolls.

Delighted, Bridget decided to start there and work her way through the rest of the store at her leisure.

Her feet slowed, hesitated, then stopped altogether. She wasn't alone in the store after all. Two small children studied the shelves of toys in complete silence. They had their backs to Bridget and were huddled close together, hands joined, bodies pressed side by side. By their size, Bridget decided they were somewhere between three and four years old.

A range of emotions sped through her, concern foremost. Their little bodies were unnaturally still as they stared upward.

Why weren't they fidgeting? Or looking for trouble? Or reaching for the toys they wanted?

Why did they seem so solemn?

The urge to gather them close and comfort them surprised Bridget, especially since she hadn't yet seen either of their faces to determine if her impressions were correct. They could simply be well-behaved children.

Where were their parents?

She looked over her shoulder. Nobody else seemed to be in the store. Concern took hold.

But then the little girl angled her head and reached up to pull one of the dolls free. Her hand fell short of its goal. The little boy whispered something in her ear then attempted to help her, but his arm was too short, as well.

Bridget couldn't stand back and watch any longer. She approached the two with slow, careful steps.

"Hello." She plucked a doll from the shelf, one with a porcelain face behind a cloud of silvery-blond hair and clothed in a lovely, pale blue dress trimmed with white. "Is this what you wanted?"

The child's eyes widened. She didn't move right away, as if afraid to touch the doll, but then she reached out and skimmed a fingertip along the sleeve.

While she carefully inspected the doll's clothing, the boy watched. Bridget took the opportunity to study both children. They had the same color hair, a soft ginger, the same striking features and the same arresting blue eyes. These two were clearly related to one another.

No, not just related. Their similar size and nearly identical features, if a bit more delicate on the girl than the boy, indicated they were twins. They were as darling and as sad as she'd suspected.

The look in their eyes captured her sympathy. This time the feeling was so strong she nearly pulled them into a comforting hug. She didn't, of course. Such a bold move might scare them.

Yet as Bridget continued looking at them she realized they reminded her of someone, someone she couldn't quite place in her mind.

She stretched the doll closer to the child. "I'm sure it'll be all right if you hold her awhile."

The girl's gaze darted over her shoulder then back again. Finally she reached out and took the doll.

At the same moment the boy took a step to his left, away from Bridget. She gave him an encouraging smile but didn't make a move in his direction.

Shifting from one foot to another, he blinked at her with large, round eyes.

Bridget lowered to her knees and placed her hands flat on her thighs. "My name is Bridget." She kept her voice soft, her tone gentle. "What's yours?"

She directed the question at both children, but the little girl chose to answer.

"I'm Olivia." She tugged on the doll's dress with tentative fingers. "And that's my brother, Caleb."

"Well, Olivia and Caleb, it's a pleasure to meet you."

"You talk funny," Caleb said, scuffing his foot back and forth on the floor in a nervous gesture.

Bridget hid a smile at the bold statement. She loved the honesty in children, how they spoke the first thing that came into their minds. There was never any doubt as to what they meant, or how they felt.

She thought of Daniel, how he'd hurt her with his change of mind and mean accusations and...

This wasn't the time to think on such things.

"Well, Caleb," she began, still smiling, "I suppose I talk funny because I'm not from around here. I just arrived in America yesterday."

"You did?"

"Oh, yes, I came over from Ireland."

His little eyes rounded even more. "Where's that?"

"All the way across the ocean." She made a grand gesture with her arm, sweeping it in a wide arc. "I sailed on a large boat, a ship called the *Annie McGee* and I—"

The front door swept open with a bang, sufficiently cutting off the rest of her words.

"Caleb, Olivia." A deep, masculine voice rang out from the front of the store. "Where are you?" There was a note of worry in the voice.

Both children's faces brightened, but they made no move to run toward the man, as Bridget would have expected. Had they come to the store without permission?

That hardly seemed likely, given their timid natures.

Well, whatever the situation, Bridget would not leave them to face their fate alone.

Reaching out, she waited for one child then the other to place their hands in hers. Only then did she rise to her full height and turn the three of them toward the front of the store as a single unit.

After the briefest of hesitations, both Olivia and then Caleb leaned in against her legs. Their tiny weight brought such a sense of completion Bridget lost her ability to breathe for a brief moment.

She'd always loved children, but this—this feeling of rightness, of being in the perfect place at the ideal time was entirely new. And thrilling, as though she'd finally come home.

"Children!" The man's hint of worry was now full of un-mistakable fear.

Yet all Bridget could think was that she knew that voice, had heard it before.

A thousand thoughts collided together in her mind. And then, as if this meeting had been destined from the beginning of time, planned by the Lord Himself, Bridget's mind grasped on to a single word swirling above the jumble in her head: *him.*

She could feel his approach, in the reverberation of his heels striking the wooden floor, each step filled with grave purpose.

He was heading her way.

But she couldn't see him yet.

And, thankfully, he couldn't see her. She needed a moment to prepare.

When the rich, masculine voice called for the children a third time, Bridget forced herself to reply. "Over here, on your right, by the toys."

The footsteps quickened.

She breathed in deeply and tightened her hold on the children. They responded in kind.

Half a heartbeat passed. And then...

He came into view. The one person Bridget hadn't been able to get out of her mind since arriving in America. William Black.

The moment his gaze connected with hers he came to a dead stop. Surprise registered in his eyes first. Then confusion. Followed by something she couldn't begin to decipher.

For several more seconds he stared at her, unmoving, not speaking.

Bridget was stuck in a similar state of shock.

Before either had a chance to recover, Olivia yanked her

hand free of Bridget's and lunged forward, her doll raised in the air. "Papa, Papa. Look what I found."

Olivia's excited words barely registered in Will's mind. He struggled to moderate his breathing and calm his thoughts. But no matter how hard he tried to focus, he couldn't fully accept that he was staring into the mesmerizing eyes of Bridget Murphy.

She was here. In Faith Glen's general store.

Holding his son's hand.

Will's stomach performed a slow, unexpected roll. Was that confusion spinning around in his gut? A sense of foreboding? Nervousness, perhaps?

"Papa. *Papa.*" Olivia tugged on his pant leg. "I'm talking to you."

Will lowered his gaze. A tiny frown creased the soft skin between Olivia's slim brows.

Sometimes, he thought with a burst of affection, his daughter could be such a serious little creature.

In an effort to calm his child's worry, or whatever had put that look on her face, he smoothed his hand over her hair. "What have you found, my darling? Show me."

"A dolly." She thrust the toy higher, a slow grin spreading across her lips. "I couldn't reach her at first. The nice lady helped me get her down from the shelf."

The nice lady. Did his daughter mean Bridget? Bridget Murphy?

Will looked up again. This time he felt an actual impact when his eyes met Bridget's. Under her soft gaze something unexpected awakened deep within him, as though a part of him had been half asleep, poised and waiting to come alive until this precise moment.

Bridget smiled. The feeling dug deeper.

"Hello, Will."

He managed a short nod. "Bridget." He could think of nothing more to say.

Needing a moment, he dropped his chin and gazed at his son. Will had never seen Caleb that at ease with a stranger. In fact, the boy was holding Bridget's hand with unmistakable confidence, as though he'd been doing so all his life.

"I see you've met my children." Will spoke past the lump in his throat.

"I have." Her gaze went blank a moment and then understanding filled her expression. The look said she'd put several missing pieces of the puzzle together in her mind. "Well, that explains it."

"Explains what, precisely?"

"Their eyes." Her voice softened. "They have your eyes."

How often had he heard that before? Too many times to count. But spoken in Bridget's soft Irish lilt, the compliment seemed to take on new meaning.

Olivia tugged on his pant leg again. "I like her, Papa."

He did, too. God help him, he liked her, too. Perhaps a bit too much. He'd been down this road before, to devastating results. Had he learned nothing from his mistakes?

Will swallowed back a wave of unease.

Unaware of his discomfort, Olivia skipped back to Bridget and took hold of her free hand.

A brief moment of silence passed. The three stood there, looking back at him with smiles on their faces. Bridget and his children looked comfortable together, happy, as if they were a family.

The sight nearly brought him to his knees.

There was no denying that Bridget Murphy, in her simple muslin dress and hair confined in a neat bun, looked the picture of a happy young mother spending the day with her children. An illusion, of course. A trick of the eye.

Again Will wondered why the woman was here in Faith Glen.

Perhaps her appearance on the scene, at this particular moment in time, was no accident, but a part of God's plan for all of them.

Is she our answer, Lord?

There was an easy way to find out. But not in front of the children. "Caleb, Olivia, have you picked out your toys yet?"

Olivia studied the blond-haired doll in her hand, looked up at Bridget, then shook her head decidedly. "I don't like this dolly anymore. I want one with brown hair—" she pointed up to Bridget "—like hers."

Although surprised, Will couldn't blame his daughter for her change in preference. Bridget had the loveliest head of hair he'd ever seen. He was sorry for the perfectly neat bun, sorrier than he should be. "Then go on and pick out a different one."

Olivia skipped off.

Caleb, however, wasn't budging from Bridget's side. He had that stubborn look on his face, the one Will knew all too well. The boy was staying put.

Before Will could decide how best to pry his son loose, Miss Murphy provided a solution of her own. "Caleb, I think I would very much enjoy a miniature boat to remind me of my trip across the ocean. Would you go pick one out for me?"

It was all the encouragement the boy needed. He rushed toward the display of toys with a promise to find her the very best one in the store.

Will's heart twisted in his chest. He hadn't seen his son that enthusiastic in a long time, maybe never.

He turned back to Bridget. She watched the children with a soft smile playing on her lips. She was really quite beautiful when she smiled like that.

The thought put Will immediately on guard.

The woman could be hiding a selfish heart behind that pleasant look. Or she could be exactly what she seemed, a lovely Irish lass worthy of his trust.

He was desperate enough to hope for the latter.

"When we met yesterday," he began, keeping his voice even, "I hadn't realized your final destination was Faith Glen."

She turned to look at him. "Nor I, you."

"You are staying with relatives?" He didn't recall any Murphys in town, but Bridget could have family living here under a different name, perhaps on her mother's side.

"No." She shook her head. "My sister and I are renting a room at Rose's Boardinghouse."

Although that didn't explain *why* she was in Faith Glen, Will nodded his understanding. "I see."

Her features suddenly shifted with concern and her cheeks turned a becoming pink. "Oh, you must think me terribly callous. I haven't yet asked you, what did you find out about your fiancée?" She touched his arm, the gesture full of compassion. "Please, tell me I was wrong about Miss Collins and that she is here in Faith Glen with you now."

As if hoping to find the woman in the store, she looked over his shoulder and scanned the immediate area behind him.

Will shoved back the despair that tried to rise within him. "Unfortunately the woman who died in the accident aboard ship was by all indications my intended." He had her baggage in his possession to prove it.

"Oh, Will." Her hand tightened on his arm. "I'm sorry for your loss."

He believed her, believed the sadness in her tone and the sympathy in her touch. Something in him, some need he hadn't known was there, wanted to rest inside all that gentle concern. If only for a moment.

He didn't dare. This wasn't about him. It had never been about him.

"Thank you for your condolences." His voice sounded as stiff as he felt. He hadn't met Bridget Collins. Her death was surreal to him. But that didn't mean he didn't feel sadness and guilt. Especially guilt.

Bridget must have sensed his shift in mood because her hand fell gently to her side. "Do your children know their new mother is de—" She cut herself off before finishing the word. "I mean, do they know Miss Collins is…gone?"

"No." He shook his head. "I thought it best not to tell them anything about her until she arrived, in case something happened on the journey over."

And something had happened, the worst possible something. Had Will not sent for Miss Collins, had he not insisted she come immediately, she might not have been in the wrong spot at the wrong time. She might still be alive today.

Forgive me, Lord, for putting the innocent woman in danger.

"Keeping your bride a secret until she arrived." Bridget's expression turned thoughtful. "That was rather wise of you."

Wise? No. He'd merely been protecting his children from the possibility of another disappointment. "Olivia and Caleb have endured enough broken promises in their short lives. I won't be responsible for adding another."

He hadn't meant to speak that plainly, regretted doing so the moment he noticed the change that came over Bridget. It was subtle, of course, and could mean anything, but she was no longer smiling.

"Would you say, then, that you are a man of your word?" She asked the question in an odd voice.

It was clear his answer mattered to her but he couldn't fathom why. "Yes. A man's word is his most valuable commodity in this life."

"I agree." Everything in her seemed to soften then, her eyes, her shoulders, even her smile. "What will you do now that you know the truth about your intended?"

He answered without hesitation. "Find another bride."

"I see."

She fell silent. As did Will. He could tell Bridget wasn't finished, though, by the way she studied him with her brows pulled together in a thoughtful expression. When she did speak again she seemed to choose her words with care. "Perhaps you should consider hiring a nanny, at least until you are able to find another bride."

"I've considered that option, but no." He gave one, decisive shake of his head. "I don't want my children getting used to someone who will eventually leave them like…" He let his words trail off.

No matter how comfortable he felt around Bridget, there were some subjects he couldn't share with her. Or anyone, for that matter. Only his mother knew the full truth behind Fanny's tragic death.

"Won't you at least consider me for the position? I have experience. Your children and I already get along. It would be a great honor to—"

"No." His tone indicated the discussion was over. His children already adored Bridget. If she took a position in his home, then changed her mind, where would that leave Olivia and Caleb? Hurt. Confused. Devastated.

The possibility of another upheaval in the twins' short lives wasn't worth the risk.

"I have considerable background as a nanny," Bridget continued. "And I could use the job. I would be willing to start immediately."

"I said no."

Her eyes widened at the vehemence in his tone. He hadn't

meant to answer so abruptly, or so harshly, but he didn't want to get anyone's hopes up, not even his own.

Bridget glanced over at Olivia and Caleb. "I don't understand why you won't consider my suggestion."

"I know. And I'm sorry." But not sorry enough to explain himself further, his secret shame was his to bear alone.

Bridget might be willing to care for his children, now, but she had no real obligation to any of them. She could suddenly change her mind. Perhaps even meet a man one day and wish to become his wife.

Although…

What if Will made a different offer than the one she'd suggested? What if he supplied her with a more permanent position in his home, one that would solve the problem of losing her to another man?

"Bridget Murphy." He captured her hand in his and held on tight. "Would you consider becoming my wife?"

Chapter Six

His wife?

William Black was asking her to marry him? With only the benefit of a two-day acquaintance? This wasn't the first time Bridget had found herself rendered speechless by this man. She doubted it would be the last.

There was more to his story. Something terrible had happened, something that had left him feeling as though he had no other choice but to hire a bride.

What Bridget didn't understand was why a man like William Black, one with many obvious qualities to recommend him, would settle only for a wife and nothing else? He had to be holding part of the story back beyond the explanation he'd already given concerning his children.

The children. Poor little Olivia and Caleb. They were so sad, so lonely.

What sort of trauma had they endured? Perhaps the trouble had something to do with their mother, as did Will's refusal to consider anything but a wife. Bridget could practically feel the tension rolling off him as he waited for her answer.

"Oh, Will. Surely, you can't be serious."

"But I am."

Bridget opened her mouth to decline his offer, politely as

possible, but he spoke over her. "You said you needed a job. What I'm offering is a much more permanent solution. I don't see the problem."

Where to start?

She stared at him, stunned by his words, but even more by the realization that part of her wanted to accept his proposal. "There are considerable problems with your request, but the first one that comes to mind is that we don't know one another."

"Most couples don't know one another on their wedding day." The way he said the words—with a clenched jaw and narrowed eyes—Bridget had to wonder what had happened in his first marriage to make him so cynical, so jaded.

Not that she didn't agree with him, at least in part. Her experience with Daniel had taught her that many men and women walked down the aisle with half their story hidden.

What had she really known of her fiancé? Not enough to predict that last, hurtful conversation with him.

A hot tingle of shame tried to steal her breath. She swallowed the sensation away.

"You said you weren't married when we met yesterday," he pointed out.

Will's tone as much as his words had her lifting her head to meet his gaze. "Yes, that's what I said."

"Has that changed?" he asked.

"No." She actually felt a smile tug at her lips. "My marital status has not changed in a day."

"Then I don't see the dilemma." He lifted a single eyebrow. "Our marriage would be a formal arrangement only, if that is what concerns you."

As though realizing he'd said quite enough, he clamped his mouth shut and waited for Bridget to speak.

Again Bridget had no idea how to respond. He offered a marriage of convenience, one in name only, as if there were no real difference between a nanny and a wife other than an exchange of vows in front of God and a handful of witnesses.

Sadly enough, had he presented his proposal in a more romantic manner, had there been hope of something more between them, at least in the future, Bridget might have been tempted to accept his offer.

Unlike Daniel, Will was a man of his word. Or so he claimed. She leaned toward believing him. She even trusted he would never hurt her intentionally. After all, his actions spoke for themselves. He'd withheld the news of his future bride from his children in case something happened. Which, of course, something had.

Bridget knew firsthand the pain that came from broken promises, the disappointment and humiliation. Will had wisely spared his children.

There was no doubt he loved Olivia and Caleb. And they adored him in return. All three of them needed someone to bring joy into their lives.

Bridget wanted to be that person. She wanted to erase those haunted expressions in their eyes, the look that never seemed to go away. But she would *not* do so as Will's wife. Ever since Daniel had left her at the altar—literally—she had promised herself only the greatest of love would induce her into matrimony. Surely she wasn't ready for that kind of love yet. Not with her heart still healing. And definitely not with a man who wanted a marriage in name only.

No. No matter how much she wanted to help this family, she could not accept Will's offer of marriage.

"I'm sorry." The words were hard to say. Bridget was not one to turn away people in need, especially children. "I simply cannot become your wife."

His jaw clenched tight. So tight, in fact, that she could see the pulse ticking in his neck.

Wanting to soothe him, Bridget reached out and touched

his arm. A jolt of awareness took hold. She quickly dropped her hand. "If you ever change your mind, I would still consider a position in your home as the children's nanny."

"No." He shook his head, his mouth a grim slash. "I won't have them grow to love you if you don't plan to stay permanently."

She had to appreciate his conviction, even if she didn't completely understand what motivated his decision. "Then I'm afraid we are at an impasse."

"So it would seem."

Bridget lowered her head again. What terrible pain had Will and his children suffered that made him want a marriage in name only? Why was he so bent on taking a wife that he would settle for nothing less?

She had no idea how to continue this strange, intimate discussion.

Thankfully, Olivia stepped into the conversational void. "Look, look, Miss Bridget, I found another dolly. And she has hair just like yours. See?"

"Well, isn't that something?" Bridget fingered the doll's pretty lavender dress, the same color as her own, then ran a hand down the brown curls that were a close match, as well.

Will reached out to the doll just as Caleb swerved past him and skidded to a stop inches short of colliding into Bridget's legs. "I found it, Miss Bridget. I found the perfect boat for you."

Smiling at the little boy's eagerness, she focused on Caleb next. In his tiny hand he held an exact eight-inch replica of the ship she'd disembarked only yesterday. The toy was made out of wood and string and had remarkably accurate detail, all the way down to the individual sails.

"Why, Caleb, that looks just like the *Annie McGee.*"

He turned it over in his hand. "Truly?"

"Oh, yes. Look. Right here—" she pointed to a spot on

the ship "—those small round white dots are windows. On a ship they're called portholes."

"Portholes," he repeated, chewing on the word a moment before turning the boat around to face her. "What's this called?"

"The wheelhouse. And this is…" She thought for a moment, decided to go simple. "The main deck."

"More," he demanded. "Show me more."

Like most boys his age, Caleb Black had an eager, inquisitive mind. He would be a joy to teach, if only his father would give her a chance. For the next few moments Bridget busied herself explaining various points of interest on the toy.

Caleb stayed alert throughout. Olivia, however, watched them with dwindling interest, the doll cradled in her arms pulling her attention away quite effectively.

As each moment passed, Bridget experienced a pang of regret. Both children were utterly charming, even in their reserve. Sensing their father's eyes on her, she turned and noted the disappointment radiating out of him, a feeling she shared.

Oh, Lord, if only…

No, there could be no *if only* in this situation. Bridget would not wed William Black, no matter how much she liked his children. Marrying a man like him, with his desire for a wife in name only, could only end in heartache for her. And for his children, as well. Possibly even for Will.

She glanced at him. His posture said it all. He'd finally accepted defeat. "Children, we should be on our way. Tell Miss Bridget goodbye."

In unison they swung to face him. Caleb spoke for them both. "But we were just starting to have fun."

"We need to check on Nene before we head out to the river."

"Nene?" Bridget asked before she could stop herself. She

usually wasn't quite so curious, but this man had asked her to become his wife. Didn't that give her certain rights?

"Nene is my mother," Will said, his tone full of quiet gravity. "Caleb gave her the name when he first started speaking."

Confused, Bridget cocked her head. "I don't understand."

"Her given name is Naomi Esther Black. She usually goes by Esther but Caleb must have heard her full name and tried to say it and—"

"Nene was what came out."

"Precisely."

A moment of understanding passed between them. And then, William Black smiled. He actually *smiled*. The gesture revealed a hidden dimple in his left cheek and Bridget's heart stuttered. She'd never met a more handsome man. For a moment she considered accepting his offer of marriage right there on the spot.

She kept her mouth firmly shut.

Farewells were said far too quickly, purchases were made for the twins, and with more sorrow than she would have expected Bridget watched the Black family troop out of the store.

At the last moment Olivia looked over her shoulder. Bridget waved. The child returned the gesture.

And then…

They were gone.

They need me. The realization slammed through her so plainly Bridget stumbled back a step. It took every ounce of willpower not to chase after them and accept Will's proposal.

Instead she took a large pull of air and went to introduce herself to the store owner.

A quarter of an hour later Bridget made her way back to the boardinghouse, her heart troubled. Hattie James, the sole proprietress of Faith Glen's general store, had been a kind, if somewhat severe older woman with iron-gray hair, weathered features and an infectious laugh. Bridget had liked the woman well enough, but her mind had been too full of William Black and his children to engage in a lengthy conversation.

If Will would just give in and accept Bridget's help, on *her* terms, maybe those children of his would smile more often.

Lord, surely something can be done.

No solution came to her, not even when she squeezed her eyes shut and prayed harder.

Head down, she rounded the last corner to the boardinghouse and nearly collided into Cameron Long.

"Oh." She reared back, nearly losing her balance. "Pardon me, Sheriff."

"My fault." Although he appeared to be leaving he changed direction and joined her on the boardinghouse's walkway, matching her step for step as they commandeered the stairs together.

Bridget couldn't help but wonder what business had brought him here on a Saturday.

Then she caught sight of Nora's face. Her sister looked very pleased with herself, happy even. Perhaps the sheriff had told her the house was theirs and they could move in right away. There was no need to travel to the County Clerk's Office after all.

For the first time since arriving in Faith Glen, Bridget let excitement settle over her. Her feet barely hit the porch as she hurried to Nora's side.

"You've had news about the house."

"Sadly, no." Nora shook her head, her gaze sweeping past Bridget a moment to land on the sheriff. She lowered her eyelashes.

"Oh." Bridget tried not to pout like an unhappy child who hadn't gotten her way.

To her surprise, when Nora lifted her head she was still smiling. "Now don't look so down, dear sister. Sheriff Long has brought other news almost as exciting."

What could possibly be as exciting as finding out they owned Laird O'Malley's house? Bridget looked from the sheriff to Nora and back again.

Neither seemed willing to take the lead in the conversation now that the subject had been broached.

"Well?" she prompted. "Won't someone tell me the news?"

"Cameron has agreed to hire one of us to cook and clean for him and his deputy on a regular basis."

Cameron was it? Nora was on a first-name basis with the sheriff already? How…intriguing.

And completely beside the point.

Bridget smoothed her hands down her skirt, unsure why she wasn't more pleased by this new bit of information. Perhaps she was still sad over the situation with Will and his children. If matters had gone her way Bridget would be bearing good news, as well.

Nevertheless with their money draining away faster than expected due to their boardinghouse stay, this job offer was a blessing, an answer to prayer. "That's very kind of you, Sheriff."

"Not so kind." He shrugged off her compliment, looking oddly embarrassed. "More like selfish. My deputy and I have been sharing the duties these past few years, to disastrous results. It's a wonder one of us hasn't killed the other."

He smiled, as though he'd told a rather funny joke.

Bridget couldn't help but smile back.

"The duties would include cleaning the living quarters and jail cells, as well as feeding any prisoners that might spend the night behind bars. Of course that's a rare occurrence," he said when Nora gasped. "There's a no-saloon ordinance and a strong Christian presence in Faith Glen. We're a peaceful community."

Bridget had already come to that conclusion after her walk this morning. But she was happy to hear her assumptions confirmed from the sheriff's own mouth.

"I'll pay a fair salary." The number he mentioned was more than fair. "But the hours will be long, sunrise to sunset."

"That's only to be expected," Bridget said, chewing on the information.

As wonderful as the offer was she had one main concern: the sweet bundle sleeping peacefully in the bassinet beside Nora.

If Will decided to change his mind and hired Bridget as his children's nanny—*oh, please, Lord*—she wasn't sure the offer would include Grace, as well. And even if it did, Nora would never give up the child for any great length of time. She'd grown uncommonly attached.

Under the circumstances it was best to make certain the matter was settled before her sister's first day of work. "Would Nora be able to bring baby Grace with her?"

The sheriff stared at her as though he didn't understand the question.

Nora looked at her with the same glazed expression in her eyes.

Bridget glanced from one to the other, wondering at their odd reaction to a simple question. Was she missing something? Had she struck some unknown point of contention between them?

Seconds ticked by. Neither Nora nor Sheriff Long would look at one another. Or Bridget for that matter.

What had happened while she'd been at the general store?

"Nora?"

Her sister moved a small step away from the sheriff,

enough to make her point without appearing rude. "I was thinking you would take the job."

"Me?" Bridget didn't bother hiding her surprise. "But you're the better cook."

"You are competent, as well."

Competent, yes, while Nora was exceptional. The sheriff and his deputy deserved the best cook possible. After all, they were the reason this peaceful community was, well, peaceful.

"Bridget, we have to consider what's best for the baby. Considering all she's been through, Grace—"

"Can come with you during the day," Cameron Long said, putting an end to the rest of Nora's argument.

Before either could change their minds, Bridget spoke first. "Then it's settled. Nora will start Tuesday." The day after they met with the county clerk and discovered the truth about Laird's house—*their* house.

"That'll be fine." The sheriff stuffed his hat on his head. "I'll see you both bright and early Monday morning."

He turned and started down the steps.

Bridget called after his retreating back. "Sheriff, wait."

He paused, but didn't turn around right away.

"Won't you consider showing us the house today?"

At that bold statement he turned slowly around, his movements precise, his expression hidden under his hat.

"There's a lot of day left," she persisted, deciding she had little to lose at this point. "Surely, there would be no harm in us taking a brief look at the house."

For a moment he seemed to debate silently with himself. Bridget shared a look with Nora. Neither dared break the silence, in case the man was using the time to rethink his earlier decision.

"Ordinarily I would agree with you." He thrust out a heavy sigh. "But there's an elderly couple in residence who've been acting as caretakers for the past seven years. For all intents and purposes, Laird's house is their home now. They have no place else to go."

Bridget gasped at the implication she heard in his words, finally understanding the man's reticence and yet offended all the same. "We would never throw an elderly couple off our property."

The Murphy sisters knew better than most what it meant to be tossed off land they'd considered their home. In their case, back in Ireland, it had been simply because the landlord decided to offer the tiny piece of property to his own kin. To suggest they would do the same was woefully incorrect.

"You go too far, Sheriff Long," Nora added, returning to the formal address as if to make a point. "We would certainly allow this couple to stay on as long as they wish, indefinitely if need be."

"That's good to know." He seemed relieved, even as his gaze darted from Nora to Bridget and back again. "But I still recommend you verify ownership before you undertake the half-mile journey to the house."

As was true the first time they'd had this conversation, Bridget sensed the sheriff was withholding information, something more than this business with the elderly caretakers, something to do with the house itself.

A sliver of panic sliced through her. Nora must have had a similar reaction because she straightened her spine even further. "What are you hiding from us, Sheriff?"

He bristled at her tone, or perhaps the overly formal use of his title. "Now don't go getting all high and mighty on me, Nora Murphy. I'm only trying to save you both added grief. At the moment the house isn't, shall we say, presentable."

Bridget didn't like the sound of that. How bad could it be? Apparently bad enough that he felt the need to warn them.

She refused to be daunted. They'd survived the potato

famine and being thrown off the land they'd called home all their lives. They could handle a house not quite presentable, especially if it was *their* house.

"Sheriff Long, please," Bridget pleaded. "We would like to see the house and decide for ourselves what sort of condition it is in."

"I see I cannot dissuade either of you." He whipped off his hat and speared his fingers through his hair. "If you insist—"

"We do."

"Then I'll take you over tomorrow, after the church service has let out."

Bridget clasped her hands together, her spirits lifting by the second. "That would be lovely."

"Yes," Nora agreed, her shoulders relaxing ever-so-slightly. "Yes, it would."

"If I were you—" he crammed his hat back on his head "—I'd hold off your excitement until you see the place."

With that simple warning Bridget knew, knew for sure, that there was something dreadfully wrong with the house. And yet, her excitement remained. If the elderly caretakers still lived there, then the structure was at least habitable.

At the moment that was good enough for her.

Chapter Seven

Will strode along the lane with two cautiously excited children in tow. His sad, despondent twins of mere hours before had lightened somehow. The solemness from before wasn't entirely gone, but now it seemed to be mingled with hope. All because of a short visit to the general store and a fortuitous meeting with a beautiful young woman.

Relief, joy, disappointment…he hadn't known it was possible to experience this many conflicting emotions all at once. Uncomfortable with the sensation, he shoved every unwanted feeling aside and focused on his children. His *happy* children, he noted.

Olivia was walking sedately, but she was smiling broadly, her new doll clutched desperately against her heart. Caleb's expression was more serious, but he darted around her, bobbing his ship in the air as though the tiny boat rode a series of invisible waves. The toy was identical to the one he'd found for Bridget.

Neither child appeared to notice the suffocating, thick heat. They were too contented.

Will wiped at the sweat on his brow and looked back over his shoulder, wondering where the pretty Irish lass was now.

Bridget Murphy had accomplished a task no one had been

able to do in over a year. She'd made his children smile with genuine pleasure on their faces.

Was it any wonder he'd asked her to marry him?

He'd acted rashly, he knew, and contemplated his own behavior with a slice of concern now that he had a moment to think clearly. The instant his eyes had landed on Bridget at the store he'd discovered the pull of attraction between them was still there, stronger than before, tugging at a hidden place deep within him that had whispered: *she's the one you've been searching for.*

His throat tightened with emotion. There was no denying she was beautiful, soft-spoken and outwardly kind. But Fanny had been all of those things when he'd first met her, too. In his wife's case, the facade of a sweet, untouched innocent had been a lie. Consequently she'd taught him never to trust a first impression, or a second or even a third.

Like Fanny, Bridget could be hiding unseemly qualities below that pretty, engaging surface of hers.

His steps faltered.

When had he become so cynical, so jaded? Had he missed all the signs of a good, honest, trustworthy woman because he'd been expecting to find a dishonest one?

Unhappy with all this introspection—Will hated introspection—he drew in a deep, slow, steadying breath and swerved around a branch on the pathway.

Stick to his original plan; that was what he must do. All he really needed in a wife was a woman who would be good to his children.

Bridget has been that, and more.

Will shoved aside the thought. She had refused his proposal and that was the end of the matter. He would start his search for another bride first thing Monday morning.

For now he would enjoy the day with his children.

After rounding the final corner to their home, the twins

raced up the stairs leading to the front door. Caleb rushed ahead of Olivia.

"Nene! Come see what Papa bought me." The little boy shouted in a high-pitched, excited voice, his words tumbling over one another. "It's a ship. And Olivia has her very own dolly with brown hair. Brown hair!"

"Well, honestly, I've never heard so much yelling in all my life." Will's mother entered the hallway, her feet shuffling slowly across the wooden floor in the way she did when her hip was bothering her. "What's all this excitement about?"

Shutting the door with a soft click, Will turned and studied his mother more closely. She appeared tired, more so than she had earlier, even with the added rest he'd provided her this morning.

He started to ask her how she was feeling, when Olivia skirted past him.

"Look, Nene." Her words flowed just as quickly out of her mouth as her brother's had. "Look at my new dolly. Isn't she pretty?"

The little girl planted a tender kiss on the porcelain cheek then thrust the doll in the air toward her grandmother.

Will's mother made a grand show of studying the toy carefully. "Oh, my, yes. She's very pretty. I especially like her long, curly, *brown* hair."

The color choice was significant. Until today, Olivia had chosen only blonde dolls for her private collection. It was clear Bridget Murphy had made an impression on his daughter. Will wasn't sure how he felt about that.

"She's not as pretty as Miss Bridget," Olivia added as she fingered the doll's hair. "But close."

"Miss Bridget? As in, Bridget…" His mother swept her shocked gaze up to Will. "Collins? Was there some mistake, and she's still ali—"

"No." Will gave a brief but fierce shake of his head, the

gesture a silent warning to hold back the rest of her questions until they were alone. "The twins met Bridget Murphy."

He put considerable emphasis on the last name, willing his mother to understand that the woman the twins had met today was not the same one he'd intended to wed.

"You met *another* Bridget?" Her voice sounded incredulous.

Will lifted a shoulder. "It's a common Irish name."

"Is it?"

Will nodded, trying not to react to the reservation he saw in his mother's eyes. From the start Esther Black had been privy to every aspect of his search for a mail-order bride. She hadn't entirely approved, she'd made that clear enough, but after what Fanny had put them all through she'd understood.

Or so she'd claimed.

When he'd come home alone the night before, she had been full of sympathy, accepting his brief, pained explanation without pressing for details.

"Am I to assume that this Bridget…*Murphy* lives here in Faith Glen?" She angled her head at a curious tilt.

"It would appear so." Will looked everywhere but directly in his mother's gaze.

"I have never heard of her," she said.

"That's because she arrived on the *Annie McGee* just yesterday."

"The *Annie McGee*?" She obviously recognized the name. "How very…interesting."

It was a mistake, Will knew, to look straight into his mother's eyes, but he did so anyway. If only to prove he had nothing to hide. Which, of course, he didn't. The fact that he'd met a young woman named Bridget, who'd traveled to America on the very boat his intended bride had boarded, was simply a strange, unexpected coincidence.

Nothing more.

"William Black." She planted a fist on her hip. "You mean to tell me—"

"Yes, mother." He cut her off midsentence. "The children and I met a woman named Bridget in the general store this afternoon. And, yes, she traveled to America from Ireland on—" he gritted his teeth *"—The. Annie. McGee."*

She considered him a moment. "But she is not the woman you—"

"She is not." He didn't explain any further, not with Olivia and Caleb staring at him with large, rounded eyes and poised ears.

His mother must have noticed the children's interest because all she said was, *"Well."*

His sentiments exactly.

He hoped that was the end of the matter. He should have known better.

"And what, may I ask, brought this other Bridget to Faith Glen?"

"I don't know." As soon as the words left his mouth, Will was reminded again that he'd acted rashly today, dangerously so. He'd proposed marriage to a woman he hardly knew and hadn't bothered to acquire the most basic particulars of her life. Such as why she'd traveled all the way across the Atlantic only to land in Faith Glen, Massachusetts.

Was her presence a coincidence, as he'd thought earlier? Or God's providence?

He didn't know.

One thing was for certain. He should have asked Bridget about herself. Not because it would have been the polite thing to do—although that was certainly part of it—but because whatever had led her to settle in their small town might have given him a clue to her character.

She might be harboring a bitter secret, or running from a terrible scandal, though he doubted either scenario. The woman hadn't shown any signs of deceit. And he knew them all.

Suddenly Will was seized with a desire to learn every detail about Bridget Murphy, small and large. He wanted to know her hopes, her dreams. What she liked to do for fun. The titles of her favorite books. Did she have a strong faith in God? Did she trust the Lord to guide her daily path? Would she—

He cut off the rest of his thoughts, reminding himself Bridget's life was none of his concern. He had more important matters in which to attend, like finding a woman to care for his children on a permanent basis. A woman willing to accept a marriage in name only.

That didn't mean he couldn't assuage his curiosity about Bridget Murphy. As the largest employer in the area, he liked to know all the citizens of his community.

Faith Glen was a small town. It wouldn't be hard to locate her again, even easier to discover what had brought her to America in the first place.

He knew exactly where to start.

Cameron Long, the local sheriff and a good friend of Will's, made it his business to meet all the newcomers in town. After church tomorrow, Will would make a trip to the jailhouse. And find out exactly what sort of woman Bridget Murphy was under that sweet, pleasant exterior.

The next morning Bridget eyed Faith Glen's only church from the bottom of the perfectly measured steps. Situated directly across the town square from the jailhouse, the white clapboard structure with its tall steeple and thin iron cross on top rose majestically under the clear azure sky.

The building practically glowed beneath the sun's warm rays, beckoning Bridget forward. She climbed the first stair without hesitation, her gaze darting from left to right, right

to left. Rows of square windows lined both sides of the wide
double doors. Sunlight polished the glass into clear, sparkling
diamonds.

Cradling a sleeping baby Grace in her arms, Nora matched
her step for step. It was a shame Flynn and Maeve had sent
their regrets and wouldn't be able to make a trip to Faith Glen
for a few more days. Bridget understood why. Flynn's home
was close by in Boston, yes, but they were newlyweds. They
deserved time alone, just the two of them, while Bridget and
Nora needed to get on with their own lives here in Faith Glen.

The moment they entered the church all heads turned
in their direction. Although the attention was unnerving,
Bridget had expected this blatant interest. She and Nora were
strangers in town. But that wouldn't be true for long. Bridget
would work hard at making friends here. Not only because
she liked meeting new people, but because Faith Glen was
her home now.

The Lord had guided them here, had protected them
throughout the journey across the ocean. Bridget had to trust
all would turn out well, if not exactly as they had planned.

She lifted up a silent prayer for courage, moved deeper
into the building and set out down the center aisle ahead of
Nora. Refusing to be intimidated by the undisguised curiosity, Bridget smiled at several individuals along the way.
Thankfully all returned the gesture.

We're a peaceful community. The sheriff's words echoed
in her mind, providing the courage she'd prayed for moments
before.

Still smiling, Bridget took another step and stopped as two
tiny voices shouted her name in unison.

"Miss Bridget," they squealed in unified delight. "Over
here. Look, we're over here."

Turning her head slightly to her right, she caught sight of
Caleb and Olivia Black two pews up. Dressed in their Sunday

best, their hair combed and eyes shining, they waved in her direction.

Bridget waved back and then took note of the only other occupant in their pew. The children's father. William Black. Or rather, Will. His gaze locked with hers and for a moment everything stopped.

Bridget blinked, her mouth opened then closed. The man's eyes were as remarkable as she remembered, the color still the same pure blue as a cloudless sky.

Holding her steady in his gaze, he smiled.

Something deep within her, some part of her that had been filled with tension since boarding the *Annie McGee* simply... let...go. Her shoulders relaxed. Her face warmed.

She quickly looked away.

"Miss Bridget," Caleb said her name in a hissed "whisper" that was nearly as loud as a shout. "Come sit with us."

"I take it you know those children?" Nora's surprise was evident in her tone.

"I met them in the general store when I went for a walk yesterday." Bridget didn't expand. Not now, not here. Someone could overhear and come to the wrong conclusion.

"That man sitting beside them," Nora said in a hushed whisper. "He looks familiar."

"It's William Black, from the docks in Boston. Remember, he was looking for his...bride."

Nora's eyes narrowed. "He's smiling at you."

"At *us*," Bridget corrected her. "He's smiling at us."

"Well, then." Nora readjusted her hold on Grace. "I say it's time for a proper introduction."

"Of course." Bridget continued to the pew where the Black family sat.

"Hello," she began. "Isn't this is a happy coincidence?"

She smiled at the children first then looked up at Will.

He'd already risen to his feet and was staring at her with such a compelling gaze her breath hitched in her throat.

"Bridget. I mean…" Will cleared his throat and glanced at Nora. "Miss Murphy. It's a pleasure to see you again."

"And you, as well." She swallowed back her expanding nerves. "This is my sister Nora. Nora, this is William Black and his children, Olivia and Caleb."

"Oh!" Olivia gasped in delight when she caught sight of the bundle in Nora's arms. "You have a baby, too. Mine's sleeping." She rocked her dolly back and forth to prove her point.

"Mine is, too." Nora laughed softly. "Her name is Grace."

"I named my baby Bridget." Olivia's face practically glowed as she turned to smile at her doll's namesake.

Bridget's heart filled with warmth and affection.

Nora shot a look in her direction, the lift of a single eyebrow indicating that explanations would be in order once they were alone.

Bridget suppressed a sigh, knowing full well she was in for another lecture, one that would surely include a list of the various complications that could arise when a person kept secrets from their older sister.

"Please, ladies, won't you join us for the service."

The invitation came from Will. There was a look of urgency in his eyes Bridget had missed earlier. A gasp worked its way up her throat and stalled. Had something happened since they'd last seen one another?

"We'd be delighted to join you," Nora answered for them both.

There was a moment of jostling and organizing and arguing among the children over who would stand next to Bridget. In the end neither did so. Olivia ended up beside Nora. Caleb settled on Will's right, while Bridget ended up on his left in the middle of the pew.

Olivia proceeded to pay homage to Grace while Caleb plopped onto the floor with his toy boat in hand. Will opened a hymnal, shifting until Bridget could see the page, as well.

As if on cue, the first strains of organ music wafted through the air. Although Will concentrated on the book in his hand, Bridget could feel his attention solely on her, as if he had something important he needed to say to her. She briefly wondered what had happened and why she wasn't more uncomfortable standing this close to him. He smelled of soap and pine. She took a deep breath, leaned in closer and promptly began singing the selected hymn.

Peace enveloped her.

The song rolled off Will's tongue in a clear, perfectly pitched baritone. Bridget's voice joined with his in flawless harmony, as though they'd been singing together all their lives.

Against her best efforts to stay focused on the song, her thoughts turned fanciful. She imagined her and Will, together, sharing their love of music with their children. Five of them, to be exact. Olivia, Caleb, another set of twins, both of them girls, a smaller boy. They would…they would…

She shook away the image, shocked at the direction of her thoughts. Had she learned nothing in the past year? She needed to guard her heart, to hold a portion of herself back, or she'd risk another heartache.

Out of the corner of her eye she glanced at Will, only to discover he was watching her in the same covert manner. Despite the tension she felt in him, something quite nice passed between them, a feeling that instilled utter contentment.

She swallowed a flash of misgiving and kept singing.

Halfway through the second hymn another person joined them in the pew, a man, his lean, muscular frame sending everyone a few steps to their right. Bridget couldn't fully see the newcomer around Nora's hat. But from her sister's quick intake of air she had a good idea who the man might be.

Sheriff Cameron Long had joined them. Bridget hadn't pegged him for the churchgoing type. She suspected Nora was the reason for his appearance, and that her sister was secretly pleased by this turn of events. Of course she would never admit to such a thing to Bridget. Maybe not even to herself.

The singing came to an end. There was another round of jostling for position. This time Caleb landed on Bridget's lap, his little cheek pressed against her shoulder. Olivia climbed over the lot of them until she settled in an identical position in her father's arms.

Bridget and Will shared a smile over his children's heads. She had to breathe in hard to gather a proper amount of air in her lungs. Truly, William Black should smile more often.

As the preacher made his way to the pulpit, Will leaned forward and inclined his head toward the additional member of their tiny group. "Cam, nice to see you here this morning." There was a hint of irony in his voice.

The sheriff grinned. "Never say never."

There was no more time for conversation before the preacher took his place. He was exactly what Bridget would have expected of an American pastor. Tall, scarecrow-thin, with gray, thinning hair, he was an ordinary-looking fellow with somewhat angular features.

His voice was surprisingly pleasant. Low, soft and compelling. Within moments Bridget found herself riveted by his every word.

When he quoted Hebrews 11:1, she sat up straighter. She'd memorized the verse back in Ireland and had recited it to herself throughout the sea voyage.

Now faith is the substance of things hoped for, the evidence of things not seen, she repeated in her mind.

She listened intently to the rest of the sermon. When making a particular point, the preacher would lower his voice. The entire congregation leaned forward, hungry for whatever bit of wisdom he was about to impart. The whole experience was quite dramatic.

Bridget slipped a quick glance in Will's direction. He appeared to be listening as intently as everyone else. It comforted her to know he took the sermon seriously.

Olivia, far too young to pay attention, spent the time quietly grooming her doll's hair. She twisted the strands into a long, messy braid that would surely end up in need of a drastic untangling. Would Will's mother's elderly fingers be able to accomplish the task?

Where was his mother, anyway? Was she sitting with friends? Had she come at all? Bridget searched the church, but had no idea what the woman looked like.

Comforted by the preacher's voice, Caleb grew heavy in her arms. She tightened her hold to keep him from slipping off her lap.

"Where there is no risk, there is no faith," the preacher said in a low, convicted voice. "Throughout the coming week I want you to consider the one thing that has been weighing heavy on your heart. And then ask yourself this question." He paused for effect. "What if I trusted this to the Lord?"

Bridget immediately thought about the deed to the house and wondered whether or not it would turn out to be legal. Would worrying make a difference in the final outcome? Of course it wouldn't.

Her mind turned to the man sitting by her side and his troubling situation. His intended bride was dead. His children were without a mother. Unable to stop herself, she risked a glance in his direction.

He appeared deep in thought. Had the sermon hit him as

it had her? With all the talk about faith and trusting the Lord would he be more open to hiring her as his children's nanny?

Dare she hope?

Oh, Lord, please—

"Let us pray." The preacher bowed his head.

Bridget closed her eyes. She desperately wanted the courage to trust the Lord in all things, especially the situation with the house and Will and his darling children and—

Organ music broke through her thoughts. Caleb hopped off her lap. Olivia immediately followed. The rest of the congregation stood more slowly and proceeded to sing the closing hymn.

All too quickly the service was over and people began filing out of the church. Several cast looks in Bridget and Nora's direction, but none stopped to speak to any of them. She supposed that was to be expected.

Once the way was clear, Sheriff Long moved out into the aisle then stepped back and motioned everyone to go on ahead of him.

The children scrambled out first then surrounded Nora and baby Grace once she made her way into the empty aisle, as well. Cameron Long stood slightly apart from the commotion and watched the interaction with a guarded, almost sad look on his face.

Before Bridget could contemplate his strange reaction, Will's voice washed over her. "Bridget, if you would be so kind, I'd like a word with you in private."

"Oh?" She spun around to face him. "I… Now?"

He touched her hand and a quiet intensity filled his gaze. "It's important."

She angled her head at him, trying desperately to read his expression.

He lowered his voice. "It concerns what we discussed in the general store yesterday."

A surge of apprehension raced through her. Was he about to make her another offer of marriage? This time with a bit more romance? If so, would she accept?

No. Of course she wouldn't. What did it matter how he approached the subject of matrimony? She'd made her wishes very clear when last they'd met, as he had made his. She would not enter a marriage of convenience, no matter what Will said or how he asked.

Surely, he knew all this.

Didn't he?

Chapter Eight

Seconds ticked by and Bridget wondered why Will wasn't speaking.

Get on with it, she nearly shouted at him. Perhaps he was waiting until the children were out of earshot. With that in mind, she made eye contact with Nora, gave a meaningful look at the twins and then angled her head in Will's direction.

Understanding the silent message, Nora steered Olivia and Caleb farther down the aisle, toward Cameron Long. Shoulders tense, lips flattened, he politely gave the twins his undivided attention. The poor man looked slightly uncomfortable, but he was making a gallant effort at hiding his reaction.

With the children occupied, Bridget turned back to Will.

The look of urgency was back in his eyes. "Will?"

"Something has occurred since we spoke yesterday, something that makes it imperative I reopen our previous discussion."

Not sure what she heard in his tone—worry, apprehension, despair?—she braided her fingers together and told herself not to panic, not to jump to conclusions. Patience was the key in situations such as these.

"You see, my mother, she has…" His words trailed off and for an instant he looked slightly helpless.

Bridget gasped. "Is she hurt? Has she been injured?"

"Nothing like that."

"Praise God."

"Yes." He blinked. "But I'm afraid she is not entirely well, either. I'm no doctor but if I had to give a diagnosis I'd say she's suffering from a case of exhaustion."

His concerned expression told Bridget what she'd already determined for herself. This man cared deeply for his family.

"My mother missed church today," he continued, his eyes filling with world-weariness. "It's the first time since my father passed."

"Oh, Will. I am sorry." Bridget reached out to him, but realizing where they were she dropped her hand before she made contact with his arm. "Has she seen a doctor?"

He shook his head. "Not yet."

An idea formulated in her mind. "I could ask Flynn to examine your mother. He is very good, very kind. He would know what to do for her."

His eyes narrowed. "Who is Flynn?"

"Flynn Gallagher," she said. When the name still didn't seem to register, she added, "The ship's doctor you met in Boston. He is my brother-in-law."

Will looked down at her with a thoughtful expression, as if he were untangling several details in his mind. "The woman who'd accompanied us in the infirmary," he said. "She is your…sister?"

"Yes, her name is Maeve."

"Maeve." He digested this a moment, then nodded. "Right, I remember now."

Bridget waited for him to continue.

"I…" He shoved a hand through his hair. "My mother is stubborn. She doesn't want to admit she isn't well. But if she is not better soon, I will insist she see a doctor."

Bridget wanted to push the matter, wanted to do whatever

she could to help, but she'd interfered enough. This wasn't her family, or her concern. At least that's what everyone kept telling her.

Nevertheless she wasn't one to walk away from anyone in need. And by the look of concern on Will's face the man was clearly in need.

"If it is agreeable with you," she began, "I would like to inform Flynn of the situation. Perhaps he could give advice without having to meet your mother."

Letting out a breath that wasn't entirely steady, he inclined his head. "Perhaps. In the meantime—" he cleared his throat blinked once, twice "—I find it necessary to do what I can to relieve my mother's daily burden."

"That is perfectly understandable," Bridget agreed.

He cleared his throat again. "Would you reconsider the offer I made to you yesterday?"

Bridget shook her head. "I'm sorry, no."

He paused, one beat, two. On the third he blew out a slow breath of air then nodded in resignation. Despite his hesitation, her answer didn't seem to surprise him. "Would you consider becoming—" he grimaced "—my children's nanny?"

At last. *At last,* Bridget thought. The man was willing to make a compromise. He was putting aside his own preferences for his mother's sake. That said a lot about his character, as well as his love for his mother.

Bridget wanted to help him. She wanted to honor this man's leap of faith with one of her own. They could work out the particulars in time.

Then what was stopping her? Why wasn't she saying yes?

Will did not like the look of indecision he saw on Bridget's face. Nor was he overly fond of the way she continued to hold to her silence long after he'd relented and asked her to become his children's nanny instead of his wife.

The arrangement had been her idea. Why wasn't she agreeing on the spot?

Finally, she broke her silence. "I'm not sure I understand. I thought you wanted a more permanent solution."

"I do. But with my mother's current health situation I don't have time to send away for another bride. I see how you are with my children, and they with you." He swallowed. "They haven't had much to smile about in the past year. But with you they seem quite…happy." He had to believe that was a good sign.

"And you'd be willing to risk me leaving them, sometime in the future, whenever that might be?"

What other choice did he have? His mother had looked beyond exhausted this morning, more than usual. At this rate he feared she wouldn't last the months it would take him to make arrangements for another mail-order bride. If she wasn't better in a few days he would send for the doctor.

"Yes, Bridget," he said her name with conviction, knowing he could no longer jeopardize his mother's health. "I am willing to take that risk."

She fell silent again, pressing her mouth into a flat line of concentration. Her gaze landed on the twins and a sigh slipped past her tight lips. "I do adore them."

Although he already knew that, hearing her say the words brought a wave of relief. "Then you will become their nanny?"

"On one condition."

He would give her whatever she wanted. Money. Gratitude. "Anything."

"I will accept the position only on a trial basis."

"A trial basis?" He didn't like the sound of that.

"Yes." She nodded her head firmly, as though she'd made

up her mind and that was the end of the discussion. "You will allow me to work for you for one full week. At the end of that time we will reevaluate the situation, before the children become overly attached."

It was a solid enough plan, except for one major flaw. The twins were already half in love with the woman. One week in her company would probably send them over the edge. They would end up devastated if she left them, even after only a week.

The answer to the problem was simple. He would give Bridget no cause to leave them. "Agreed."

She smiled and his heart picked up speed, making him feel as though he were running a race with no end in sight.

"Can you begin tomorrow?"

She opened her mouth to respond, then shut it just as quickly. "Wait here a moment."

He gave her retreating back a nod.

She hurried out of the pew and approached her sister, pulling her slightly away from Cam and the children. The two women whispered together for several moments. Will took the opportunity to study Bridget in greater detail. She'd donned the same dress she'd worn the first day they met, a striking concoction with ruffles and gold ribbon streamers at the elbows. She'd pinned her hair on top of her head and, as always, several long tendrils had already escaped.

Her hair really was quite glorious. It was no wonder Olivia had chosen a doll with the same color.

Unaware of his inspection, Bridget called Cam over next. Her sister returned to the twins. More whispering ensued. Cam nodded a few times, then touched her arm and smiled reassuringly.

Seeing the ease in which the two conversed, something dark and ugly swept through Will. With their heads bent close together, Cam and Bridget looked completely in tune with one another.

An ugly memory surfaced. Will remembered the way Fanny had been with other men, one in particular. He remembered her outrageous flirting, the way she'd—

No. Will stopped his train of thought abruptly. Bridget was not Fanny. Cam was not that other man. All signs pointed to the fact that the pretty Irish immigrant was a woman of integrity. Although, she was rather friendly with Cam. And they were both unattached.

Perhaps a one-week trial was a good idea, after all. Will could use the time to ferret out Bridget's true intentions. If she turned out to be just like Fanny, he would send her packing.

If she was nothing like his dead wife, then he would…he would…

See what came next.

He narrowed his eyes, wondering what was taking so long. What was she discussing so secretively with Cam?

Bridget eventually stepped away from the other man, spoke to Olivia and Caleb a moment then approached Will once again.

"Yes." She gave him a winning smile. "I can start tomorrow morning."

Relief spread through him, the emotion so strong it threw him back a step. He swallowed, hard, and focused on calming his raging pulse before speaking again. "Excellent." He rattled off his address.

She smiled.

"And where are you living?" At her lifted eyebrow, he explained, "I ask so I can make arrangements to pick you up in the morning."

"Not to worry." She looked over her shoulder, her smile

still firmly in place. "Sheriff Long has agreed to drop me off on his way out of town."

The dark emotion he'd suppressed earlier spread through Will again. *One week,* he reminded himself. He had one full week to discover if Bridget Murphy was a woman he could trust around his children. "Then it's settled."

"Lovely." She clasped her hands tightly together.

Unable to stop himself, he touched her braided fingers. "Thank you, Bridget."

"You're welcome, Will." She held his gaze a moment. "Do you wish to tell the children about our arrangement, or may I?"

He hadn't thought that far ahead. He was still trying to process the fact that this woman would be in his home, everyday, helping to raise his children. Not as their mother, he reminded himself, but as their nanny. "You may do the honors."

Her eyes brightened and before two complete heartbeats passed she was stooping in front of Caleb and Olivia. After a brief conversation, the children squealed in delight and then launched themselves into Bridget's outstretched arms. Laughing, she hugged them tightly to her.

In that moment Will knew he'd made the right decision— for his children.

But what about for himself? Had he just made the biggest mistake of his life, hiring a woman he knew so little about? Or would this turn out to be the best decision he'd ever made?

At this point only the Lord knew for sure.

William Black left with his children soon after the hugging and smiling and laughing subsided, with the understandable excuse that he needed to check on his mother. Bridget watched their departure, tossing waves to the children and then staring after them long past the time they'd disappeared around the corner.

"The twins are darling," Nora said from behind her.

"Yes, they are."

Coming around to face her, Nora studied her.

Bridget knew that look in her sister's eyes. "Speak, Nora. Just say whatever it is you have on your mind."

"All right. I will. Are you certain you want to work for William Black? He seems rather…severe."

Severe? Yes, perhaps he was. But today Bridget had gained a bit more insight into what drove the man. Not only did he love his family, his concern for them took precedence over his own preferences.

A wistful ache pulsed through her. What would it be like to have a man care for her so completely, so sacrificially? Daniel had always been more concerned with appearances than Bridget herself. Why hadn't she realized that sooner?

"If Will seems severe," she said in his defense, "it's because he's worried about his children." She decided to keep his mother's health crisis to herself for now. At least until she consulted Flynn. "I want this job, Nora. Truly, I do."

Her sister didn't appear entirely convinced. "If you are certain."

"I am." Bridget quickly changed the subject. "Oh, Nora, just think. We're to get our first glimpse of our new home this afternoon."

The house was theirs, she told herself firmly. She wouldn't allow herself to think otherwise. Determining the legality of the deed was only a formality.

Smiling at last, Nora ran the tip of her finger over Grace's cheek. The baby cooed softly in return. "It's all rather exciting, isn't it?"

"Oh, aye, it is."

They made their way down the church steps just as Cameron Long broke away from a young couple and ambled toward them.

"Well, ladies. I'm at your disposal for the rest of the day." He swept the hat off his head and bowed grandly. The gentlemanly gesture encompassed both of them, but his eyes kept straying to Nora. "Do you want to head to the house now, or later this afternoon?"

"Now," they chimed as one.

"Right, then." His lips curved in a lopsided grin. "Follow me."

He guided them toward a rickety wagon with an empty flatbed in the back. He apologized for the rustic accommodations, explaining that the three of them would have to share the lone seat up front. "It might be a bit cramped," he warned.

"It'll be fine," Bridget said for them both, not wanting to give him any reason to change his mind.

Once they were settled on the hard seat, Nora and baby Grace first, then Bridget, the sheriff rounded the wagon and climbed on board, as well. A series of creaks and groans met the additional weight. Shifting forward, he released the brake. A flick of his wrist and they were off.

"If you ladies don't mind," he said, "I need to stop by the jail before we head out of town."

The request sent a wave of impatience sweeping through Bridget, one she firmly clapped into submission. What was one more delay at this point in their journey?

Thankfully the trek around the square took no time at all.

"Hey, Ben," the sheriff called as he drew the wagon to a halt, gruff affection in his voice. "Get out here, you old coot, and meet Faith Glen's newest residents."

"I'm coming. I'm coming." The door to the jailhouse swung open and an older gentleman sauntered onto the planked sidewalk. He had a pleasant, ruddy complexion, a full shock of white hair and wore a badge clipped to his chest.

Bridget guessed him to be in his late sixties and immediately noted how his dark brown eyes gleamed with mischief and good humor.

"Don't tell me these lovely young women are the Murphy sisters." He spoke with a pleasant, if somewhat thick Irish accent. The familiar brogue reminded Bridget of home.

Nostalgia tried to overwhelm her, a sensation that felt as bittersweet as it did unexpected. Oh, how she missed the people of Castleville and the comfort that came from relationships built over a lifetime.

Refusing to allow her melancholy to ruin this special day, Bridget blinked away the memories and forced a smile on her face. This was not a time for looking back, but for focusing on what lay ahead.

"Ben." Cameron Long jumped to the ground and slapped the man on the back. "Meet Nora and Bridget Murphy. Ladies, this is Ben MacDuff, the former sheriff of Faith Glen and now my acting deputy."

Without waiting for any of them to respond, he disappeared around the corner of the building with a cryptic explanation of needing to gather a few things.

While he was gone, Nora introduced Grace to the deputy sheriff. As he admired the baby, Bridget said to his bent head, "Deputy MacDuff, I was wondering—"

"Now let's get something straight right now, young lady. I don't answer to no formal title." He winked at her, the gesture taking away the sting of his words. "Everyone calls me Ben."

"Oh, well, then, Ben." She winked at him in return. "Did you know Laird O'Malley?"

"Know him?" He yanked off his hat and slapped his thigh with the brim. "Yeah, I knew him. Met him the day he arrived here from Ireland. I was the town sheriff back then."

"Will you tell us about him?" Nora asked.

Ben shrugged. "Not much to tell. He kept mostly to himself. Guess he weren't the type for interacting with others, if you know what I mean."

Bridget's heart sank. Laird O'Malley had been a recluse. Had he been so in love with their mother, so heartbroken she hadn't returned his feelings that he'd shut himself off from the world? Or had that just been his nature? Either way...

"How sad," she whispered.

Ben shrugged again. "It was what it was."

Cameron Long returned with a large basket in his arms, the contents covered with a colorless muslin cloth. He loaded the basket in the flatbed then strode toward his deputy with ground-eating strides. "You're in charge while I'm gone."

"I figured as much." Eyeing Nora and Bridget, he said, "Now don't you two go worrying about that old house. You're in good hands with Cameron. The boy will sort this out for you in good time."

A chill slid down Bridget's spine. What, exactly, did *the boy* have to sort out? The confusion over the deed? Or was Ben referring to something else, something more specific to the house itself?

Before she could voice her questions the sheriff released the brake, picked up the reins and they were on their way again.

Bridget waved to Ben over her shoulder.

Silence filled the majority of the ride through town. They eventually turned off the main road and began winding their way down a path overgrown with underbrush and scrub. As the wagon bumped along the lane their horse's tail idly swished at the flies swarming around his flanks.

Bridget fanned herself with her hand, her pitiful efforts useless in the rising midday heat. There was no breeze. Yet despite the hot, still air, birds chirped a happy tune from their perches in the towering trees up above. The smell of grass mingled with the fragrant flowers in bloom.

An idyllic scene, to be sure. Yet Bridget could find no joy in the moment. Not only was the heavy underbrush growing thicker with each step the horse took, her nerves were winning the battle over her attempt to remain hopeful.

No. Bridget refused to allow her apprehension to get the best of her. Whatever they found at the end of the lane, she would consider it an additional blessing among the many they'd already received since leaving Ireland.

A month ago they'd faced destitution. But now Maeve was married to a good, honorable man. Bridget and Nora had acquired jobs perfectly suited to their talents. The Lord had guided their path every step of the way.

Her optimism firmly in place, Bridget held her breath with eager anticipation. The wagon rounded a small bend and…

"Oh, my," she gasped, shaking her head blindly. The house, the very reason for their journey to America was…it was…

A disaster.

Chapter Nine

Oh, my. Oh, my. Oh, my. The words continued echoing in Bridget's mind, making coherent thought impossible.

She shaded her eyes from the sun and took in what amounted to years of neglect. The roof sagged, leaning dangerously off-center and slightly to the right. Loose shingles hung haphazardly in places. The paint, once white but now a faded gray, was peeling off in various places, giving the entire structure a chaotic, patchwork feel.

They had traveled all the way from Ireland with so much hope in their hearts for—this?

A disaster, she repeated to herself. The house was a complete and utter disaster.

Speechless, Bridget drew in a shaky breath and lifted up a silent prayer. It seemed better than crying.

Drawing her bottom lip between her teeth, she looked to her right, saw a garden overrun with weeds. There was a rickety old bench sitting under a large shade tree that had a sign tacked to its trunk. The sign read—she leaned forward—Colleen's Garden. Bridget blinked back tears. Laird O'Malley had planted a flower garden for their mother. How—sweet.

Off to her left she spotted a structure that looked like a barn, a barn that had seen better days a decade ago. A scrawny cow grazed on a patch of grass nearby and a few chickens scratched in the dirt.

As the wagon slowed to a stop Bridget took her first look at the rich, black soil beneath the wheels and smiled for the first time since arriving. The fertile dirt would produce food abundantly, with a bit of hard work on their part. Bridget was not afraid of hard work. Neither was Nora.

"This isn't so bad," she said aloud, warming to the burst of ideas swimming in her head now. A bit of paint, a few new shingles, a lot of weeding and they would have a fine home to call their own.

"Not bad?" Nora swung her wide-eyed gaze in her direction. "It's impossible."

"I did warn you," Sheriff Long said under his breath as he set the brake and hopped to the ground.

Ignoring him, Bridget scrambled down as well and grabbed a handful of the black dirt. "Look at this soil, Nora. It'll grow whatever we plant."

Nora made a face, her unhappy expression indicating she was not feeling nearly as hopeful as Bridget.

Undaunted, Bridget turned her gaze to the house. "We'll give it a good cleaning, weed that garden over there then take stock of what repairs need addressing first." She shaded her eyes again. "We'll take this one step at a time. Isn't that what you always say, Nora? One step at a time?"

"Yes, Bridget, that's what I always say." Nora studied the dilapidated structure. "The house must have been truly lovely at one time."

"And it will be again," Bridget said, remembering the sermon from this morning, the part about trusting their greatest burdens to the Lord. Yes, that's exactly what they would do in this situation. "Faith, Nora. We just need a little faith."

"And a lot of elbow grease," she mumbled.

Bridget laughed. "Precisely. One step at a time, dear sister.

Now come." She reached for Grace so Nora could climb down from the wagon. "Let's go inside and introduce ourselves to the Coulters."

She handed back the baby and started off.

"Wait." The sheriff's voice stopped her midstep. While she'd been busy convincing Nora all was well, he'd retrieved the basket from the bed of the wagon and had rounded back to the front once again. "Let me lead the way."

The stoop wasn't much, just a few steps on a raised slab. Nevertheless the sheriff tested each stair before he motioned for them to follow. They trooped up the steps single file, Nora and Grace bringing up the rear.

"Agnes?" he called out, shifting his load so he could tap on the door frame. "You home?"

A small, thin voice responded to his question. "Come on in, Cameron. I'm back in the kitchen."

He elbowed past the door and then held it open with his shoulder so Bridget and Nora could enter ahead of him.

Once inside Bridget came to the unfortunate realization that the interior had been equally neglected. The walls were stark, with chipped paint their only adornment. The carpets were threadbare, holes literally worn in places.

The furniture, what little there was, also sported holes in the tattered upholstery. At least the room was clean, not a dust mite in sight. That said something about the Coulters. They might be elderly, and probably didn't have many resources, but they were doing their best.

The sheriff led them through the sparse room, steering them toward the back of the house. Impressions slid over one another. Faded paint, broken furniture, torn rugs, there was little to recommend the place.

And yet Bridget saw the possibilities.

The rooms were clean and spacious, the windows positioned to allow the light in but not the summer heat. Laird

O'Malley had thought through the design with an eye for functionality. Paint, a bit of pretty wallpaper and a few new pieces of furniture would do wonders.

They ended their short jaunt in a spacious kitchen. Shoving past Bridget, Nora laughed in delight and made straight for the large black iron stove. Bridget understood her sister's pleasure. They'd only had a fireplace in their home in Ireland.

Glancing around the room, Bridget's gaze landed on a frail-looking woman sitting at a sizable table in the middle of the room. Her fingers slowly shelled beans. She looked painfully thin and wore a dress as threadbare as the rugs in the front room. Lines spiked around her pursed lips, giving her a look of suppressed pain.

Bridget smiled gently. "You must be Agnes Coulter."

"That's me," came the uneven reply. She didn't make any move to stand.

Still smiling, Bridget sat down in one of the empty chairs next to her. "I'm Bridget Murphy and that's my sister Nora. The baby she's carrying is Grace."

"Murphy." The woman's eyes lit with recognition, and something else. Wariness, perhaps? "Would that mean you're Colleen's daughters?"

"Well, yes. Yes, we are." Bridget reached out and touched the woman's bony hand, the skin practically translucent over the thin purple veins running across the knuckles. "You know about our mother?"

She focused on her bowl of beans. "Laird spoke of her often, especially in the end."

Bridget squeezed her hand gently. "Then you must know about the deed he sent her."

She nodded. "You've come to claim the house."

"Yes—" she gentled her voice even further "—but since we both have jobs in town we'll need your help running the place."

A deep clearing of a throat preceded an elderly man's entrance. He shuffled into the room, his gait sporting a decided limp. His hair was a wild white cloud around his face. His eyes were a rheumy blue.

"So," he began, his narrowed eyes landing on first Nora and the baby then Bridget. "You've finally come to push us out."

"No." Bridget jumped to her feet. "On the contrary, we want you to stay on as before. We need you to help us care for the house."

While we care for you, she wanted to add but knew by the mutinous look in his eyes she would insult him if she did. She'd met many like him in Ireland, men who had endured the potato famine and had come away proud and humbled, the kind who would rather die by their own effort than live on someone else's charity.

"Please," Nora added. "We want you to live in this house with us and carry on as before. Nothing need change."

"Nothing," Bridget reiterated. "Except you'll have two extra pairs of hands to put this place back to rights."

"I warn you," he said, then drew in a shuddering breath. "There's a lot of heavy work ahead."

Bridget heard the hoarseness in his grizzled voice, the pride behind his words. He was obviously ashamed the house had gotten away from him. She wanted to ease his worry, to help him see they weren't here to judge him or his efforts. "We've lived through famine and drought. We aren't afraid of hard times or hard work."

Arms folded over his chest, he assessed her then Nora then Bridget again with a noncommittal aloofness. Despite his gruff exterior, Bridget saw a good man who took pride in his work, one who took his role of caretaker seriously. "You will stay on, won't you?" she asked.

"I suppose."

"Splendid."

Cameron Long, silent throughout this exchange, stepped forward and set the basket in his arms on the table with a loud thump. "I brought you some things, Agnes."

The woman bristled, the bowl of beans in her lap bobbling. "You know we don't need your charity."

"Who said this is charity?" He gave her one of his big, friendly smiles. "You'll pay me back when you're able."

The comment solidified what Bridget already knew about Cameron Long. He was a kind, down-to-earth man with a generous heart.

Agnes's eyes filled with unshed tears. "You're a good boy," she said, patting his hand.

He dropped a kiss on the top of her head. "Anything for my favorite girl."

"Oh, honestly," she shoved at him with a surprising burst of energy. Setting aside her bowl, she rummaged through the contents, her smile wobbling. "Coffee, flour, sugar, eggs." She looked up at her husband, then quickly thrust her hand back into the basket. "A cured ham."

Nora took charge, wordlessly handing Grace over to Bridget. "Let me put these supplies away and fix us all something to eat."

While she went to work, Bridget took baby Grace and sat back at the table. "That cow outside, is she a milk cow by chance?"

Agnes nodded. "She is."

Bridget caught Nora's eye and smiled. Fresh milk would be readily available for the baby. It was another blessing to add to their list.

With that matter solved Bridget proceeded to entertain everyone with tales from their trip across the Atlantic. She told them about the widow Mrs. Fitzwilliam, her search for her missing stepgranddaughter and, of course, the McCorkle brothers. She highlighted how Maeve's quick thinking had saved little Emmett's life. Halfway through the story, the sheriff cut her off. "You mean to say, the other two boys stowed away on the ship?"

His expression reminded Bridget he was a lawman first, a friend second. "Yes," she said carefully. "Flynn, the ship's doctor, had taken Emmett on board before they could come forward. They had to follow or be left behind. And besides, they couldn't let their brother sail to America without them."

She didn't add that the boys' original intent had been to stow away together, all three of them, before the injury changed their plans. Best not to get anyone in trouble. "Once Dr. Gallagher found out about the other two boys, he put them to work around the ship so they could earn their passage."

The sheriff lifted a single eyebrow. "That was certainly resourceful of Dr. Gallagher."

"Kindhearted, too." Bridget rose, hoping to end the conversation there. She should probably set the table, but wasn't sure what to do with Grace.

Agnes offered the perfect solution. "May I hold her?"

"Of course." Bridget surrendered the baby then went to help Nora.

Once the meal was served, and everyone was sitting at the table, conversation flowed easily. Talk turned to a local mill, the Huntley-something-or-other. Bridget hadn't caught the full name. Assuming they were speaking about the mill she'd seen on her way into town, she asked, "What sort of mill is it?"

"A chocolate mill," Agnes said, her eyes gleaming. "It's been in the area for nearly seventy-five years, begun by one of Faith Glen's founders, Reginald Black."

She straightened at the name. "Black? Any relation to William Black?"

"Absolutely," the sheriff said. "Your new employer owns

the largest mill in the area. He ships his chocolate cakes all over the world, the kind used for baking."

James joined the conversation, his hard voice of earlier softened now. "The Huntley-Black chocolate also makes the best warm cocoa I've ever tasted."

Bridget digested this new information. She wasn't surprised to discover Will was a successful business owner. Even in his desperation to find a mother for his children, he'd had an air of confidence that indicated a man used to being in charge.

Which begged the question: Why had he chosen to send all the way to Ireland for a bride? What had driven him to settle for a marriage in name only instead of seeking a love match?

The sensible voice in her head warned her to reconsider working for William Black. There were too many unanswered questions surrounding him.

Her heart told her he needed her help. Bridget knew she would go with her heart, as always.

Decision made, she spent the rest of their visit getting to know her future housemates better.

Too excited to sleep, Bridget clambered out of bed early the next morning. Night had yet to surrender fully to dawn. Shadows still flickered across the floor at her bare feet.

She loved this time of the morning, when everything seemed possible. By the afternoon she and Nora would have their answer about the deed. A formality, she reminded herself. Nothing more. There would be work ahead of them, *hard* work, and she looked forward to every aching muscle.

Dressing quickly, she chose serviceability over style. She would be spending her day with two three-year-olds. That meant short attention spans on their part, exhaustion on hers and flat-out good fun for them all.

Bridget did not attest to the common notion that children should be kept inside and out of mischief. Children, in her mind, should be children. She remembered her own youth, how she and her sisters had spent hours fishing and digging for buried treasure with the Donnelly boys.

With impatience making her fingers fumble, she managed to lace up her boots after only two tries. She then twisted her hair into a single braid down her back and after a quick breakfast, rushed out of the house.

Nora was already waiting for her on the porch, leaning against the wall as she fed Grace.

"Am I late?" Bridget asked, skidding to a stop then hopping on one foot to regain her balance.

"Actually, you're early."

Relieved, she sank onto the top step. "We have a big day ahead of us."

"Our very own new beginning," Nora added.

"You scared?" she asked over her shoulder, smiling.

"A little. But excited, too."

"Scared and excited, that describes how I'm feeling perfectly."

Bridget closed her eyes and lifted up a silent prayer of thanksgiving. God had brought them here safely. He'd blessed Maeve with a doting husband, and had provided both Bridget and Nora with a means to earn money. They would eventually restore the house Laird O'Malley had built for their mother. In the process they would provide a safe home for James and Agnes Coulter, as well as themselves.

Thank You, Lord, she whispered in her mind. *May Your blessings continue. I pray You use me as Your instrument to tend to the children in my care.*

She opened her eyes just as Cameron Long drew his rickety wagon to a halt in front of the boardinghouse.

"You ladies look especially lovely this morning." He included Bridget in the quick sweep of his gaze, but his eyes lingered on Nora, as they seemed to do often.

Bridget hid a smile behind her hand. Her sister did look especially pretty this morning. Her dark hair gleamed in the early-morning sun, the soft light shooting gold threads through the rich brown. She'd wrapped Grace in a blue swaddling blanket, the softer tone a nice contrast to her darker dress.

After making it clear they were to call him Cam or Cameron, not sheriff, the short trek to Will's house was made in companionable silence. By the time *Cameron* reined in his horse, Bridget was blinking up in wonder at the most beautiful house she had ever seen.

There were rows of windows on three full stories. The first and second floors were identical to one another. Each had five sets of windows and shutters. The top level could possibly be an attic? Or maybe a loft?

It was a large home, meant for a large family, a dream manifested in brick and mortar and seventy-five-year-old wood.

Suddenly overcome with a moment of sorrow, Bridget had to look away. She feared something dreadful had stolen the happiness William Black and his children deserved.

Unaware of her change in mood, Cameron helped her to the ground with a smile. Just as she steadied herself the front door flung open and a pair of loud squeals erupted in the air.

"Miss Bridget!"

Two tiny blurs bulleted down the walkway. Little Olivia stopped short of running into Bridget. Caleb, on the other hand, slammed into her legs, nearly toppling them both.

Cameron steadied Bridget with a hand on her arm. She steadied Caleb in the same manner.

Disaster avoided.

She smiled her thanks to the tall man then focused her attention on her new charges. Their faces were full of joy and they practically bounced in place.

"We've been up for hours," Caleb said.

"Hours and hours," Olivia added.

Heart in her throat, Bridget laid a hand on both their heads, ruffled the matching light auburn hair, and then sighed. She was completely and utterly doomed. Her affection for these two children was quickly outdistancing her ability to remember she'd agreed to work for Will only on a trial basis.

Who had she been kidding with that stipulation? She was here to stay.

Cameron's voice broke through her thoughts. "Your sister and I will be gone most of the day." He climbed back into the wagon, acknowledged the man striding down the walkway with a hitch of his chin, then turned back to Bridget. "Ben will be at the jail all day. Let him know if you need anything in our absence."

"I'll be fine," she assured them both.

Fighting to contain a surge of anxiety as the wagon rolled away, Bridget offered up a silent prayer that all would go well at the County Clerk's Office.

"Miss Bridget." Olivia tugged on her skirt, her shoulders rocking back and forth in a little girl dance. "What are we going to do today? Tell me. Tell me."

"Oh, we're going to do lots of things."

"Like what?" Caleb demanded eagerly.

Bridget leaned over and placed her hands on her knees. "You'll have to wait and see."

"All right, children. Don't crowd your new nanny." Will's voice slid over her like a cool splash of water.

Feeling her cheeks warm in response, Bridget raised her gaze to his. "Hello, Will."

"Hello." He stared into her eyes a moment, and then— finally—he smiled.

The sky tilted, the ground shifted beneath her feet, her equilibrium shattered. With very little effort William Black could hook her heart just as thoroughly as his children had.

She'd never felt this drawn to a man. Not even Daniel had been able to steal her breath so completely.

Still holding her gaze, Will took her arm. "Come, Bridget." His eyes said things she had no idea how to interpret. "Come and meet my mother."

She looked up toward the house, only just now noticing an older woman standing in the doorway, her smile wide and full of welcome. A beautiful woman despite her advancing years, Esther Black wore a light pink dress with a lace collar and matching cuffs. The pretty, soft color set off her white hair and blue, blue eyes. A lovely woman, to be sure, but there was no mistaking the exhaustion in her gaze and the tight lines of fatigue around her mouth.

I was right to come here and serve this family.

Chapter Ten

Hand pressed lightly on her arm, Will directed Bridget toward his house, his chest rising and falling in perfect rhythm with his heartbeat. As impossible as it would seem, the woman was more stunning than he remembered.

Her smile had nearly knocked him off his feet. And when their glances had met, then melded, there had been a tangible impact in his gut, the kind that made him think of things he had no right thinking, like maybe Bridget could become more than his children's nanny.

And...

She wasn't his, he reminded himself sternly. The woman was Olivia and Caleb's temporary nanny, here on a trial basis.

One week. Will had one full week to determine if he could trust her in his home and with his children.

The twins, their excitement still in full force, rushed ahead of them then flanked their grandmother. All three smiles were larger than Will had seen in months.

Bridget had better not break their hearts. *Or mine.*

The thought made Will scowl. "Mother." His voice came out gruffer than he'd intended. "I'd like you to meet Bridget Murphy." He turned to the woman by his side. "Bridget, this is my mother, Esther Black."

Bridget favored his mother with a smile that Will wanted for himself.

He looked quickly away.

"It's a pleasure to meet you, Mrs. Black." Bridget's soft lilting accent washed over him. Surely no woman with a voice like that could be dishonest.

"Welcome, Bridget." Taking the children's hands in hers, his mother stepped backward. "We're very pleased to have you in our home."

Already running late and suddenly needing vast amounts of air, Will gathered the papers and ledgers he'd left in the entryway. "Mother, I'll leave you to help Bridget settle in this morning."

"Of course." She walked toward him and then pecked him on the cheek. "What time will you be home tonight?"

"Early enough to escort Bridget to the boardinghouse."

"Oh," Bridget said. "I'm sure that won't be necessary. Cameron said this was a peaceful town. Surely I could walk the short distance."

Will felt an odd pang at her words. Whether from her casual reference to Cam or her refusal of his offer, he couldn't say.

"Nevertheless." He held her gaze, warning her that the subject was not up for discussion. "I will walk you home this evening. No matter how peaceful our community might be, I won't have you on the streets alone."

She studied him a moment, a glint of pleasure in her eyes. "That is very good of you."

Deciding the matter was settled, he kissed both the children, nodded to his mother and Bridget then left the house as the rest of his family tugged the new nanny into the next room.

One of the last things he heard was the woman's delighted gasp. "You have a piano."

His mother's inevitable response came next. "Do you play, dear?"

"I haven't had the pleasure in a while, not since—"

Not wanting to hear the rest of Bridget's answer, Will shut the door behind him with a decided snap. Fanny had played the piano exceptionally well. Her talent had been one of the things that had drawn him to her. He'd wrongfully equated her love of music with a depth of character that had not been there.

He'd been disappointed to discover she'd played to win favor and for no other reason. Music in his childhood home had been for joy, yes, but was also a way to worship the Lord.

Fanny hadn't wanted anything to do with God, or with Will, as it turned out. After the birth of the twins he'd hoped she'd change her mind, on both counts.

He'd been deluding himself, on both counts.

Fanny had continued avoiding church. She'd craved the life she'd left behind in Boston, and had sought it out as soon as the children were weaned. Wishing to see her happy, Will had encouraged her to visit her friends. He'd counted on her missing the children, possibly even him.

Instead her day trips had grown longer, turning into weeks. Then she had…

He shook the rest of his thoughts away and steered his carriage the final rise to the mill.

In the end Fanny had taught him a very valuable lesson. Never again would he be fooled by a pretty face. *Never again.*

Bridget folded her arms across her waist, leaned a shoulder against the wall and watched her new charges nap peacefully in their beds. They looked sweetly innocent in their sleep, their little faces relaxed and carefree. A soft, rhythmic snore slipped out of Caleb while Olivia mumbled something incoherent then snuggled deeper under her blanket.

Bridget smiled with pleasure. The twins were completely worn out, as children should be after a day of vigorous activity.

The hours had flown by this morning and she was ever grateful. With Caleb and Olivia occupying most of her time, and nearly all of her thoughts, she'd found little opportunity to fret over what Nora and Cameron might—or might not— discover at the County Clerk's Office.

Just as well. Bridget had learned long ago that no matter how much she worried about a situation, the outcome never changed. *Fear not.* Wasn't that most common command in the Bible? Didn't the Lord promise to feed and care for His flock, always?

With that in mind, Bridget focused on the sleeping children once again.

Like most three-year-olds, Olivia and Caleb had active, inquisitive minds and were ready to play any game she suggested. But unlike other children their age, there were moments when they possessed an unnatural reserve. It was as if they feared upsetting Bridget. But why? If only she knew the reason behind their restraint.

She needed more information and, sensing their mother's death was at the heart of the problem, decided to start by finding out what had really happened to the woman.

Satisfied the children were resting peacefully, Bridget pulled the door shut and went in search of Esther Black. The housekeeper told her she could find the older woman in the front parlor.

Bridget stopped in the doorway and waited a moment, watching Esther pour tea into a cup. She looked rested from her own nap, which was exactly what Bridget had hoped. One of her goals had been to relieve this kind woman's burden, and it appeared she was making progress. Bridget would still consult Flynn, but for now she stepped into the parlor.

"The children are asleep," she said.

Esther looked up, smiled and then signaled her to take the empty seat across from her. "Join me, please."

Once Bridget was settled, Esther set a teacup in front of her. "I know I've said this countless times since you arrived this morning, but I'm going to say it again. You are a blessing to us, Bridget Murphy, a true blessing."

Bridget felt her cheeks warm. "Oh, Esther, I've had a wonderful day. The children are utterly charming." A burst of longing shot through her, reminding her how desperately she wanted children of her own. "I'm quite taken with them."

"And there's no denying they adore you, as well." Esther busied herself pouring tea into both cups. She seemed relaxed, but from the furrow on her brow Bridget sensed she had something more to say, perhaps something concerning the children's mother? Dare she hope it would be this easy to gather the information she wanted?

"I understand," Esther began, "that you traveled to America on the same ship as Will's intended."

Surprised and slightly uncomfortable at the direction of conversation, Bridget clasped her hands tightly together in her lap. "Well, yes, I did."

"Did you know her, then?" Esther kept her eyes on the tea service. "Would she have been a good mother to the children?"

Something in the other woman's manner, the way she kept her gaze slightly averted, led Bridget to believe Will's mother hadn't been in full agreement with his decision to "hire" a bride.

It would have been nice to have alleviated Esther's concerns, to have informed her that the woman with which Will had corresponded was worthy of him and the children. Unfortunately Bridget couldn't say for sure. "I'm afraid I never met her."

Esther fell silent, evidently taking a moment to process the information. When she continued looking down at the table, Bridget decided to ease the tension in the air and shift the conversation back to the children.

"The twins are very sweet, but they often seem…a bit…" she searched for the proper word "…subdued."

"It's been a hard year for them."

To hear her concerns spoken aloud, in that sad tone, well, her stomach twisted in sorrow.

"I'm sorry." She reached out to touch Esther's hand and squeezed gently. "For all of you."

Acknowledging her sympathy with a slight incline of her head, Esther pulled her hand free and then scooted a plate of scones in Bridget's direction.

She ignored the pretty pastries. "I assume the children's mother died a year ago?"

"That's correct."

Bridget waited for her to say more but, yet again, Esther didn't give any further details. Instead she made a grand show of buttering a fresh scone and handing it to Bridget.

Accepting the pastry out of politeness more than hunger, she took a bite. As the buttery goodness melted on her tongue, she wondered all the more what had happened to Will's wife. Something tragic? Heartbreaking, perhaps? "The children never mention their mother."

"They don't remember her."

How odd, Bridget thought. Although Olivia and Caleb were young, not yet four, most children their age had memories from when they were much younger.

Should she continue questioning Will's mother? No, Bridget decided. She'd pried enough for one day. Time would reveal the answers she needed.

"Esther, would it be acceptable if I played the piano for

the children when they wake from their nap? Maybe I could teach them a song?"

She peered over her shoulder into the other room as she spoke. The gleaming instrument was the finest she'd ever seen. Bridget desperately wanted to test the keys and determine for herself if the sound matched the piano's exquisite beauty. She loved music and would enjoy sharing her fondness with the children.

Esther's gaze shifted to the piano. After a moment of silent contemplation, she gave one firm nod. "I think teaching the children to sing a song is a grand idea."

With such an enthusiastic answer it was a wonder the woman had taken so long to consider her response. What had been behind her initial hesitation? Bridget wondered.

She wouldn't ask. She'd been nosy enough for one day. Tomorrow morning she would take the children outside to enjoy the fresh air. But today, oh, today, there would be music in this house.

Smiling in satisfaction, Bridget leaned back in her chair and took another bite of her scone.

With his paperwork complete, Will decided to check on the day's production. As he made his way to the main floor of the mill, he reflected over all he and his ancestors had accomplished in seventy-five years. When his grandfather had founded the company he'd been an educated man, a doctor by trade, with absolutely no desire to practice medicine. Upon meeting an Irish immigrant, Liam Huntley, a man who'd been an expert in making chocolate, Reginald Black had struck upon the idea of a chocolate mill.

Within a few years the mill became a phenomenal success, even surviving the American Revolution when cocoa beans had been difficult to acquire.

Will's father had inherited the business upon Reginald's

HOW TO VALIDATE YOUR
EDITOR'S FREE GIFTS!
"THANK YOU"

1 Peel off the FREE GIFTS SEAL from the front cover. Place it in the space provided at right. This automatically entitles you to receive two free books and two exciting surprise gifts.

2 Send back this card and you'll get 2 Love Inspired® Historical books. These books are worth $11.50 in the U.S. or $13.50 in Canada, but are yours absolutely FREE!

3 There's no catch. You're under no obligation to buy anything. We charge nothing—ZERO—for your first shipment. And you don't have to make any minimum number of purchases—not even one!

4 We call this line Love Inspired Historical because every month you'll receive books that are filled with inspirational historical romance. This series is filled with engaging stories of romance, adventure and faith set in historical periods from biblical times to World War II. You'll like the convenience of getting them delivered to your home well before they are in stores. And you'll love our discount prices, too!

5 We hope that after receiving your free books you'll want to remain a subscriber. But the choice is yours—to continue or cancel, anytime at all! So why not take us up on our invitation, with no risk of any kind. You'll be glad you did!

6 And remember...just for validating your Editor's Free Gifts Offer, we'll send you 2 books and 2 gifts, *ABSOLUTELY FREE!*

YOURS FREE!
We'll send you two fabulous surprise gifts (worth about $10) absolutely FREE, simply for accepting our no-risk offer!

The Editor's "Thank You" Free Gifts Include:

- Two inspirational historical romance books
- Two exciting surprise gifts

PLACE FREE GIFTS SEAL HERE

I have placed my Editor's "thank you" Free Gifts seal in the space provided above. Please send me the 2 FREE books and 2 FREE gifts for which I qualify. I understand that I am under no obligation to purchase anything further, as explained on the opposite page.

102/302 IDL FNLR

Please Print

FIRST NAME

LAST NAME

ADDRESS

APT.#   CITY

STATE/PROV.   ZIP/POSTAL CODE

The Reader Service—Here's How It Works:

Accepting your 2 free books and 2 free gifts (gifts valued at approximately $10.00) places you under no obligation to buy anything. You may keep the books and gifts and return the shipping statement marked "cancel." If you do not cancel, about a month later we will send you 4 additional books and bill you just $4.49 each in the U.S. or $4.99 each in Canada. That is a savings of at least 22% off the cover price. It's quite a bargain! Shipping and handling is just 50¢ per book in the U.S. and 75¢ per book in Canada.* You may cancel at any time, but if you choose to continue, every month we'll send you 4 more books, which you may either purchase at the discount price or return to us and cancel your subscription.

*Terms and prices subject to change without notice. Prices do not include applicable taxes. Sales tax applicable in N.Y. Canadian residents will be charged applicable taxes. Offer not valid in Quebec. All orders subject to credit approval. Credit or debit balances in a customer's account(s) may be offset by any other outstanding balance owed by or to the customer. Please allow 4 to 6 weeks for delivery. Offer available while quantities last.

▲ If offer card is missing write to: The Reader Service, P.O. Box 1867, Buffalo, NY 14240-1867 or visit www.ReaderService.com ▲

BUSINESS REPLY MAIL
FIRST-CLASS MAIL   PERMIT NO. 717   BUFFALO, NY

POSTAGE WILL BE PAID BY ADDRESSEE

THE READER SERVICE
PO BOX 1867
BUFFALO NY 14240-9952

NO POSTAGE
NECESSARY
IF MAILED
IN THE
UNITED STATES

death. Will had taken over ten years later. In his hands Huntley-Black chocolate was now available all across the country. In order to meet the increasing demand, Will had moved the business to this larger facility five years ago, right after his marriage to Fanny. The conversion had demanded long, sixteen-hour days.

Perhaps Fanny had felt neglected and that was the reason she'd strayed. Perhaps she'd missed her friends and family, as she'd claimed. Or perhaps she'd simply been bored and that had led to her poor decisions.

Will would never know for sure why his wife had sought another man's affections. Even now, at the thought of the resulting tragedy, anger and guilt burned deep.

Looking back, he wasn't sure he'd fought hard enough to bring Fanny home. When he'd finally gone to fetch her he'd been too late. Why hadn't he sought her out sooner?

What did that say about *his* character?

Will shook away his unsettling thoughts with a swift jerk of his head and focused on his surroundings once more. Still in the grips of a dangerous heat wave, the day had grown uncommonly hot, the interior of the building twice as sweltering.

But despite the heat, the atmosphere inside the mill was congenial. Noise and chatter filled the air, mingling with the sound of grinding millstones crushing the newest shipment of cocoa beans into powder. Farther down the line the powder was heated into a thick syrup. Still farther down, workers poured the syrup into molds to make hard cakes that would eventually be sold under the name Black's Best Chocolate.

Although the cakes were used for baking or grated into hot milk to make a sweetened beverage, Will was working with his best chocolatiers to create a new product that would contain a higher sugar content. His children, both lovers of sweets, were his inspiration.

At the thought of Caleb and Olivia, Will's mind wandered to their new nanny. Bridget Murphy. Had she been sent to them straight from heaven?

Will shut his eyes momentarily and prayed. *Lord, let it be so.*

Focusing once more on his surroundings, he looked around the main floor of operation. The men and women were hard at work. He employed most of the Irish immigrants who lived in the area and liked to think he treated them fairly. But chocolate making was hot, grueling work, especially in the midst of a heat wave.

Combing a hand through his sweat-dampened hair, he went in search of his foreman, a middle-aged man with strong arms and a ready smile. "Joe. A word."

"Mr. Black." Joe stepped away from the millstone and greeted him with his no-nonsense tone and sharp manner. "Any news on the shipment of my nuts?" Joe always called cocoa beans nuts.

"The ship left South America on schedule. If the weather holds it will arrive in Boston Harbor sometime next week."

Wiping the sweat from his brow with a muscled forearm, Joe let out a relieved puff of air. "Not a moment too soon."

Will silently agreed. Business was so good they were running out of Joe's *nuts* at an alarming rate. "How we doing for today's production?"

"Ahead of schedule."

As Will expected. Joseph Ferguson was an excellent, efficient foreman who managed to inspire his workers to new heights of excellence.

Nodding his approval, Will pulled out his watch and checked the time. Four in the afternoon. Early still, but not alarmingly so. "Let's call it a day. Send everyone home."

Knowing better than to second-guess the decision, Joe made the announcement.

A loud cheer rose up from the workers.

"Joe, you go on home, too." He clapped the shorter man on the back. "Enjoy your family." Advice Will planned to take himself.

"You got it, boss."

Several workers thanked him personally as he made his way back to his office to retrieve his papers and other belongings. He thanked them in return for their continued hard work.

His gratitude was genuine. Many of the residents of Faith Glen thought of the Irish immigrants as intruders, outsiders. Will saw them as honest, honorable, hard-working people, which had been the primary reason he'd sent to Ireland for a bride.

A cold, ruthless wave of guilt spread through him. Bridget Collins deserved better than what he'd provided her. She'd suffered a terrible ending, death at sea, all because she'd been looking for the better life he'd promised to provide her in America.

Even as he thought of his bride with sadness, his mind steered toward another female immigrant, the one who'd kindly stepped in, if only temporarily, to assist Will and his family while he determined what to do next.

He wondered what Bridget and the children were up to this very minute. Were they playing, laughing, having a good time together?

He quickened his pace, eager to hurry home and see for himself.

Less than a half hour later, Will stood frozen on the front steps just outside his house, struck immobile by the music wafting past the open windows. Then he noticed the sounds of laughter, and high-pitched, childish joy. He'd forgotten those sounds. For a moment he simply closed his eyes and allowed the music to wash over him.

Then more unwanted memories slammed into him, the kind he'd suppressed for a full year but seemed to be coming at him at an alarming rate these days. When he'd met Fanny at a dinner party in Boston she'd been playing a piano. The owner of a shipping company Will commissioned to import his cocoa beans had invited him to his home, under the guise of discussing business. But Richard Osmond had had another agenda in mind. He'd wanted Will to meet his daughter, Fanny.

Will had been smitten from the start. Fanny had been beautiful, talented, the most refined woman he'd ever met. And she'd played the piano with flair, indicating a passionate, enthusiastic nature.

The attraction had not been one-sided, no matter what Fanny had later claimed. She'd been equally enthralled with Will, and had gone out of her way to win him.

Their courtship had been a blur. They'd attended the opera, the theater and countless parties. Will had found the social whirlwind amusing, primarily because he'd known he was too dedicated to his business and his employees to have continued the extravagant lifestyle beyond that initial burst.

Just like the partygoing, happiness hadn't lasted long in his marriage either, less than a year. Pain and anger had replaced what Will had thought was love. Shouting had replaced the music in his home. Joy had all but disappeared.

Now, standing on the front stoop, listening to the sound of his children singing and laughing, Will realized how much he'd missed the music.

He wanted to be a part of it now. He prayed the memories, or at least the worst of them, stayed away so he could simply enjoy the moment with his children. And his mother. And, of course, Bridget.

Bracing himself, he twisted the doorknob and shoved inside the house. The music was louder in the entryway, jollier, his children's laughter happier.

Will swallowed past a lump in his throat.

Not wanting to interrupt just yet, he held perfectly still, listening. He recognized Bridget's soft, lyrical tone as she led the song. Her voice has been just as sweet in church yesterday. And now his children, with Bridget's urging, were attempting one of his favorite nursery songs from childhood.

He mouthed the words along with them. *How does my Lady's garden grow? In silver bells, and cockle shells and pretty maids all in a row.*

Caleb was pretty shaky of the first part of the song, but he had the last line down. His voice rose to a near shout as he sang, "All in a *row!*"

The music stopped, only to be replaced by clapping. "Oh, well done," his mother said with unmistakable glee.

The children giggled in response. "Again," Caleb demanded. "Let's sing it again."

Heart suddenly lighter than he could ever remember, Will wanted to be a part of the fun. He entered the room.

His gaze landed on his mother first. She was sitting in a chair facing the piano, still clapping her hands in enthusiastic approval. She looked remarkably refreshed.

He felt his eyes burn with relief, then quickly looked away.

Thankfully Bridget hadn't seen him yet, nor had his children. Sitting on either side of her on the piano bench, the twins were hugging her fiercely. Both of their spindly arms wrapped tightly around her waist.

For her part Bridget alternated between kissing their heads and praising their singing. A portion of a long-forgotten verse from Isaiah came to mind. *They shall obtain gladness and joy; and sorrow and mourning shall flee away.*

Will cleared his throat.

Bridget snapped her head up. Their gazes met and held. Her eyes shone with emotion, and then…

She smiled. Directly at him.

Will felt himself suffocating until he managed to drag in a gasping tug of air.

He'd once thought a woman could only be considered beautiful if her hair was perfectly coiffed and she was clothed in fashionable attire.

But now, *now,* Will realized he'd been woefully incorrect in that assumption. There was nothing more appealing than the sight of wild, untamed hair escaping from a long, thick braid, and nothing more striking than his children's arms wrapped around the waist of Bridget Murphy.

The scene was enough to give any man pause, especially a man with Will's disastrous marital history and determination to avoid a second mistake for his children's sake. Yet as he continued to stare into Bridget's pretty eyes he felt a sudden release. For that single, solitary moment in time he was free. Free from the anger and guilt of the past. Free to start over.

Free.

Chapter Eleven

With Will's intense gaze locked with hers, something very strange and unfamiliar began to swell in Bridget's stomach. Her lips parted in surprise.

The way Will was looking at her. It—it was so—enthralling.

Her arms automatically tightened around the children. Both squirmed in response, Caleb more than Olivia, but neither let go of her waist. They clung to her, their little cheeks pressed to her ribs.

Bridget dipped her head and whispered, "Your da is home."

Squealing with pleasure, they simultaneously jumped off the bench and rushed for their father. They shoved one another, jockeying to be the first one to cross the short distance.

Caleb, the stronger of the two, won the harmless competition.

"Papa." He vaulted himself against his father's leg. "You're home early."

"Papa, Papa." Olivia hopped from one foot to the other, raising her voice to be heard over her brother. "Miss Bridget taught us a song."

With excruciating tenderness in his eyes, Will touched his

daughter's cheek. "I heard." He lowered to his haunches so his gaze was level with hers. "You sounded wonderful."

"Miss Bridget said we get to learn another song tomorrow," Caleb declared. "After we play some games outside."

"Splendid." Will's face broke into a wide grin. The gesture took ten years off his face and made him appear far more relaxed than Bridget had ever seen him.

The man was dangerously handsome, especially when he smiled so tenderly. Captivated, she filled her gaze with his face, his shoulders, his hair. She couldn't stop staring at him.

Talking over one another, the children told their father about the various adventures of their day.

Reminding them to take turns, Will sat on the ground and allowed them to crawl into his lap.

The children chattered on.

"And then she made us take a nap," Caleb said, wrinkling his nose in disgust.

Will laughed deep in his throat. "I never liked naps, either."

Olivia tugged frantically on his sleeve. "Papa, Papa. I learned how to braid my dolly's hair."

Will nodded solemnly. "A most important skill for a young lady."

"That's what Miss Bridget said."

The three of them looked so happy, and so very different from the sad little family she'd met in the general store two days ago. Was this change due to her influence? Had the Lord brought her to this home, at this precise moment in time, to make a difference for this family, to help them overcome their grief and sorrow?

If that was true, why did Bridget feel as though she was the one receiving the blessing? The smiles, the giggles, the relaxed shoulders on the far-too-serious man, *these* were her rewards. Her eyes stung with gratitude.

Thank You, Lord. Thank You for bringing me to this home and to this family.

Looking away before a tear escaped, Bridget caught Esther's eye. The older woman smiled brilliantly at her, her own eyes shining.

Several moments passed before the children finally wound down. Will untangled himself and rose to his feet. Olivia skipped back to Bridget and plopped onto the bench next to her. The little girl leaned against her and released a dramatic sigh of pleasure. Bridget wrapped her arm around the child's tiny shoulders. It felt natural to have Olivia with her, while Caleb stayed close to his father's side.

Bridget felt a pang at the sight the two made. Man and boy, father and son, the perfect statement of family.

She felt a tug on her heart, a painful yearning that dug all the way to her soul. *If only they were mine.*

Her breath hitched as the thought whispered through her. She swallowed, knowing her wish could never come true. Will didn't want a real family, he wanted a wife in name only.

Bridget wanted so much more. She wanted it all. Love, family, *forever*—someday. When her heart had healed from all the damage Daniel had done.

"Papa?" Caleb tugged on his father's hand. "Can we keep her?"

Will looked down at his son. "Keep who?"

"Miss Bridget." Caleb pointed in her direction. "Can we keep her for forever and ever?"

A pause.

"Oh, can we, Papa?" Olivia hopped off the stool and ran back to her father. *"Can we?"*

Will whipped his gaze to Bridget's, his eyes perfectly unreadable. For a long, tense moment they simply stared at one another. It was a question neither was prepared to answer.

Will cleared his throat. "It's only been a day, Cal. We don't..." he swallowed "...need to..."

"Decide anything just yet," Esther finished for him.

Asserting herself, the older woman stood and then crossed the room with surprising agility. *"Now."* She put a hand on each child's shoulder. "Let's get you two washed up for supper while your father and Miss Bridget have a quiet moment to talk about the day."

The childish arguments began at once, proving just how far the children had come in one day. When Bridget had met the twins in the general store, neither would have raised their voices, much less protested a direct command. She wondered if their father realized the magnitude of the change in them.

One day. Nothing more than a handful of hours in Bridget Murphy's care and his children were already acting like... children. Will was so pleased he didn't have the heart to reprimand them for their whining.

His mother had no such qualms. "That's enough, both of you." Her voice had taken on the stern yet loving tone he remembered from his own childhood. "Upstairs, now."

Will recovered quickly from his stupor. "Do as your grandmother tells you."

Both children grumbled then trooped out of the room with slumped shoulders. He resisted the urge to call them back and hug them until those forlorn looks disappeared. No matter how pleased he was to see their very normal behavior, he couldn't reward disobedience.

Once they were out of earshot, he turned back to face Bridget. "You have won over my children completely."

She smiled at the empty doorway, a look of gratification lighting her eyes. "I'm afraid it's the other way around. They are very charming."

As are you.

He refrained from saying the words aloud. Barely. She was amazingly beautiful even with her disheveled appearance, and it was very distracting.

As though reading his mind, she smoothed an unsteady hand down her hair. The gesture drew his attention to her glorious face. The dark, loose waves were a perfect contrast to the flawless alabaster skin. A woman shouldn't be that stunning after wrangling two three-year-olds all day.

Will shook his head, only just realizing the heavy silence that had fallen between them.

This awkwardness would not do. Perhaps a change of scenery would help matters. "I would like to hear how the day went from your perspective," he began, pleased his tone was easy and businesslike. "Would you do me the honor of a short walk along the lane?"

"That would be lovely, Will."

The way she said his name in that soft Irish lilt made his steps falter. Recovering quickly, he strode to the entryway, waited for her to join him and then opened the door so she could lead the way onto the front steps.

As she passed by him, Will breathed in her scent, a blend of lavender and fresh air. She carried herself with poise and dignity, and not for the first time, he wondered about her background. Where she came from. Why she'd left her home. What her plans were now that she was in Faith Glen.

Determining how best to start the conversation, he directed her down the lane toward the town square. The afternoon heat hadn't yet dissipated, but there was a pleasant breeze kicking up.

"Tell me about your life back in Ireland."

She didn't answer him right away. And as he stared at her he realized her expression wasn't merely sad. It was grief stricken, as though she was working to hold back painful memories.

"You've lost someone recently," he said softly, wishing he could wipe away her sorrow but understanding there wasn't much he could do. Death was final.

"My da."

"And your mother? What about her?"

"She died ten years prior, during a terrible influenza epidemic."

"I'm sorry." He knew his words were woefully inadequate, but she graciously accepted his condolences with a nod.

"At Da's funeral Reverend Larkin promised we would see him again someday in a heavenly place, a place where there will be no more hunger or sickness."

The preacher at his father's funeral had said something similar. "That must have been a comfort."

"Not at the time." She pressed a fisted hand to her midriff and sniffed back what sounded like the beginnings of a sob. "Especially since we'd been turned out of the only house we'd ever known that very same day."

"How…" He wanted to say criminal, but he didn't know the particulars so he swallowed back the word and said, "That must have been terrifying."

"Terrifying? Yes, I suppose it was, but it was also grossly unfair. We'd worked the land alongside Da for years. It wasn't right, what Mr. Bantry did, kicking us off the land without warning. Maeve, my youngest sister, was the most upset."

"The one married to Flynn Gallagher, the doctor on the *Annie McGee?*"

"That's the one." A distant smile spread across her lips. "Maeve said 'May God turn Bantry's heart, and if He doesn't turn his heart, may He turn Bantry's ankle, so we'll know him by his limping.'"

Will let out a short bark of laughter. "Can't say I blame her, under the circumstances."

Bridget bit her bottom lip as though trying to keep from

smiling, or perhaps frowning. "She wasn't feeling very charitable at the time. None of us were."

If Will ever traveled to Ireland he would find Mr. Bantry and tell him exactly what he thought of the man's treatment of the Murphy sisters. Not usually prone to violence, Will felt a strong urge to punch the other man in the face. And then he would…

Best not to continue the rest of his thought.

"So you were tossed out of the only home you ever knew." Anger made his voice come out harder than he intended. He drew a breath. "And then the three of you decided to come to America."

The courage and faith required to make such a journey had Will admiring Bridget Murphy and her sisters all the more.

"Not at first." The distant expression filled her gaze once again and Will sensed she was no longer with him but back in Ireland. "When we started to pack our belongings Nora found a faded daguerreotype of our dear mother in an old worn frame. Behind the likeness we found a letter from a man named Laird O'Malley and a drawing of a home with a beautiful garden beside it."

Recognizing the name, Will stopped walking. "A Laird O'Malley settled here in Faith Glen a few years after I was born."

"That would be the same man." She looked up at him with shining eyes. "He told our ma that he would always love her, that he'd built a house that he would keep waiting for her. He put the deed to his home in our mother's name."

Will nodding in understanding, then resumed walking, matching his stride to her slower pace. "So you decided to come to America for the home awaiting you here."

The move only made sense, yet he still admired the courage it took the sisters to leave everything they knew behind and set off for a foreign land.

"We had enough money to live on for a month or buy three tickets to America." She smiled at him. "As I'm sure you have already guessed, we bought the tickets and placed ourselves in the Lord's care."

Her smile was enough to make his steps falter.

"Unfortunately when we arrived three days ago Sheriff Long said the house wasn't legally ours until we verified our deed against the one filed in the County Clerk's Office. He promised it was just a formality and agreed to travel to the county seat with us himself."

"Sounds like Cam."

"He and Nora left this morning, after dropping me off at your house. They took baby Grace with them."

Will silently wondered how Cam was coping with a woman and an infant in tow. It was a well-known fact that the big bad sheriff of Faith Glen was uncomfortable around children, especially babies. Will could see Cam squirming now, tugging on his collar and doing his best to pretend Grace didn't exist.

Will's smile faded as an image of Laird's house flashed in his mind. James Coulter had hurt his hip a few years back. The old man hadn't been the same since, but refused to admit he couldn't take care of his own home. As a result the house had fallen into a state of disrepair. Will had never liked the idea of the elderly couple residing in the house in its current condition. He liked the idea of Bridget joining them even less.

"Have you seen the house yet?"

"I'm afraid so." She stumbled over a small branch. He reached out, holding her steady until she caught her balance. Once she was walking once more, he let her go then offered his arm.

She accepted his assistance without question, as if they'd made this walk countless times before. The easiness he felt with her should have left him unsettled. Instead the rightness of the moment made speech impossible for several seconds.

Will forced himself to concentrate on the conversation once more. "So if I understand you correctly, you will know sometime later today if the deed you possess to Laird's house is legal?"

Her fingers flexed on his arm. "Aye, that's the way of it."

Although she'd been very forthright in all her answers, Will sensed Bridget was holding something back, a personal piece of her story she didn't feel comfortable sharing with him. "Any regrets leaving Ireland?"

"Not many." Her response came quickly, perhaps a bit too quickly. "I miss some of the people."

Some of the people, or one in particular? A man, perhaps? Just as he opened his mouth to ask, a mangy dog came into view. The hound stood several yards ahead of them on the path, his shoulders hunched in a slightly aggressive stance. Burrs and twigs were caught in his coat.

Will shifted in front of Bridget and put himself in the direct path of the animal. He rose to his full height and stared hard at the dog. Bridget's safety was in his hands, now.

The dog hunched lower and added an insistent bark, bark, bark in the process.

Will balanced his weight evenly on both feet, holding steady, ready for a sudden attack, prepared to strike if necessary.

He had the situation under control, or so he thought, until Bridget got it in her mind to join the scuffle. Speaking in a soft, sweet tone, she moved out from behind Will and told the mutt he was a "pretty boy."

"Stay back," he warned her, punctuating his command with an outstretched arm that barred her way.

She stepped around him, just as the dog flattened his ears against his head and increased the volume of his barks.

"Aren't you a sweet boy?" she cooed as though she were talking to an infant. "We aren't here to hurt you, you know."

Will knew better than to make any sudden move, but he couldn't stand by and watch Bridget step straight into danger. Filing through several possible scenarios, he eased toward Bridget. "You need to get behind me again so I can—"

"He's afraid of you," she whispered, her eyes still on the agitated animal. "Isn't that right, little doggy? The big bad man is scaring you."

"Little doggy," Will muttered under his breath. "He's at least seventy pounds." And was some sort of mixed breed with black, brown and possibly white fur. It was hard to tell under all the dirt.

Bridget took a tentative step forward.

The dog's ears lifted, just a bit, enough to tell Will that Bridget's tactic was working.

"That's right, boyo." She took another step. "I'm not going to hurt you."

The ears relaxed some more and then *boyo* belly-crawled toward her.

She stuck out her hand, slowly. "That's it."

The dog inched forward again.

This painful process of belly-crawl and soft encouragement went on for several minutes. At last, the animal raised himself to all fours then sniffed Bridget's hand tentatively.

Another moment passed and the mangy tail started wagging.

If Will hadn't been there to witness the full exchange, he would have never believed it possible. Bridget Murphy had won over a skittish dog in a matter of minutes. And she didn't look a bit concerned the outcome could have been less pleasant.

"You've done this before," he said, aware his voice was full of awe.

"Maybe a time or two." She smiled at the dog. "Put your hand out, slowly," she told Will, "so he can get a hold of your scent and know you aren't a threat."

"Who says I'm not a threat?"

"I do." She gave him a look that grabbed at his heart and tugged. In that moment Will would have done anything she asked of him. He'd never really understood Delilah's hold over Samson. Until now. A woman's smile was her most powerful weapon, and a man's ultimate doom.

"Go on," Bridget urged. "Make friends. Or we won't be able to continue our walk."

Knowing she was right, Will did as she suggested. One inch at a time, he stuck out his hand.

The dog dutifully sniffed and then licked his knuckles. Boyo was friendly enough, if a bit jumpy. Who could blame him? It was obvious the creature had been neglected and, Will narrowed his eyes, starved. A burst of indignation filled his heart. No creature should suffer ill-treatment like that.

"He needs food," Will said, eyeing the emaciated frame, and the matted fur. "And a bath." He contemplated a way to accomplish both tasks without putting his children in danger when the sound of a wagon wheel crunching over gravel sounded in the distance.

The dog flattened his ears against his head, looked over his shoulder and then shot off like a bullet toward the forest.

"He's gone," Bridget said with a sigh. "What a shame."

Will wasn't so sure.

As much as it pained him to admit it, even in the privacy of his own mind, he didn't much like sharing Bridget's affections with a dog. He knew he had no claim on her. She was merely company. He liked her. Perhaps too much.

She's your children's nanny, he reminded himself.

Why couldn't he keep that straight in his head?

Chapter Twelve

Soon after the dog disappeared into the woods, leaving a row of trampled wildflowers in his wake, Bridget heard the grind of wagon wheels approaching from the distance. Had the skittish animal heard the sound as well and sensed a threat? Had that been the cause for his hasty departure?

Whatever the reason, Bridget was sad to see him run off. Like Will said, he needed food and a bath, in that order.

Perhaps the animal would return. If he did, she would work to keep him close, then she would go about getting the poor dear some food.

Pleased by the thought, she felt a smile spread across her lips. But in the next moment her mind faltered and she paused to absorb what had just happened. Sensing danger, Will had put himself between Bridget and the dog. He'd been willing to sacrifice his safety for hers.

She wasn't used to that sort of care and protection from anyone other than her family and didn't know how she felt about it. Pleased, to be sure, but also uncomfortable and confused. Bridget took care of others. They did not take care of her.

The polite thing to do would be to acknowledge Will's gallant behavior. She studied his profile. The sudden despair of knowing he would never be hers, not truly, lent urgency to her words. "Thank you, Will."

He turned to face her. "Pardon me?"

His strong jaw was shaded with dark stubble. She wanted to reach up and touch, to feel the rough prickles on her fingertips. She clenched her hand into a fist. "I... Thank you for trying to protect me from the dog."

He continued to stare at her.

"He could have been feral," she added.

Will blinked very slowly, his silvery-pale eyes filled with strangled emotion as he took her hand in his. "Praise God he wasn't."

"Yes, praise God." Instead of pulling her hand free she braided her fingers through his.

Something quite lovely passed between them, a moment of complete contentment that went beyond words. But instead of feeling delighted by the sensation, a wistful sadness crept through her. Will wanted the kind of wife she could never be for him, or for any man.

She dropped her gaze and sighed. She would not—*would not, would not, would not*—allow herself to want what she could never have.

Another moment passed and then someone shouted her name. "Bridget. Oh, Bridget, we have news. Good news."

Reluctantly pulling her hand free from Will's comforting grip, Bridget turned toward an approaching wagon. Cameron Long and Nora and baby Grace had returned.

Bridget had no doubt what that news was.

She should be beside herself with joy. Yet the sight of her sister with that wide smile spread across her face roused the most curious reaction. Annoyance. She was actually annoyed Nora had returned at this very moment. The strange, unexpected reaction constricted her lungs and she thought impatiently, *Why am I not more pleased?*

"Stop fretting, Bridget. Everything will work out fine." Will punctuated his statement by reaching out and giving her hand a gentle squeeze. An immediate sense of relief spread through her entire body.

She swallowed back her misgivings and looked up again, calling upon the faith that had brought her to this crucial moment in time. Bridget had been the most hopeful of all her sisters about this venture to America. She'd certainly felt the most confident when Nora and Maeve had wavered. Why was she not happier now?

What was causing her reservation?

Cameron pulled the wagon to a stop, nodded a silent greeting to Will, then smiled down at Bridget. "You will be pleased to know that all went according to plan."

She turned her gaze to Nora and lifted a questioning eyebrow.

"It's true," Nora said, her smile as radiant as Bridget had ever seen. "We own Laird O'Malley's house, free and clear."

Feeling oddly placid by the news, Bridget nodded. "So the deed is legal."

"That's what I just said."

At last—*at last*—Bridget's stomach gave a delighted leap. "Oh, Nora, this is wonderful news."

"I was wondering when you'd say that."

Hopes and dreams tangled together in her mind, weaving into a beautiful tapestry of possibilities. Bridget paused to sort through one wonderful reality after another. For the first time in her life her future was secure.

There was much work ahead, but she and Nora would be repairing their own home and toiling on their own land.

It was all quite exciting.

She was suddenly aware of the man standing beside her, his silent presence far more comforting than she would have thought possible from a man she'd only met three days ago. She turned to face him again.

He smiled.

"You will want to go with your sister and discuss your next step." Although the words were uttered in a light vein, Will's eyes were alert, questioning.

"Not yet. The children will be expecting me." More than that, she wanted to see them through their suppertime and then read to them before they went to bed. Somewhere during the day the twins had stopped being a duty and had become her joy.

"Stay with your sister, Bridget. You have much to plan. I'll tell the children where you've gone. They'll understand."

Bridget wasn't nearly as confident. But what bothered her most wasn't what Will had just said but rather that he'd spoken in such a stunningly offhanded manner, as if he was used to making up other people's minds for them.

"No, Will. I appreciate the offer but I will return home with you." She took a deep breath and held her ground. "And only leave once the children are in bed."

He opened to his mouth to argue.

She cut him off with a raised hand. "And that's the end of the matter."

There was a flash of something in his eyes, something akin to amusement, as though he'd just come to a sudden realization that was a welcome discovery. "If that's what you want."

"It is."

"Then I'll make sure you are safely returned to the boardinghouse after the children are settled for the night."

Now that they had come to an understanding, Bridget wanted to make sure Nora was comfortable with her decision. Not that it would matter, but she didn't want her sister to feel abandoned. "You will be all right without me for a little while longer, yes?"

"Go on, Bridget, and take care of your charges." There was an odd note in her voice, an indulgent consideration that wasn't typical for Nora. There were also questions in her eyes, none of which Bridget knew how to answer just yet. Suddenly, a few more hours with the Black family seemed very attractive.

"We'll talk later tonight," she said in an even voice, hoping to send Nora on her way.

"Yes, Bridget," Nora replied, rearranging the baby in her arms. "We will talk later." Now *that* was the tone Bridget expected from her older sister, the quiet warning that promised much would be discussed once the two of them were finally alone.

When a heavy silence descended over their tiny group, Cameron took charge. He bid a friendly farewell to both Bridget and Will, and then asked if Nora was ready. She nodded.

The wagon rolled away with Nora gazing back over her shoulder. The insistent look in her eyes was enough to give Bridget pause. But not enough to make her think she'd made a mistake by staying with Will. Putting him and the children ahead of her desire to make plans for her own future seemed the right thing to do.

In that moment, she realized the Black family had already become a part of her heart. She prayed they didn't break it.

Several hours later Will sat in a chair beside Caleb's bed while Bridget's lilting voice filled the room. She read from the twin's favorite book, *Mother Goose's Melody.*

Will closed his eyes and listened. Her inflection was different than his mother's had been when she'd read to him as a child, yet just as soothing. Transfixing, even.

He opened his eyes and found himself watching Bridget's lips move as she spoke. She was achingly beautiful and something tugged at his heart. A breeze fluttered the curtains, creating a soft, pleasant feel to an already tender moment. Will tried not to read too much into the situation. Bridget was reciting nursery rhymes to his children as part of her job, nothing more.

Perched on the edge of Olivia's bed, near the foot, book spread across her lap, Bridget paused, looked up and caught him watching her. Holding his gaze, she continued narrating the story of Mary and her little lamb. All the while her beautiful eyes searched his, her gaze full of profound gentleness. No woman had ever looked at him that way before, certainly not Fanny. He swallowed a wave of unease.

She mercifully looked back to her book.

On surprisingly unsteady legs Will quietly left the room. Two steps into the hallway his mother grabbed his arm. He started to speak but she shook her head and pulled him away from the children's bedroom.

There was no sound in the house except the distant melody of Bridget's voice.

"I don't know where you found her, son, but that Bridget Murphy is a treasure."

He shot a look over his shoulder, a rueful affection filling him. "Yes, she is."

"She told me a little about how she ended up in Faith Glen. If you ask me—"

"Which I didn't."

"If you ask me," she repeated with deliberate slowness, "I'd say Bridget's appearance at such a time as this is a sure sign the Lord has smiled on our family at last."

Will didn't argue the point. Why would he? Hadn't he already decided that Bridget was indeed a gift from God?

Yet even as he silently admitted that he liked her, maybe even trusted her, discomfort spread through him.

Bridget was not a permanent fixture in his home, nor would she ever be. Her position was only temporary and still on a trial basis. She could still change her mind at the end of the week, and there was nothing Will could do about it.

Or was there?

What if he gave her no reason to leave? What if he gave her every reason to stay?

"…then she managed to coax Caleb into taking a nap, after she'd astonishingly convinced Olivia to hand over her unwanted crackers when Caleb had run out of his."

Will shook his head, only just realizing his mother had been speaking the entire time he'd been thinking about Bridget.

"What did you just say?" He thought he heard something about a nap and crackers? Did Bridget let the twins eat crackers in their beds?

"It was nothing important, just a little something about the children." A knowing smile hovered on his mother's lips, then spread into a grin as she looked over his shoulder. "Bridget, dear, are you finished reading already?"

"I am. The children are sound asleep."

Hearing the satisfaction in her voice, Will turned around, hoping to get a glimpse of her smile. What he saw were drooping eyelids. "You're tired."

"Only a little." She released a soft laugh. What a wonderful sound, he thought, light and throaty. "I've had an amazing day."

Will liked knowing she'd found pleasure in her position with his family. "Let's get you to the boardinghouse at once, or you'll be too exhausted to return in the morning."

He lifted up a silent prayer that this woman would continue as his children's nanny. And then another that she was as trustworthy as she seemed.

After she said good-night to his mother, Will escorted Bridget outside then drew to a stop at the end of the walkway. "Wait here while I bring the carriage around."

She placed a hand to his arm. "It's such a lovely evening, Will, and the boardinghouse is so close. Let's walk."

"You aren't too tired?"

"Not at all. The fresh air has quite restored me."

"Well, then, Bridget, allow me to walk you home."

Bridget and Will made their way down the lane in companionable silence, turning together at the bend. Enjoying the sounds of the night and the unique smells that were familiar yet also foreign, she took a deep breath. The same sweet scent she'd smelled that first carriage ride into town filled her nose. "That aroma, is it from your mill?"

"It's the chocolate syrup, the byproduct of the melted cocoa powder." A smile tugged at his lips. "I'm so used to the smell I forget it's there."

She suddenly wanted to know more about his work, about how he spent his days. "Tell me how you make chocolate."

As he described the process, she could picture him in his mill, his shirtsleeves rolled up, his powerful arms pouring cocoa beans between the millstones. She suspected he was a fair employer, one who expected the best out of his workers without demanding the impossible. When he explained the grueling process of heating the powder into syrup, she stopped him. "So you closed the mill early today because of the unbearable heat?"

"Partly, yes." He shrugged, looking a bit sheepish. "But I also wanted to see how you and the children were making out."

"You mean you wanted to check on me."

"I did." He paused a beat. "As well as the children and my mother."

Bridget wasn't offended by his admission—well, only a little. A man like William Black would want to ensure his loved ones were in good hands. How could she find fault in that? "You care very much for your family."

"I do." His tone was light but his eyes had taken on a very serious gleam. This was a man who would sacrifice everything for his family, even his life. Once again she experienced a strong desire to be cherished so completely, to enjoy the same care and concern that Will bestowed upon his kin. Earlier, he'd stepped up to protect her, but that had likely just been chivalry. What would it be like to have his devotion, his love?

Did she want those things from him, in particular, or would any man do?

It was a question she shouldn't ask herself, not now. Perhaps not ever. Will had made his intentions clear. Perhaps the death of his wife had left no more room in his heart for romantic love again.

Bridget looked down at her feet, swallowed three times, each time the beating of her heart grew louder in her head.

"We're here."

She looked up, having lost track of their route. "So we are."

Will set a hand on her shoulder and turned her to face him. "Thank you, Bridget." He reached up and touched her cheek. "Thank you for giving my children a lovely day and my mother a much-needed break."

Compelled, she leaned into his hand, trying not to sigh. It was all quite disturbing, this pull she felt for a man she hardly knew.

"It was a joy working in your home today," she said, desperately needing to remind herself she was this man's employee.

He dropped his hand to his side. "Would you like me to fetch you in the morning?"

What a lovely offer and completely unnecessary. "No. I can walk the two-and-a-half blocks on my own."

He took a step away from her. The added distance between them felt like a chasm. "Then I will see you in the morning."

"Good night, Will."

"Good night."

As she watched him turn and leave, Bridget remembered she was working for him only on a trial basis.

Why had she made such a condition? She didn't want to leave his employ. She adored the twins, and Esther, too. The thought of walking away from any of them—or from Will— brought physical pain.

There was a simple solution to the problem. She would give Will no reason to ask her to leave. She would make herself so indispensible he wouldn't be able to live without her.

Smiling at the thought, she turned and walked up the boardinghouse steps. She froze midway. Nora was waiting for her. "You just missed Flynn and Maeve."

"I'm sorry for that. How are they faring?"

"As well as two blissfully in love people can manage."

Bridget smiled. "The poor dears."

Nora laughed. "Flynn is considering the idea of opening a medical practice in Faith Glen and maybe even building a house so he and Maeve can be closer to us."

"Oh, Nora." Bridget clasped her hands together in excitement. They'd talked of this before, of Flynn and Maeve eventually making Faith Glen their home. But to hear it confirmed made Bridget's heart fill with joy. "That's wonderful news."

No longer smiling, Nora acknowledged her words with a distracted nod. "They plan to return for another visit Sunday afternoon. Flynn wants to check out Laird O'Malley's house before we move in."

"You mean *our* house."

"Yes." Nora nodded in satisfaction. "*Our* house."

"That's very kind of him." Bridget relaxed, but just as she commandeered the last step uneasiness stirred within her. Nora was alone.

"Where's Grace?" She caught her breath inside a gasp. "Did Maeve take her? Has someone come forward to claim her?"

"No, no." Nora waved off her concern with a flick of her wrist. "Rose is watching the baby."

Confused, Bridget continued forward, walking through the shadows that were dark pools of gray at her feet. "Why is Rose watching Grace at this late hour?"

"I wanted to talk to you, Bridget, without any chance of distractions cutting off our conversation."

That didn't sound good.

"Has something happened since we last saw one another?" Her mind went immediately to the deed, then shot to the house, rounded back toward the elderly caretakers. "Is it the house? The Coulters? The deed itself?"

"Come, Bridget." Nora took her arm and directed her to one of the rocking chairs. "Sit."

She did as requested, primarily because she had no other choice. Nora was pressing down on her shoulders.

She landed on the seat with a plop.

Towering over her, Nora planted her fists on her hips and scowled.

Bridget shuddered at the look in her sister's eyes. A lecture was in the making and, quite frankly, she wasn't in the mood. She'd had a long day, a happy one but long nonetheless. All she wanted to do was go to bed and relive the precious moments in her mind.

Bridget leveled a challenging gaze on her sister. "Out with it, Nora."

"I want to talk to you about William Black."

Bridget pretended surprise, then adopted an innocent expression. "Why do you want to talk about my employer?"

"Don't pretend you don't know what I mean. You've been uncommonly concerned with his situation, and that worries me."

Bristling, Bridget jerked her chin. "He's had a rough go of it lately."

"I realize that." Nora lowered in front of her and placed her hands on Bridget's knees. "You like him, don't you?"

"He's a good man," she allowed, refusing to give her sister any more ammunition than necessary. "*And* a fair boss."

"That's right. You're his children's nanny, Bridget. You need to remember that very important point."

"What are you implying?" It was a rhetorical question. They both knew what Nora meant.

Sighing, Nora settled in the chair next to her and began rocking. They were both quiet a moment, each lost in their own thoughts.

"Bridget." Nora took her hand and squeezed. "You give your heart so freely. *Too* freely, I fear. After what Daniel did to you, I couldn't bear watching you go through that pain again."

The mention of her former fiancé took her by surprise and she flinched. "What does Daniel have to do with Will?"

"Everything." Nora released her hand. "You were devastated for months after he left you at the altar."

Of course she'd been devastated. She'd planned to make a life with Daniel McGrath. She'd thought he'd shared her same hopes and dreams, as well as her desire to serve the Lord. She'd been wrong, so terribly wrong. Daniel hadn't wanted Bridget to serve the Lord; he'd wanted her to serve him.

She still wasn't sure what hurt more. His rejection or the way he'd broken things off, minutes before the ceremony.

"That was a year ago, Nora. I'm fine, now." As soon as the words left her mouth Bridget realized they were true. She wasn't devastated by Daniel's change of heart, not anymore. In fact, had she married him she wouldn't have left Ireland. She wouldn't have met Will and his family. She wouldn't—

"I don't want to see you hurt again," Nora reiterated, shoving her hair off her face. "Daniel was a selfish man, only concerned with his own interests. I fear your new employer is no different."

"Will is *nothing* like Daniel."

"Isn't he?"

"No." She shook her head vehemently. "You have no right making assumptions like that. Will cares for his family and puts their needs above his own." That alone made him different from Daniel.

"What about your needs, Bridget? Does he put your needs first?"

It was an unfair question. "I'm his children's nanny, my needs aren't important."

"Oh, but they are. Bridget, listen to me." Nora's mouth tightened. "You've always put others first, yourself last."

"What's wrong with that? Aren't we supposed to be humble and consider others better than ourselves? Isn't that the message in your favorite Bible verse, Philippians 2:3?"

By Nora's scowl, Bridget knew she'd hit her mark. "I won't deny that your tender, giving spirit is your greatest gift. But I see the way you are with William Black, the way you look at him. Bridget, you're headed for another heartache."

Now Bridget was angry. Nora had no right to lecture her on this matter. She didn't know all the facts. "I'll not quit my job because of something that may or may not happen in the future. No—" she held up her hand to keep her sister from interrupting "—let me finish."

Nora clamped her lips tightly shut.

"I've made a promise to William Black to care for his motherless children until he can find another woman to marry. I will follow through with my promise." And if she harbored a secret hope, deep in a hidden place in her heart, that things might work out differently, well that was none of her sister's concern.

Feeling the tiniest bit guilty for holding back a portion of the truth, Bridget rose from the chair and lifted her nose in the air. "And that's the end of it. I'll not discuss this again with you, Nora."

Finished having her say, she marched toward the boarding-house, head still high. No one told Bridget Murphy she was wrong to serve a family in need. Not even her older sister.

"Bridget, wait."

She stopped with her hand on the doorknob.

"Don't you want to talk about our new house and all we have ahead of us? We need to plan our next step and we need to do so together."

Nora wasn't exactly apologizing for her meddling, but Bridget knew the change of subject was an olive branch none-theless.

It was also the perfect topic to erase Bridget's annoyance. Excited about the possibilities that lay ahead of them, she returned to her abandoned rocking chair. "I have some initial thoughts."

Nora smiled. "I'd love to hear them."

Chapter Thirteen

Hoping to catch Will before he left for the day, Bridget arrived at his house early the next morning. She caught him on the front stoop, just as he pulled two sleepy-eyed children into his arms. Laughing at something Caleb mumbled in his ear, he kissed them both on their tiny heads.

Caught up in the moment, Bridget's throat clogged with emotion. The unmistakable love and affection in Will's voice as he told his children to mind their new nanny made the backs of her eyes sting. She placed her fingertips to her eyelids and swallowed hard, praying the moment would pass before any of them noticed her watching them.

Too late. Olivia shrieked her name. "Miss Bridget, you're here!"

Straightening, Will pivoted around to face her. His lips spread into a welcoming smile.

Her reaction was immediate. Everything ground to a halt inside her, her breath, her heartbeat, her ability to think. And then an ache of longing tore through her, one that nearly brought her to her knees.

Bridget was a talker by nature, or, at least, she'd always thought that to be true about herself. But around this man, with his marvelous eyes and intense love for his children, she found herself speechless all too often. Today was no exception.

Caleb rescued her as he sped around his father and catapulted himself into her arms. She had to move quickly to keep from dropping him. Bobbling under his additional weight, she laughed. "Hello, Caleb."

The little boy rubbed his cheek against her shoulder. "Good morning, Miss Bridget." So heartfelt, so sweet.

"I think he likes you," Will said over her head.

"It's a mutual affection."

He chuckled. "I see that."

Setting the child on the ground, she smiled up at her new boss. She felt an actual impact when their gazes met. "I'm glad I caught you."

"You are?" His voice sounded pleased.

"My sister and I have decided to move into Laird O'Malley's house, I mean *our* house, Sunday afternoon." She wasn't sure why she felt the need to inform him of her plans. He was only her employer. His confused expression indicated he was wondering the same thing. She paused, collecting her thoughts. "I just wanted you to know I don't plan to ask for a day off."

"I would have given it to you if you'd asked."

Of course he would have. "Nevertheless." She smiled despite her nerves. "I thought you should know."

"Thank you." He reached down and picked up a large leather case that she guessed was designed to house important papers. "I'll be home early again tonight."

And with that he was striding away from them, tossing one last goodbye over his shoulder.

Staring after him, her throat thick with emotion, Bridget smoothed a hand down her hair and breathed in deeply.

Caleb yanked on her skirt, practically vibrating with little-boy eagerness. "What are we going to do today? Can we play tag?"

Not to be left out of the planning, Olivia pulled on Bridget's skirt from the other side. "I want to see the baby again, the one you had with you at church."

After much discussion and a bit of arguing between the twins it was decided they would do both, a rousing game of tag followed by a short visit to the Sheriff's Office to see how Nora and baby Grace were coping. "But before we start the fun and games we're going to march back inside, eat our breakfast and then practice our letters."

A chorus of mild-mannered grumbles followed her statement, but they obeyed.

By the time they were on the road to Nora's place of employment, Bridget had learned several interesting things about her new charges. They had exceptional patience for three-year-olds, never once fidgeting during their lesson, and their minds were like sponges. They remembered whatever she taught them after the first telling. The Black children were a pleasure to teach.

Holding their hands, Bridget drew up short at the sight that filled her gaze. A familiar young man was talking to Sheriff Long on the walkway outside the jail.

What was Gavin McCorkle doing in Faith Glen? He was supposed to be in Boston with his brothers and Mrs. Fitzwilliam. Had something happened? No, he didn't appear upset. He was quite animated, gesturing wildly with his hands as he spoke.

"Gavin? Gavin McCorkle?" She closed the distance between them. "Is that really you?"

"Miss Bridget." His face split into a grin, his blue eyes enormous in his freckled face. "I was just telling the sheriff about our journey across the ocean with you and your sisters. And he was telling me about your new jobs."

He paused, looked down. His grin widened. "This must be Caleb and Olivia Black."

"You know our names?" Caleb asked, his round little face full of wonder.

"I sure do."

"You talk like Miss Bridget. Did you come over on a ship, too? Like this one?" Caleb lifted the boat in his hand.

"Would you look at that?" Gavin gave a low, appreciative whistle. "It's the *Annie McGee* herself."

Caleb giggled, clearly delighted by the attention from the older boy. While he rattled off the various points of interest on the model boat he now knew by heart, Bridget looked over at Cameron Long.

The sheriff was leaning against a post in a leisurely manner, seemingly relieved Gavin was otherwise occupied. She hid a smile. From what she remembered of the oldest McCorkle brother, Gavin could be very enthusiastic when telling a story.

"Hello, Cameron," she said, giving him a sympathetic smile.

He tipped his hat. "Bridget, always a pleasure."

"Is my sister inside?"

"Yep." He pushed away from the post and gave Olivia an awkward pat on the head. "Nora's tidying the jail."

"Oh." Bridget hadn't fully thought through this impromptu visit and now she wasn't sure she should expose the children to an actual jailhouse.

"The jail cells are empty." He lowered his voice for her ears only. "Olivia and Caleb have been inside before."

"Well, then," she breathed in an audible sigh of relief, "very good."

Deciding she'd been ignored long enough, Olivia scooted in between Bridget and the sheriff. "Is baby Grace inside, too?"

"She sure is," he confirmed with a slightly caged look. The man really was uncomfortable around children.

"Can we go see the baby now?" Olivia pleaded. "Please? Oh, please?"

"In a moment." Bridget placed her hand on the girl's shoulder. "You'll have to be patient a little while longer."

Lower lip jutting out, Olivia gave a long-suffering sigh then plopped onto the bench outside the jailhouse, her doll cradled in her arms.

"As nice as it is to see you, I have to run out to the Phelps's place before lunch." Cameron looked down at Olivia then lowered his voice even further. "Mrs. Phelps claims someone tried to break into her barn last night."

Bridget swallowed back a gasp. "I thought you said this was a peaceful community."

"It is." He gave her an assuring smile. "She probably heard a raccoon rustling around, or maybe a stray dog."

Remembering the skittish animal she and Will had come across last evening, Bridget relaxed. "That makes sense."

He tipped his hat again, said goodbye to Gavin and the children, then was gone.

Once he turned the corner, Bridget returned her attention to the oldest McCorkle brother. "Gavin," she said softly. "I still don't know what you're doing in Faith Glen."

Smiling at Caleb, he handed the toy back to the boy then stood to address Bridget's question. "Mrs. Fitzwilliam sent me to find out how you and Miss Nora are settling into your new home."

Although the widow's interest in them was heartwarming, it made little sense. Yes, they'd created a bond aboard ship, but the older woman was far above the Murphy sisters' station. "I half expected her to forget us by now."

"No, don't say that, Miss Bridget. Don't even think it." Gavin shook his head vehemently. "Mrs. Fitzwilliam has been very worried about all of you, even baby Grace. I'm not to return home without a full report."

Home. Bridget couldn't help but smile. The way Gavin said the word alleviated any remaining doubts she might have had about the boy's future.

"I'm also to let you know," he continued, "that she's successfully hired a private detective to search for Mary."

"Oh. Yes, of course." Bridget's cheeks grew warm. She'd been so caught up in her own life she'd nearly forgotten about Mrs. Fitzwilliam's worry over her missing stepgranddaughter. "Has she had news, then?"

"None, so far." Gavin broke eye contact a moment. "It seems the girl has vanished into thin air."

"How disappointing."

"Yes, very."

Out of the corner of her eye Bridget watched Caleb set his boat beside his sister then jump from one plank to the next, reciting the alphabet as he went.

"But Mrs. Fitzwilliam has hired the best detective in Boston. We're very hopeful she'll find Mary soon."

Gavin sounded as concerned as his benefactor. Mrs. Fitzwilliam had obviously taken the McCorkle brothers into her heart, but so had they taken her into theirs. It was a lovely ending to a rocky beginning for all four of them.

"You are looking very well, Gavin." She paused to eye his clothing. The trousers and shirt were a far better quality than the ones he and his brothers had worn aboard the *Annie McGee*.

Blushing under the inspection, Gavin scuffed the toe of his boot on the sidewalk. "Mrs. Fitzwilliam has been very good to me and my brothers."

"I'm glad to hear it."

"She's even gone so far as to enroll me in school," he said, sighing heavily, his tone falling short of pleased. "She says it's important I better myself with an education."

"That seems like wise advice," Bridget said carefully, not sure what she heard in his voice. "Gavin, do you not wish to attend school?"

He shrugged. "I was never good with books. I'd rather be a lawman—" he looked over his shoulder in the direction Cameron had taken out of town "—maybe even a sheriff one day."

It took little imagination for Bridget to picture Gavin in the role. The boy had a very strong sense of right and wrong and knew how to protect others, as evidenced by the care he'd given his younger brothers. Yes, she could see him one day becoming a deputy. "Have you told Mrs. Fitzwilliam any of this?"

"A hundred times." He shrugged again. "She won't listen, says I'm far too smart to waste time on such a lowly endeavor."

Now *that* sounded like the high-handed widow Bridget remembered. Before she could comment any further Caleb hopped onto the plank next to Gavin, stopping mere inches from slamming into him. "I know how to say the entire alphabet," he declared, his little chest puffed out with pride. "Want to hear?"

Gavin ruffled his hair, seemingly fine with the change of topic. "Sure do."

Three verses later, minus a few letters in the middle, Bridget decided it was time to move along. "Come, children. You, too, Gavin. Let's find out how my sister and baby Grace are making out."

"At last." Olivia hopped to her feet, her eyes thrilled. The little girl was the first to enter the building, the rest of their tiny group following closely behind.

Since the first day Bridget had begun working in his home, Will had found a multitude of reasons to alter his daily routine. He'd closed the mill hours ahead of schedule—and only partially because of the stifling heat. He'd returned twice under the guise of having left important papers behind. He'd eventually quit making excuses and journeyed home to eat lunch with Bridget and the rest of his family.

And thus, as the noon hour approached on the fifth day of Bridget's employment, Will walked home with a smile on his face. Today was the end of her one-week trial. He would definitely be asking her to stay on.

Whistling the song she'd taught the children last night, he headed for the front door. Childish giggles dancing on the wind had him redirecting his steps toward the backyard. A familiar bark had him increasing his pace to a dead run.

When Will rounded the side of the house he froze.

Happy chaos reigned in the backyard of the Black home. It wasn't long before a laugh bubbled in his throat, begging for release. He let it come, let it flow out of him with welcome force.

Bridget had somehow managed to entice the mangy mutt they'd encountered earlier in the week into a tub of soapy water. The dog splashed around, tossing his head in the air, sending suds flying.

In their attempt to help, the children were as wet as the animal. Even Bridget hadn't escaped the madness. Her dress was half-soaked while her hair clung in wet tendrils around her face. She'd never looked more beautiful.

He watched her try to form some semblance of order amidst the bedlam. Or rather she tried and failed. Somehow, he didn't think she meant to succeed.

Will wanted to join the fun, but he wasn't sure adding another person to the fray was wise.

The dog settled the matter by jumping out of the tub and barreling straight for him. There was only time for impressions before his arms were filled with wet, wiggling fur. If an animal could smile, Will was certain this one was doing so, a big, loopy grin that included a hanging tongue. The same tongue that swiped across his face.

He laughed again. His suit was probably ruined, but all he could think was: *She's done it again. Bridget has charmed yet another unsuspecting creature.* At this rate the whole town would be under her influence in a month.

Looking over the dog's head, he caught her eye.

Her returning smile was enough to stop his breath.

"All right, boyo," he said, desperate to regain control over his emotions. "Let's get you back in the tub."

Will set the animal on the ground, clapped his hands and set out. The dog obediently followed.

"Papa," Caleb shouted. "We found a dog." He pointed unnecessarily to the wet animal practically dancing beside him.

Bridget gave Will immediate assurance that his children hadn't been in harm's way. Of that he had no doubt. Not when he remembered the night they'd first encountered the dog and how quickly she'd soothed the nervous animal's fears.

Bending over, Will lifted the dog in his arms and set him in the tub once more. "Where did you find him?"

"Actually…" Bridget poured a bucket of water over the animal's soapy fur "…he found us."

A wide spray of water and suds shot through the air as the dog shook, and then shook again. Giggling, Olivia opened her arms and twirled under the impromptu waterfall. Caleb jumped up and down in his own version of the same dance.

Feeling unusually lighthearted himself, Will swiped water droplets off his face. "I'm sure there's a story behind this."

"Oh, there is," Bridget agreed, repeating the rinsing process.

Better prepared this time, Will took a step back before the animal shook himself free of the excess water.

By the third dousing every family member was as wet

as the dog. No one seemed to mind, not even Bridget. She seemed entirely oblivious to her disheveled state. And that made her all the more stunning in Will's mind. Her face was bright and happy and incredibly beautiful.

He took another step back and nearly trampled over his tiny daughter. He caught her before she fell to the ground. Then, on a sudden whim, lifted her high in the air and spun her in circles. Around and around and around. She squealed in delight, kicking her legs wildly.

"Again," she demanded. "Do it again."

Will spun her around in the opposite direction.

The moment he set Olivia on the ground, Caleb lifted his arms. "My turn."

Laughing, Will obliged his son, tossing the little boy over his shoulder after the third spin. He hopped around a bit then lowered him to the ground.

Once his feet were steady Caleb rushed back to the dog, now a very calm animal who was stoically enduring a vigorous toweling off from Bridget.

"Can we keep him, Papa?"

"Please, can we?" Olivia echoed.

"I have a feeling the matter is already settled." When both children simply stared at him, he clarified. "Yes, you may keep him, as long as he stays outside."

A chorus of cheers rose in the air. Sensing something significant had just occurred, the dog joined in the fun with a blissful *bark, bark, bark.* An impromptu celebration ensued.

Two children, one dog, lots of happiness.

Unable to remember a time he'd seen either of his children this uninhibited and natural, or when he'd felt this full of joy, Will glanced over at Bridget. Gratitude filled him. She had her head down, her hands busy pouring out the tub water onto the lawn.

Needing to thank her, he walked over to her, took her hand

in his and laced their fingers together. Her soft intake of air was the only sign of her reaction to his bold move. He tightened his hold.

"You've done it again," he whispered.

She swung a startled glance up to his and then carefully drew her hand free. "I…I didn't mean to force the issue. The dog isn't a danger. He's—"

Will stopped the rest of her words with a finger to her lips. "I'm not angry."

Her mouth parted in surprise.

She looked so sweet, so innocent. So—kissable. He breathed in a sliver of hot summer air and nearly gave in to the urge to press his lips to her very attractive mouth.

She's your children's nanny, Will. Their. Nanny.

His instincts warned him to keep his distance, to remember why Bridget was in his home and that she'd refused to be his bride. She would not welcome his kiss—that had been made quite clear. "I better go change my clothes."

She said nothing, simply stared at him. Her hair hung loose around her face, the brown locks shot with red fire from the sun. The warm July air wafted between them and, still, she remained silent, blinking up at him as though deciphering a puzzle.

His arms itched to gather her close. He stepped back instead, and did so again for good measure. Each inch pulled him away from her, away from the temptation of doing something both of them might regret. Because no matter how many times he told himself this woman wasn't his, a rebellious part of him refused to accept that fact.

He turned on his heel and strode quickly to the house. His mother met him at the door. "My goodness, son, you're soaked through."

"Mother," he said in way of greeting, then rested his gaze upon her face. The purple shadows beneath her eyes were all but gone, the tight lines around her mouth smoothed away. "You look…" he searched for the proper word "…refreshed."

"Oh, I am." She ran a hand over her hair. "The daily naps Bridget insists I take have restored my tired old bones beyond my wildest hopes."

Once again Will found himself in Bridget Murphy's debt. Five days in his home and she'd worked wonders. His children were happy. His mother was no longer exhausted and he, well, *he* needed to change out of his wet clothes. He started off.

"Will, before you go."

He turned back around. "Yes?"

"Did you know Bridget and her sister are planning to move into Laird O'Malley's house Sunday afternoon?"

"She told me about the plans several days ago." And since that time he'd spent countless quantities of wasted breath trying to dissuade her from moving in so soon. But her excitement had been too great and she'd refused to listen to his arguments.

Although he'd eventually given up the fight, he still wasn't pleased with the idea of her living in that ramshackle house without a proper inspection first.

"I think you should assist the Murphy sisters with their move."

He'd like nothing better. It would give him a chance to check out the structure, assess any damage. But there was a problem, two of them to be exact. "The children—"

"Should stay home with me."

"Are you sure you're up to it?"

It was the precise wrong thing to say. "William Nathanial Black. I am not dead yet." Tiny as she was, his mother looked rather fierce. "I am quite capable of watching my grandchildren for a few hours."

He'd insulted her. That hadn't been his plan. "Of course you're capable."

"Then it's settled." Her tone brooked no argument.

"Yes." Will gave her one solemn nod of his head. "If Bridget wants my help moving into her new home, then I will be at her disposal the entire afternoon."

"Wonderful. Now go." She gave him a mock scowl, followed by a little shove. "You're dripping all over my clean floor and adding extra work for the housekeeper."

"So sorry." He strode swiftly down the hallway, thinking his day couldn't get much better.

Chapter Fourteen

Bridget was still disheveled, but thankfully composed by the time Will returned in a fresh set of clean, dry clothes. He looked handsome as ever, even with damp hair. She had to fight to regain her equilibrium all over again. There'd been a moment earlier, right before he'd gone inside, when she'd thought he might kiss her. He hadn't, of course. But now her insides were all quivering and she was struggling with an array of complicated, baffling emotions.

Her eyes met his from across the lawn and her stomach performed a slow, unexpected roll. Will was looking at her in that special way of his, as if he truly saw her, and she *truly* mattered to him.

Her cheeks grew warm and her hand lifted to her face. She brushed back a tangle of wet curls flopping across her eyes.

The dog caught sight of Will, did a few hops of joy and then raced straight for him.

"No," Bridget yelled after the animal. "No jumping."

Undeterred, the dog continued toward his target, but then he skidded to a stop, dropped to the ground at Will's feet and executed a quick flip, stopping once his feet were in the air and his belly was exposed.

Will gave the white fur a brisk rub. "You miserable mutt,

spoiled already." He looked up, glanced around him, focused on Bridget. "Where are the children?"

"Upstairs with your mother." She angled her head toward the house. "Esther offered to bathe them while I clean up out here. He likes you," she said, indicating the happy dog at his feet.

"Have you named him yet?"

"I was thinking we could call him Winston, or maybe Gus, or, perhaps—" she narrowed her eyes and thought about the animal's propensity for uprooting bushes "—Digger."

"Digger, huh?" Will laughed, the sound a rich, hearty baritone. "I'm afraid to ask."

"Best that you don't."

They shared a smile.

Will straightened, the dog all but forgotten. "Bridget, about our agreement..." His words trailed off.

She tried not to stiffen at the sound of his serious tone. Needing something to do with her hands, she called the dog over and rested her fingertips on his head. "Our... agreement?"

Eyes dark and somber, Will stepped closer. "I'd like you to stay on as the children's nanny. For however long we can have you."

"Oh." That ridiculous stipulation of hers. How could she have forgotten? Perhaps because she felt so much a part of this family already, as if the matter had been settled long ago.

"I'd like to stay on." She stroked first one then the other of Digger's silky ears. "I'd like that very much."

"Then we're in agreement."

"We are."

His gaze dropped to her mouth.

Her lips trembled in response.

He drew in a long, hard pull of air. "There is one other matter I wish to discuss with you."

Her hand stilled on the dog. She swallowed and then ran her fingernails down his back.

Will's gaze followed the gesture. "I'd like to offer my assistance to you and your sister Sunday afternoon."

"You want to help us move?"

He must have sensed her surprise because his lips twisted in a grimace. "Is that so hard to believe?"

"No, but—" she pulled her hand back to her side "—what about the children? I don't think it would be wise to bring them out just yet."

She didn't add that she feared for their safety. That would only open up yet another conversation about her decision to live in a house that wasn't quite sound.

"My mother will watch them for us."

For us. Bridget's heart danced a happy jig against her ribs. Did he realize how that sounded?

She had to turn away so he wouldn't see the joy that surely must be in her eyes. They had more than enough hands already committed to the move. Nora, herself, Maeve, Flynn, even Cameron Long had agreed to be available for most of the afternoon.

Nevertheless Bridget found herself saying, "I would love for you to assist us on Sunday. Thank you for offering."

"No, Bridget, thank you." He reached out and placed a finger under her chin, adding pressure until she looked in his direction. "Thank you for bringing happiness back into this home."

"You're welcome, Will." She tried to keep her voice easy and bright, but the tension building inside her was like nothing she'd ever experienced. She was both hot and cold at the same time, all shivery inside and out.

Oh, Lord, what's happening to me? What is this strange, new feeling?

Will dropped his hand and shifted slightly away. "I better return to work."

"As should I."

"I'll be home at the usual time tonight." He reached down, acknowledged the dog with a quick pat then was gone.

Trying not to sigh, Bridget watched his retreating back until he disappeared around the house.

You like him, Nora had accused. "Oh, Nora," Bridget whispered to the spot Will had just vacated. "You have no idea how much."

Sunday afternoon brought rain, the kind of hard, pile-driving sheets of water that created mud puddles and bad tempers. And to think, the morning had started off so well. The sun had shone brightly in the sky. The church service had been both inspiring and moving, with another fitting sermon on faith and trusting the Lord.

God was trying to tell her something and Bridget was listening. Her future was in the Lord's hands. She simply had to have faith that all would turn out for the best, no matter what obstacles came her way.

Just like the week before, Bridget and Nora had sat with Will and the children in their pew. Esther had joined them, as had Cameron Long and—this one shocked them all—Deputy MacDuff.

More stunning still, Ben had spent most of the service whispering softly with Will's mother. Evidently the two were friends, *good* friends. It had been nice to see Esther smiling so liberally. When she'd giggled at something Ben had said to her, Will had caught Bridget's eye and grinned. He was clearly enjoying his mother's transformation.

With such a stellar beginning to the day, Bridget refused to be put off by the ill weather now. They were moving into their new house this afternoon and nothing, not even a little rain—all right, a large downpour—was going to stop them.

"It's just water, Nora," Bridget insisted when her sister grumbled a third time in less than a minute. "So we get a bit wet. We've been through worse."

"That's certainly true." Nora snapped open her umbrella and stepped out into the rain. Rolling thunder marked her progress to Flynn's carriage, where Maeve was already waiting with baby Grace in her arms.

Bridget followed her sister a moment later, picking her way carefully down the walk as she avoided first one puddle and then another. Raindrops fell in tidy rivulets from the points of her umbrella. Instead of feeling annoyed, she experienced a surge of excitement. Will had arranged to meet them out at the house. She was happy he would share this new beginning with her.

Flynn met Nora at the end of the walkway. Seemingly unaware of the rain falling down on his head, he took her arm.

"Is this all of your belongings?" He hitched his chin toward the top of the carriage where he'd finished tying off the second of their two trunks.

"That's it," Nora said.

"Then we should head out to the house without further delay." Although Flynn appeared somewhat impatient to be off, he helped Nora into the carriage then turned and took Bridget's arm.

Instead of allowing him to hand her into the carriage behind Nora she pulled out of his reach. "Flynn, wait."

Water dripping down his face, he gave her a questioning look.

"I have something I wish to ask of you, a favor, of sorts." When he didn't respond, she continued, "It's about my employer's mother."

"Your...employer." Flynn frowned, his expression no

longer patient but somewhat stern. "You are speaking of William Black, the man from the docks, the one looking for his *bride*."

Her brother-in-law's face took on a troubled expression, and Bridget doubted it was because of the rain pounding down on his head. What exactly had Nora told him about Will?

She wasn't sure she wanted to know. "Would you mind examining Will's mother before you and Maeve leave for Boston later today?"

The doctor slid firmly into place. "Is she ill?"

"No. At least she seems well enough." In fact, now that Bridget thought about it, Esther had glowed with good health this morning in church. "However, she recently suffered what I believe was a bad case of exhaustion. It wouldn't hurt to make sure she's as well as she seems."

"If it's important to you then—"

"Oh, it is. Very important."

"Then how can I refuse? Now if that's all, let's get you out of the rain." He took her arm and steered her toward the carriage. This time, Bridget went willingly.

Once the women were settled inside, Flynn shut the door behind her with a firm snap. A moment later the carriage gave a hard jolt then rolled smoothly forward.

Nora chattered happily with Maeve, sharing details about their stay in the boardinghouse and the lovely people they'd met. "Oh," she said, cutting herself off in midsentence. "I haven't told you yet. Gavin McCorkle came to visit us this week."

"Gavin was in Faith Glen?" Maeve's surprise sounded in her voice. "Were his brothers and Mrs. Fitzwilliam with him?"

"No, he came alone."

"He came all the way to Faith Glen, by himself?" Maeve asked, wiping a droplet of water off the baby's blanket.

Bridget joined the conversation, explaining how the boy had stopped by the jailhouse. "According to Gavin," she added, "Mrs. Fitzwilliam has hired a private detective to locate her missing stepgranddaughter."

Maeve digested this information, her expression thoughtful. "The widow is certainly a woman of her word."

"And very determined, too. I predict she'll locate Mary within the month."

All three sisters nodded in agreement.

"What I don't understand—" Maeve sat up straighter "—is how did Gavin end up at the jailhouse? Why didn't he try the boardinghouse first?"

"As it turns out," Bridget said and let out a little laugh, "Gavin is interested in becoming a lawman one day."

"Oh. Yes." Maeve nodded. "I can see that."

"Bridget said the same thing," Nora confirmed in her big-sister voice. "And we all know she's very insightful about these sorts of things."

"That she is." Maeve pressed her toe to Bridget's and gave her an unreadable smile. "So tell me about your new job. Are the Black children better behaved than the Atwater girls?"

Something in Maeve's voice made Bridget bristle. "Why don't you ask Nora about her job?"

"I did earlier, when you were speaking with Flynn in the rain." Maeve rolled her eyes. "She said it was fine."

If Nora hadn't felt the need to expand, then neither would Bridget. "My job is fine, too."

Maeve sighed dramatically. "If you won't talk about your job, then tell me about William Black." Her voice held mild curiosity, an obvious ruse to cover the fact that she was mining for information. "From what I remember of the man, he seemed a bit severe."

That was the same word Nora had used when she'd described Will. He was many things, but severe he was not. He was kind, generous, loyal and honorable to the bone. Plus, there was no doubt he loved his children dearly and shared in all their joys and excitement.

Closing her eyes, Bridget called to mind an image of him rolling on the floor with the twins, and another of him tossing a stick for Digger to chase after, and one more of him sitting in a chair far too small for his frame while he listened to Bridget read to the children.

Severe? No, her sisters were wrong. Will was…he was… remarkable.

"When you first met him—" she began, feeling the need to defend him "—of course he seemed intense. He was concerned about his intended."

"That must have been it." Looking unconvinced, Maeve smoothed her fingertip across one of Grace's eyebrows. "What about his mother? How are you getting on with her?"

"Actually rather well." Before her sister could continue with her questions, Bridget added, "And I adore the children most of all. Stop worrying, Maeve, I'm quite happy with my position in Will's home."

Maeve's expression sharpened. "If you say so."

"I say so."

Grace chose that moment to let out an earsplitting wail.

Now that, Bridget thought with a large sense of relief, was the perfect ending to Maeve's not-too-subtle inquisition. They spent the rest of the ride discussing Grace's care and what was being done to find her parents.

By the time Flynn directed the carriage onto the road leading to Laird's house, the rain had stopped and sunbeams cut bold lines through several seams in the clouds.

Bridget looked out the window, bracing herself with a hand

on the seat as they bumped and splashed along the unkempt path. Mosquitoes buzzed in her ears and she noticed gnats swarming in clumps around the puddles.

"You might want to cover Grace," Bridget warned, turning back to glance at her sisters. "The rain has brought out the insects." She swatted at a fly hovering close to her nose.

"I'll take care of it." Nora reached out her arms and took the baby from Maeve before settling a swaddling cloth around her tiny body.

Once the carriage came to a halt Bridget jumped to the ground ahead of everyone else. Steam rose off a nearby puddle and snaked around her feet.

Shrugging off the heat, she looked around her. Will's carriage sat off to her left, looking quite empty. Wondering where he could be, she turned to face the house. He was standing on the stoop, his arms hanging loosely by his sides.

The moment their eyes met something flared to life in his face, a look that Bridget knew was reserved solely for her.

She experienced a ridiculous urge to run to him. He was so different from any man she'd ever known, strong, principled and very, very masculine.

A ray of sunlight caught on his hair, streaking a hint of gold through the black. He seemed to be silently calling her to him.

She started forward, slowly, inch by methodical inch.

"Well, I say." Maeve tugged her to a halt. "I'm a bit scandalized."

"What?" Bridget yanked her gaze away from Will. "Why?"

"That man on the stoop is looking at you rather—" she lowered her voice to a whisper "—*warmly* for an employer looking at his nanny."

"*Maeve.*"

"Now don't go acting all outraged on me, Bridget Murphy. You're looking at him in the very same manner."

"I...I..." she sputtered and gasped and sputtered some more. "You can't possibly know... That is, I'm not..."

"Oh, stop it." Maeve slapped her arm affectionately. "You know exactly what I mean."

Unfortunately Bridget did know. She'd been staring at Will like a lovesick cow. "Please tell me I wasn't batting my eyelashes."

"Not quite, but close."

Bridget gasped.

"I'm only teasing you." Maeve patted her hand in a show of sisterly solidarity. "Now, come along, Bridget. I believe proper introductions are in order."

"You've already met Will, back in Boston. Remember?"

"Ah, yes, but I'm afraid we must begin anew. In fact, after what I just saw pass between you two..." Maeve gave her a haughty stare that rivaled any Mrs. Fitzwilliam had bestowed on them "...it's imperative I become better acquainted with your...employer."

Chapter Fifteen

Will had no idea what her sister said to Bridget, but he sensed it had something to do with him. Watching the two with their heads bent so closely together he saw the family resemblance at once.

Although Bridget's hair was darker and she was taller by a few inches, both women shared delicate bone structure and the same remarkable shape to their eyes. Their creamy, alabaster skin and symmetrical features reminded Will of Olivia's porcelain dolls.

They were both stunning women, but Bridget's beauty was softer, giving her a more approachable air.

The oldest sister joined them and the three locked arms. There was no mistaking the bold picture they made. Sisters, kith and kin, *family.* Remarkable women who had endured hardships together, and had not only survived their trials but had flourished. Their unity reminded Will of the Scripture from Ecclesiastes, *a threefold cord is not quickly broken.*

Bridget stood between the other two, arms linked with her sisters, her eyes seeking his a second time.

When their gazes met again, he smiled.

She lowered her head and sighed. He liked her reaction. It made him feel very masculine and more than a little possessive. She was becoming a part of his life in ways he'd never imagined. He thought of her when he first woke in the morning and right before he drifted off to sleep at night.

He knew something important was happening between them, something he didn't want to analyze too closely just yet. She hadn't committed to him, had refused his proposal. She could leave him at any time. He had to remember that.

Enough stalling. Will started down the steps, just as Bridget broke away from her sisters. She met him halfway across the lawn.

"Thank you for coming today." Her hands twisted in the fabric of her skirt.

Was she nervous? Around him?

A prickly feeling tingled in his fingertips. They itched to touch her, to soothe away her anxiousness. He placed his hand on her arm. "I'm happy to help."

A movement behind her caught his attention and he looked over Bridget's shoulder. Her sisters were watching them intently, with what looked like suspicion in their eyes. He arched a brow, both annoyed and pleased by their loyalty. These women understood family, better than most.

Not wishing to upset anyone, he dropped his hand and took a step back. "The Coulters are inside, waiting for you to tell them if they should move out of their room to another smaller one upstairs."

Bridget's gaze snapped to his. "No. Oh, no. We don't expect them to move. I must speak with them at once." She hurried into the house, leaving him to stare after her.

Nora started forward as well, the baby tucked securely in her arms. She stopped next to Will and glowered at him. "What did you say to upset my sister?"

Her obvious concern for Bridget took away any annoyance on his part. It was good to know her family valued her as much as she deserved. "James and Agnes are waiting to be told where to move. I think they may have misunderstood your intentions."

"Oh, no." She hurried toward the house behind Bridget. Watching her rush off, he realized he hadn't told her about the cakes of chocolate he'd brought for her to use in her baking.

"Well." The third sister joined him at the bottom of the stairs and gave him a rueful smile. "You certainly have a way with women, Mr. Black."

He glanced over his shoulder, trying not to flinch when the door slammed behind Nora. "One would think I'd insulted them."

"One would think." Although her words came out flat and unemotional, this youngest Murphy sister regarded him with an amused twinkle in her eye. She seemed to understand his confusion. "What, precisely, did you say to them?"

"I merely told them that the Coulters are awaiting their instructions as to where to move their belongings." He lifted a helpless shoulder.

"Ah." Her eyes filled with wisdom far beyond her years. "That would do it."

He lifted an eyebrow, still confused.

The woman patted his arm in a gesture that fell just short of patronizing. "After what we went through those last few days in Ireland neither of my sisters would subject the Coulters to a similar misfortune."

At last Will understood. Bridget had told him about their Irish landlord's actions. Considering what they'd suffered, they would never expect the Coulters to relocate, not even to a different room in the house.

Maeve patted his arm again, this time with more affection. "I had better go check on my sisters and the worried caretakers."

"That might be wise."

She walked past him, eyes fixed on the house. She climbed

the steps a bit slower than her sisters had, but Will caught the urgency in her gaze. If he'd suspected otherwise, he now knew the truth. All three Murphy sisters were godly, kind-hearted women who put the needs of others ahead of their own.

Evaluating the collection of emotions churning in his gut, Will decided one very important fact. He'd been blessed to have met Bridget Murphy. She was a special woman, born in a special family. He wasn't sure he'd ever be the same for knowing her, and was glad for the opportunity. What he would do next to make the most of that opportunity required some considerable thought.

For now, he set out toward the black, well-made carriage sitting a hundred feet away from his own. He eyed the man standing beside it, the one he'd met in Boston, the one who had declared his intended bride officially dead.

Flynn Gallagher watched his approach with an unreadable expression.

At the moment Will wasn't in the mood for a lengthy conversation with the other man. He'd just as soon forget about their last meeting, at least for today. "Put me to work."

Flynn met his gaze, smiled at last and then clasped him on the back in the universal male gesture of welcome. "Gladly, my good man."

While they were still unraveling the ropes, Cameron Long rode up on his horse. "Want another pair of hands?" he called out.

"Absolutely," they said as one.

Cam jumped down and then looped his horse's reins over a tree branch near a patch of wet grass. The steed lowered his head and happily munched away. Introductions were made and the men took on the task of unloading the Murphy sisters' belongings.

Discussing the wonders of female packing habits—all the

while marveling at how even women of modest means could collect a multitude of unnecessary items—the three men proceeded to unload bags, trunks and carrying cases.

They worked as a well-oiled team, as though they'd been toiling together for a lifetime. Will had a strange sense of homecoming, as though he'd finally found his place in the world.

That didn't make sense. He'd worked in his family's mill since he was a boy, had always known his future was there, making chocolate, providing jobs for others. Today, however, he'd been given a glimpse of something else, something equally permanent yet altogether different. Bridget Murphy was at the center, drawing him close, calling to a part of him long dormant that yearned for a richer sense of family in his life.

Uncomfortable with the sensation, he picked up a large trunk and made his way to the house without stopping.

Once inside he shifted his load and waited for instructions. Bridget pointed him in the direction of the staircase. "That goes in the first room on the right."

After a short nod he headed up the stairs, keeping his eyes cast down as he went. The house was clean, but the structure needed considerable repair. He avoided the third, fifth and seventh step. All three were warped and might not hold his weight. He wasn't sure about the rest. He would have to take a closer look. Before he left today, Will promised himself he would fix them and any other hazards that might appear.

With that in mind, he placed the trunk in the appointed room and then went in search of the other two men. He found them at the carriage, unloading the last of the bags.

"We have a problem," he said without preamble.

They both lifted their heads, but Flynn spoke up first. "What sort of problem?"

Will opened his mouth to explain then stopped himself.

"Not here, where we might be overheard by the women. Over there."

He directed them toward a large shade tree where a neglected bench sat under a sign that read Colleen's Garden. He started to prop his foot on the bench then stopped himself. Like many of the stairs, the crumbling wood probably wouldn't hold his weight. "The house needs some immediate repairs."

Cam's eyebrows slammed together. The gesture gave him a ruthless look. "What kind of *immediate* repairs are we talking about?"

"You were in the house for all of five minutes," Flynn pointed out before Will could answer Cam's question. "How could you possibly know that?"

"Five minutes was long enough to discover that three of the stairs leading to the second floor are ready to collapse." Will shuddered at the thought of Bridget navigating them at night, without the benefit of decent lighting.

"I don't like the sound of that." Flynn looked up at the house, his eyes filled with concern.

Good, the man should be worried. He was Bridget's brother-in-law, her family. That made her safety his concern, too. But no matter how Flynn handled the situation, Will wasn't going to allow Bridget to live in a house where she could get hurt merely making her way up the stairs to her bedroom.

"What else?" This question came from Cam. He looked as worried as Flynn. "Is the kitchen safe?"

"I'm sure there are other points of concern, but as Flynn pointed out I was only inside a few minutes."

"Then our first step is to decide what's what." By the look on his face it was obvious Cam's mind was already working on a plan of action. "Once we decide which of the repairs need immediate attention we'll have a better idea where to start."

It was a solid suggestion, smart and logical. "And if we discover anything life threatening," Will added, "the women won't be staying here tonight."

Cam flattened his lips into a grim line. "Agreed."

Walking shoulder to shoulder, they took off toward the house. Two steps out Flynn moved into their direct path.

"Whoa, gentlemen, now wait just a moment." Feet splayed, he crossed his arms over his chest and held steady. "Not that I don't agree with you, in principle, but you boys are forgetting one very important point."

"What's that?" they asked in tandem.

"Other than my wife, Bridget and Nora Murphy are two of the most intractable women I know."

"What do you mean by intractable?" Cam asked in his most inflexible lawman voice. The unspoken message was that he could hold his own against a stubborn woman.

Flynn widened his stance. "You have to understand. The Murphy sisters have been single-minded about this house from the day they left Ireland. Now that it's theirs, you won't be able to convince them to leave tonight, maybe not ever."

Although deep in his gut Will feared Flynn was right, he also knew he had his own stubborn streak, especially when it came to protecting what was his. And like it or not, Bridget worked in his home now. That made her one of his.

"Intractable?" Will repeated the descriptor the other man had used to define Bridget and her sister. "We'll just see about that."

"No." Bridget planted her fists on her hips and frowned at Will. How could he ask such a thing? When he knew how important this house was to her? "I am not leaving my own home. Don't ask me again."

"I'm not asking you." He towered over her, his face an immovable slab of hard angles and firm lines. "I'm telling you."

"Is that right?" She resisted the urge to stomp her foot. "Well, then, don't *tell* me again."

He softened his gaze and reached to her.

She took a step back. His hand fell away.

"Why are you being so stubborn?" He seemed genuinely confused by her resistance.

That hurt more than his words. "You know how important this house is to me."

"Bridget, listen to me. It's not safe." He spoke slowly, all impatient energy and suppressed power flickering across his face and tightening his lips.

She didn't want to be angry at him, and yet she was, very much so. "It's safe enough for the Coulters." She looked over her shoulder, as though searching out the elderly couple to prove her point. "If you're so concerned, why not insist they leave, as well?"

"They live in the bedroom off the kitchen." He moved closer toward her, his entire bearing begging her to give in.

Despite her annoyance at him, Bridget was captured by the fluid way he moved, the masculine vitality that encircled him. "What does the location of their room have to do with anything?"

"The first floor is sound enough." He spoke through a tight jaw. "It's the second floor that needs considerable repairs, especially the steps. I won't have you risking your neck every time you climb up to your room."

His explanation was not given smoothly, but with a rough sincerity that told her he wasn't trying to order her about as she'd first suspected. He was genuinely worried about her.

"You're concerned for my safety," she said, unable to hide the awe in her voice. No man other than her da had ever put her safety first, not like this, not to the point of arguing with her.

"Of course I'm concerned." He blew out a frustrated hiss, the sound reminding her he was a man used to taking charge. "I'll fix the stairs before I leave and Cam is already up on the roof mending the largest hole and—"

"Flynn is repairing the back stoop," she finished for him. "If you three complete those tasks today then I don't see what the problem is with Nora and me staying the night."

He frowned. "The *problem* is that there could be other hazards we've missed."

"There aren't any missed hazards." She raised her hand to stop him from interrupting. "I know this because you three men have been in and out of this house at least fifty times, up and down the stairs, scrambling on and off the roof, mumbling every step of the way."

"I can't let you stay in this house until I know it is completely safe."

She relished his fierce protectiveness for a brief moment. Will was so handsome, staring down at her with that stubborn, worried look in his eyes. Bridget felt a pleasant little ache in her stomach, a bone-deep yearning that she stifled. "You know the house is safe, or at least safe enough for Nora and me to live here with the Coulters."

He was shaking his head before she finished speaking. "I'm still not satisfied."

Now he was just being difficult. If she wasn't so flattered she might be frustrated with this stubborn streak of his. "*Like I said,* you, Flynn and Cam have investigated every square inch of this place, ten times over."

"Nevertheless…"

"Would it make you feel any better if I agreed to sleep down here on the first floor tonight?"

"No."

No? *No?* "If you don't want me living here, then what do you suggest?"

"I suggest—" he flashed her one of his bone-melting smiles that made her knees go weak "—you move into my house."

Chapter Sixteen

Bridget felt something akin to pins and needles running down her spine. Will wanted her to move into his home, as though she were a part of his family. A flush of warmth rose inside her, the sensation strengthening and thickening until she couldn't take a decent breath.

She tamped down her reaction and spoke with great calm. "I simply don't know what to say to such an offer."

"Say yes."

A sigh worked its way up her throat. "Absolutely not." But what a lovely, impossible request, one she had to squash at once, before she gave in. "My moving into your home, no matter the reason, would only confuse the twins."

He fell silent. His thoughtful scowl made her wonder if he even realized what he'd just asked of her. No, the request wasn't scandalous. Not when she considered the fact that his mother and children lived under the same roof as him. Bridget would simply be a live-in nanny, an employee and nothing more.

Except...

It would be much more for her. Somewhere in the past week she'd grown to care for this man, as much as she cared for his children and his mother. William Black mattered to her, in a way she didn't want to analyze too closely, not until she was alone. One thing she knew for certain, to capitulate to his request now, no matter how sound his reasoning might be, would be far too dangerous for her heart.

"You're right," he said at last, speaking over her heartbeat drumming in her ears. "I can't risk the children's welfare like that. I will take you back to the boardinghouse."

Oh, no. No, no, no. "You most certainly will not."

"Bridget—"

"Rose rented out our room already. Nora and I must stay here tonight." She softened her voice. "There is no other answer."

His hand slipped up her arm, past her shoulder, stilled just shy of touching the back of her neck. "I don't want you in danger, not for a moment."

He dropped his hand.

Even without his touch, Bridget felt enveloped by warmth and noted with some surprise that she was finding it hard to form words in her mind. She brushed shaky hands down her skirt. Why had the Lord brought this man into her life, when there seemed to be so many obstacles standing between them? "I appreciate that you are worried, Will, I do. But I will be quite fine here with Nora and the Coulters."

"I cannot persuade you otherwise?"

"No."

His lips flattened. "You are a stubborn woman, Bridget Murphy."

She felt a twinge of tenderness for him. "So I've been told."

"You realize—" he took her hand and then braided their fingers loosely together "—that you have already turned down three of my requests in our short acquaintance."

"Yes, I have." She fought desperately to keep from touching him in return, from reaching up with her free hand and smoothing away his frown. "But never for a frivolous reason."

That earned her a smile. "No, never for a frivolous reason." His gaze turned serious, alarmingly so. "One day, Bridget Murphy, you will say yes to me."

She had no doubt of that. She only prayed that when she did it was to the right question.

"If you are determined to stay in this house tonight I had better continue working on the stairs." He ran his thumb over her knuckles before releasing her hand. "Twilight is fast approaching."

Without another word he strode around the corner and mounted the steps.

Bridget blinked after him, wondering what had just happened. There had been hidden meaning in their words, a promise to one another that had been silently understood, on a soul-deep level. She was still staring after him when she heard someone approach from behind. The light, airy footsteps warned her that the newcomer was her younger sister Maeve.

"He likes you," she said, her voice full of satisfaction and perhaps a small amount of amusement.

Bridget swung around to glare at her sister. Maeve was never one to judge, but still, to know that her sister had been eavesdropping on her and Will unsettled Bridget. "You were spying on us?"

"I couldn't hear anything, not with all that hammering coming from the roof." Maeve looked at the ceiling as if to make her point more succinctly. "And I averted my eyes once I realized you were having…a moment."

"Is that so?"

"I am a model of discretion." She waved her hand in a graceful arc. "I saw nothing out of the ordinary here."

There was an unfamiliar ball of something in Bridget's

stomach, something that felt similar to panic. What if her sisters didn't like Will? Nora seemed to disapprove of him—did Maeve agree? And what if *he* didn't like *them?*

"Maeve," she began, considering her words carefully. She didn't want to alarm her sister, but she needed to know. "What do you think of Will?"

"What I think, is that we should have this conversation somewhere private." Maeve hooked her arm through Bridget's and steered her outside toward the overgrown garden. Bridget felt herself relax.

They made their way toward the tree indicating the entrance to Colleen's garden. The path was overrun with weeds, but it was clear this had once been a lovely spot.

There was a rickety old bench in the middle of the garden. Weeds were growing up its legs, tangling into a knot of twisted branches. The wood looked full of splinters and far too wobbly to support either of them.

Apparently Maeve agreed because she paced to the large oak tree and leaned against its massive trunk. "Now where were we?"

"You were about to tell me what you think of Will."

"Ah, yes." She tapped a finger to her chin. "But you must realize, my opinion isn't the one that matters. What do *you* think of the man?"

Bridget swallowed back her first response. She'd been about to give Maeve a superficial answer, something trite. But playing coy was an exercise in futility. Maeve knew her too well and would see through any attempt on Bridget's part to evade the truth.

"I think," she said, firming her shoulders and lifting her chin a fraction higher, "that William Black is the best man I have ever met."

"You are in love with him."

Was she? Was it too soon to tell? Or entirely too late? "I… No… Maybe." *Probably.*

"But, Bridget, from what I understand he is only looking for a woman to be the mother of his children, nothing more."

Maeve was certainly well-informed. Nora must have filled her in during her first visit to Faith Glen, when Bridget had stayed late at Will's to read bedtime stories to the children. When she'd put his family and their needs above her own.

In a matter of days the Black family had become a part of her heart. The children. Esther. Even Will. *Especially* Will.

She might very well be in love with him.

"Oh, Maeve." She tried to smile, but emotion drenched her throat. "What does it matter whether I'm in love with the man or not? He's made it clear he only wants a marriage of convenience, one in name only, and I will settle for nothing less than an earth-shattering love."

"Oh, dear."

Indeed.

The sun had dipped dangerously low toward the horizon before Will felt comfortable enough to deem the house fit for Bridget, her sister and baby Grace to stay the night. Surveying his handiwork, he set down the hammer, rose and proceeded to test each stair one at a time.

Once he was satisfied, he went in search of Bridget. He heard the Coulters speaking with someone in the kitchen, but couldn't make out their words. The cooing noises indicated the baby was back there, as well. Will looked in and saw the older couple smiling over the child, playing with her tiny feet and hands.

Bridget was not with them.

Before either of the Coulters noticed him, he moved back into the hallway, ran his hand along the paint-chipped wall.

They would have to address the decor eventually, but for now they had to focus on the basic structure before winter set in.

Will hadn't wanted to let Bridget win their argument this afternoon, hadn't wanted her to stay here until the house was completely put to rights. But she'd convinced him with the one point he'd been unable to deny. He couldn't move her into his home and risk confusing his children.

His entire family adored her. She had charmed him as well, somehow slipping below his defenses against his best efforts to remain guarded. She was fast sliding her way into his heart.

A hot ball of unease spun in his gut. Will didn't want to lose Bridget. And not just for his children's sake, but for his own, as well.

He longed for her, actually yearned to—

A twinge of unease had him slowing his steps. He'd made a promise to Bridget Collins months ago, and had planned to marry her without the benefit of meeting her. He'd nearly forgotten all about her. Shouldn't he be mourning the woman, at least a while longer? Yet a little over a week after discovering the terrible details of her death Will was falling for Bridget Murphy.

Lord, what does that say about me?

"Will?"

He reared back, his heart slamming in his chest. "Bridget," he said on a spurt of air, bracing his stance so he didn't run into her. "I didn't see you standing there."

"I only just arrived." She hovered in the doorway, her hazel eyes a vivid green mixed with golden brown. Her lips curved into a smile. "You were deep in thought."

"Got a lot on my mind." He spread his hands in a helpless gesture. "I was thinking about…the mill."

She gave him a dubious look but didn't question him. "The others are ready to leave. I've arranged to have Flynn stop at your house to check on your mother before he and Maeve return to Boston." She moved closer. "But only if that's agreeable to you."

Will gazed at her a moment, mesmerized. He suddenly understood why men wrote poetry. "You asked your brother-in-law to examine my mother?"

"He is a very good doctor, I assure you." She lowered her chin, breaking eye contact. "Although I believe Esther is feeling much better I thought it couldn't hurt to collect an expert opinion on the matter."

Staring at her bent head, Will experienced a sudden wave of tenderness followed by a strong desire to pull her into his arms and hold her close. In the next breath he gave in to the temptation and drew her against him, resting his cheek against her soft hair.

She relaxed in his embrace and all he could think was how good she felt, soft yet solid, yielding yet strong.

"Thank you, Bridget." His throat grew tighter, clogging with some unnamed emotion until he had to force the rest of the words past his stiff lips. "Thank you for caring about my mother."

"I care about all of you." She splayed her fingers against his chest and rested her cheek on his shoulder. "So very much."

There was a wistful note in her voice and his arms tightened around her. "I know."

Of its own accord, one of his fingers twined in her hair, the silky locks smooth against his skin. He went motionless, all but his hand. His heart pounded in his chest.

"Bridget?" A deep, masculine voice called from the back of the house. "Are you in here?"

Reluctantly, slowly, Will disentangled his hand from her hair and set her away from him. He took a second step to provide a safe enough distance to keep from pulling her back to him again.

Bridget blinked up at him, her eyes slightly glazed. Then she sighed deep in her throat. Will liked that rich, throaty sound. He liked it a lot.

"Bridget?"

Still looking somewhat bemused, she glanced over her shoulder and called out, "I'm in the hallway with Will." She sounded short of breath.

Will suffered a similar affliction.

Several loud, purposeful footsteps later and Flynn Gallagher entered the tiny space. Eyes narrowed, he looked from Will to Bridget then back again.

"Maeve and I are ready to depart." He spoke in a tone full of silent warning Will had no problem interpreting. "I'll need you to lead the way to your house."

"Certainly." He held the other man's stare without flinching. "I'll meet you outside in a moment."

Flynn looked ready to argue, but then shook his head and left without another word.

"Well," Bridget said, "that was a bit awkward."

Will felt a smile tug at his lips and almost fell in love with her right then. Leave it to Bridget to state the obvious in such a matter-of-fact manner, as though she was speaking about nothing more important than the weather.

Despite reminding himself to keep up his guard, he felt something deep in his soul shift, a softening. "Your brother-in-law is rightfully protective of you."

She laughed. "So it would seem."

"Come." He took her hand without thinking, the gesture as natural as breathing. "We should join the others outside, before we give Dr. Gallagher cause to come searching for you again."

"Heaven forbid."

They walked hand-in-hand down the corridor, as easy with one another as though they'd been together for years. Like a couple. It was a stunning realization that had Will pulling his grip free of hers before they stepped outside.

Cheeks turning a becoming pink, Bridget rushed ahead of him and took the baby from her younger sister. She positioned the bundle in her arms and turned to face him. "I'll see you first thing in the morning."

Glad for the squirming shield between them, he nodded. "Tomorrow."

He gave Flynn a brief nod, tossed out a few general directions to his home and then headed for his own carriage.

After climbing aboard, he lifted the horse's reins in his hands and patiently waited for Flynn to do the same. He let go of the reins after several moments passed, realizing he wasn't going anywhere just yet. Bridget and her younger sister were in the midst of a lengthy goodbye.

Her older sister was off to his right, under a large shade tree, poking her finger into Cam's chest. The woman did not look happy. In fact, as Will leaned forward for a better look, he realized her face was scrunched into a frown.

Cam, seemingly unaffected by the woman's obvious frustration, suddenly threw his head back and let out a belly laugh. Whereby Nora swung around and stomped off, her hands balled into two tight fists. Cam immediately stopped laughing and gaped after her retreating back in utter astonishment.

Good old Cam, Will thought with a shake of his head, *charming the ladies like always.* Clearly, the sheriff of Faith Glen needed a few lessons on how to talk to women. Not that Will was the one to school him on the subject. He wasn't much better, as evidenced by his inability to talk Bridget into leaving this ramshackle house tonight.

As he caught Will's eyes on him, a dark scowl spread

across Cam's face. He pushed away from the tree and headed in his direction. "You got something to say to me?"

"Just watching the show." Will grinned. "What was that about, anyway?"

"It was the strangest thing." Cam shrugged. "Nora suggested I hire some eighteen-year-old kid I met last week, one of the passengers she knew aboard ship."

"And you laughed at her." Will shook his head. "Badly done, my friend."

"I thought she was fooling with me." Cam slapped his hat against his thigh. "But she really wants me to hire the boy on as my deputy."

"You already have a deputy."

"Yeah, that's what I told her." He ran a hand through his hair. "That's when the finger poking began."

Will tried not to smile at his friend. Focusing on the practical points of the discussion helped. "Can Faith Glen afford another deputy?"

"The city can barely afford Ben."

Cam looked about as miserable as Will had ever seen him. Despite his gruff exterior the man hated letting people down. Will gave it one week, maybe two before Cam was in possession of a new deputy sheriff. And if the city couldn't pay, Cam would do so out of his own pocket. "I'm confident you'll work it out."

"Yeah, I will. *Right now.*" He strode purposely toward the house.

Watching him go, Will almost pitied Nora Murphy. She was about to discover the consequences of walking away from Cameron Long when he wasn't finished having his say. But after watching their previous interaction Will figured she could hold her own.

He turned back to check on the others.

Bridget pulled out of her sister's embrace. The fading sun

caught her hair just right, hugging her in a ray of soft, golden light. The effect was so stunning Will had to swallow back the sudden lump clogging in his throat. She looked beautiful with the overgrown garden as a backdrop, approachable as always, yet warmer and more inviting than before they'd met in the hallway.

They'd crossed a line in their relationship and Will wasn't altogether sorry for it.

But if he allowed the pretty Irish lass to squirm her way deeper into his life there would be unforeseen repercussions. He had his children to think of, as well as his mother and a load of dark memories that made it necessary to guard his heart more carefully than other men.

Yet for one brief moment when she turned her head and smiled over at him, all Will could think was: *Yes.*

Flynn Gallagher sauntered into Will's study an hour later. Will wasn't surprised the doctor was alone. The man's pretty wife had lured the twins into a game of marbles as soon as they'd arrived.

After being shooed out of his mother's room while Flynn conducted his examination, Will had taken the opportunity to review a stack of invoices. Now, as Flynn shut the door behind him, Will shoved the pile aside and looked up expectantly.

"Your mother is extremely healthy for a woman her age." He flashed a broad smile. "Correction, she's extremely healthy for a woman of any age."

Will's heart contracted in relief. "So she is out of the woods at last."

Flynn moved deeper into the room, his gaze lingering a moment on the dog sleeping contentedly on a makeshift bed of worn blankets. Will glanced ruefully at the snoring animal. So much for his stipulation that Digger remain out of doors.

"I didn't say your mother was out of the woods," Flynn corrected. "I said she was healthy."

Will rose, came around the desk, every movement precise and controlled. "What, exactly, does that mean?"

"It means that you must ensure she continues eating regular meals and resting whenever she's tired. Under no circumstances should she overtax herself."

Good advice, in theory. But Esther Black was a stubborn woman. "How will I know if she's overdone it?"

"I'll leave a list of the signs to look for."

"Good. Anything else I should know?"

"No. However—" the doctor stuffed his hands in his pockets and leaned back on his heels "—I can't stress enough the importance of rest."

Mulling this over, Will nodded. "So I need to bully her."

Flynn chuckled. "If that's what it takes, yes."

"Fair enough." Rubbing a hand down his face, Will wondered why he wasn't more relieved by this report. His mother had been suffering from a simple case of exhaustion. This was good news, yet something in him couldn't let go and rejoice.

Flynn reached down and ruffled Digger's fur. "Your mother claims she's been feeling better ever since Bridget became the children's nanny."

"Your sister-in-law's influence on my family has been nothing short of remarkable."

And that, Will realized, was the problem. His mother's recovery was directly due to Bridget's appearance on the scene. If they lost her, or if Will ran her off, the Black household would fall apart again.

His family had become completely dependent on Bridget Murphy. His children adored her. His mother was growing stronger by the day. Even the stray dog owed his position in the household to her.

As if to punctuate this last point, Digger kicked out in his sleep and gurgled a sort of happy dog laugh.

"What about you?" Flynn asked, his voice no longer sounding like a doctor but a protective older brother. "Has Bridget made an impact on you, as well?"

Will had no idea what to say. Not because he was hedging, or stalling, but because he simply had *no idea what to say.* "There are many ways to answer that question."

"How about going with the truth."

The truth. Bridget deserved nothing less. "Yes, she's impacted me, as well. More than I thought possible."

Flynn's piercing stare seemed to probe all the way down to his soul. "I have one final question for you."

Bracing himself, Will nodded.

"What are your intentions toward my sister?"

Astonished at his reaction to the question, Will had to fight back a rush of tangled emotions twisting through him— anger, guilt, hope, despair. His roving gaze landed on Bridget Collins' baggage.

Flynn's gaze followed his, and then narrowed in recognition. No wonder, the doctor had been the one to sign Miss Collins's luggage over to Will.

"Just one week ago you were set to marry another woman, a woman you'd sent all the way to Ireland for." The man's face was full of hard, intense lines. "You cannot be thinking of replacing her with my sister-in-law."

When spoken that plainly, in that flat tone, Will realized the terrible repercussion of his attempt to "hire" a bride. He should have never sent for Bridget Collins, no matter how desperate he'd been. He should have had more faith and allowed the Lord to reveal his next step. Instead, Will had taken matters into his own hands.

"No," he said at last. "It is not my intention to replace my intended bride with your sister-in-law."

"Then what is your plan?"

A valid question, one he could have answered a week ago but not today. "I...don't know."

Flynn moved closer, continuing forward until he was standing toe to toe with Will, his arms crossed over his chest in angry deviance. "You better decide soon."

An unspoken warning hung in the air between them.

Although Will knew Flynn was right—he did need to decide what he was going to do about Bridget—he bristled at the man's aggressive stance. "And if I don't make up my mind?"

"I'll take her away from you, and Faith Glen, if need be. I'll move her to Boston, anything to prevent her from being hurt again."

"Again?" Will picked up on the word like a dog on point. "Who hurt Bridget?" He nearly grabbed the man by his lapels. "Tell me."

As though realizing he'd said too much, Flynn stepped back, hands spread in a show of capitulation. "I can say no more. It's not my story to share."

"Tell me."

"It happened a year ago, back in Ireland, before I knew her." Flynn took another step back. "I don't know all the details, only the main points. What I do know is that it was quite a scandal, and...she was devastated."

Dread chased across his spine. Will knew all about scandal, the pain, the whispers and, yes, even the devastation. What had Bridget endured? "Tell me what happened."

No longer on the offense, Flynn gave him a sympathetic grimace, as though he knew the information he was about to share would change everything.

"Bridget was left at the altar."

Chapter Seventeen

When Cameron Long dropped Bridget at Will's house the next morning before proceeding to the jail house with Nora, Bridget discovered Will had already left for the day. Disappointment spread through her and all she could do was stare at Esther in silent regret. She'd arrived early for the sole purpose of seeing Will again.

"Bridget, dear." Esther crossed to her and set a hand on her arm. "Are you ill? You look pale."

She forced a smile onto her lips. "I'm perfectly well."

She lied, of course. She wasn't well. She was full of frustration and sadness and a strange sense of loss. She'd wanted to see Will this morning, needed to assure herself they were still on the same easy terms as yesterday. When he'd pulled her into his arms, and buried his face in her hair, and then whispered his gratitude in that sweet, gruff, serious tone of his.

"Bridget?"

"I… There is nothing wrong…I just…"

Thankfully the sound of doggy toenails clicking on the floor spared her from responding further. She dropped to her knees and flung her arms around the animal. "Digger, my big furry friend," she said a tad too brightly. "Good morning."

Caleb and Olivia rounded the corner next. Bridget opened her arms wider to include the two sleepy-eyed, rumple-haired children. Next thing she knew the four of them were rolling on the floor. It was a very inelegant, undignified moment, but when she swept a glance in Esther's direction the older woman was smiling at the four of them.

After another moment of play, Bridget scrambled to her feet, leaving the children and the dog to finish the game without her. Afraid to assess the damage, she ran a hand down her hair. Most of her curls had fallen free of her bun. Sighing in resignation, she pulled out the rest of her pins and let her hair tumble past her shoulders.

"We're going to do something different today," she declared, clapping her hands a few times to gain the children's attention.

They looked up at her, their little faces expectant. Caleb spoke for them both. "We are? What?"

"A picnic."

Heads tilted at a confused angle, they simply stared at her. Had they never been on a picnic? How sad. "We're going to eat our lunch outside, on a blanket under a tree, *and*—" she had a stroke of genius "—we're going to steal your father away from the mill so he can join us."

"What a lovely idea," Esther said, pressing a corner of her apron to her eyes. "He'll like that."

Caleb jumped to his feet. "Can we eat by the river?"

Pleased by his excitement, Bridget nodded enthusiastically. "I think that can be arranged, unless your father has another suggestion."

"I'll bring my boat, just in case."

"Splendid idea."

"Can Digger come, too?" Olivia was still on the floor with the dog, her arm looped across his shoulders.

Bridget smiled softly at the child. "It wouldn't be a family picnic without him." She turned her smile onto Esther. "Will you join us, as well?"

"I think I'll stay home and rest."

At the strange note in Esther's voice, a terrible thought came to Bridget's mind. Flynn had been here last night. Had he found something wrong, something concerning Esther's health? She was desperate to ask, but not in front of the twins.

"Children, I need you to go back to your rooms and wait for me." She used her firm, no-nonsense voice. "I'll be there in a moment to help you pick out your clothes for the day."

They opened their mouths to grumble.

Bridget spoke over them. "It's important you wear the right clothing for our adventure."

Showing his displeasure at being sent away, Caleb scuffed the floor with his foot. Olivia sighed heavily. But they soon turned on their little feet and shuffled toward their room. Digger followed in their wake.

Once she was certain the children were out of earshot, Bridget got straight to the point. "Esther, when Dr. Gallagher came by last night, did he find—" she stopped herself, not quite sure how to phrase the question "—something wrong?"

"Oh, no, dear. I am quite well." Esther waved a dismissive hand. "I'm healthy as a horse, according to the doctor."

That didn't sound like something Flynn would say. "If that's true then why won't you come on the picnic with us?"

"Because..." Esther fiddled with her apron, not quite meeting her gaze. "I have other plans."

Other plans? In all the time Bridget had worked in this home, Esther had never had *other plans.* "You do? With whom?"

"A friend." When she continued avoiding direct eye contact, Bridget couldn't help but wonder about the identity of Esther's friend.

It wasn't any of her business, of course. Yet she liked

Will's mother and worried about her. The older woman seemed to be hiding something, something secret.

It is none of your business, Bridget reminded herself. "If you are certain—"

"I am."

"Then I won't press any further."

A loud bang came from the other side of the house and was followed by an equally loud bark.

Esther looked positively relieved by the interruption. "That doesn't sound good."

Bridget sighed. "I had better go see what's happened."

"Very wise, my dear." Esther practically shoved her out of the room.

Bridget shifted out from under her hands and touched the older woman's arm. "You are truly feeling well?"

"Yes, Bridget." She patted the hand on her arm. "I am well, but I thank you for worrying. It's very kind of you."

"I care about you, Esther." It was the simple truth.

"I know, dear. You are a sweet girl and I—"

Another louder bang rang out, practically rattling the windows. And then came a very loud, very heavy thud.

"Miss Bridgeeet," Caleb shouted at the top of his lungs. "Come quick. Digger broke Olivia's chair."

"Oh, my." She released Esther's arm and hurried off.

The moment Will spied Bridget and the twins standing in the doorway of his office his heart tumbled in his chest. The picture they made personified family, a very happy, normal one.

The mangy dog leaning against Bridget's leg added the final touch to an already perfect scene. In fact, the mutt looked healthier than ever, and he appeared to be grinning at Will as if to say: *Look what we have, old boy, a real, genuine family of our own, isn't it grand?*

Yes, it was grand. And Will felt something move through him he hadn't experienced in years. Happiness. The kind he wasn't sure he deserved.

"What's all this?" he asked in a hoarse voice.

"We've come to take you on a picnic," Bridget declared, her eyes shining bright.

Staring into that beautiful, mesmerizing gaze, Will was tempted to pull her into his arms and bury his face in her hair as he had yesterday afternoon. How could any man leave such a kindhearted, lovely woman at the altar?

For the third time in his life, Will felt the urge to punch another man. The first had been Harcourt Smythe, Fanny's lover, the man she'd abandoned her family for. The second, Bridget's Irish landlord. Now when he thought about the pain and humiliation Bridget must have suffered from her fiancé's callousness, he wanted to inflict permanent damage to the rogue's face. Will wasn't normally prone to violence. Or so he'd always thought.

Swallowing back his rising fury, he lowered his gaze, locking it on the basket hanging from her arm. She carried a blanket tucked up under the other.

A picnic. Bridget wanted him to join them on a picnic.

He ran a hand down his face, drew in a hard breath. He thought briefly of praying, but he wasn't sure what he should lift up to the Lord. A prayer of thanksgiving for bringing this woman into his life? A prayer for strength so he could remember his goal wasn't to find a woman for himself, but to provide stability for his children?

Or perhaps he should just let down his guard for a few precious hours and enjoy time with his family.

"You haven't eaten already, have you?" Bridget's question brought him back to the matter at hand.

"No, I haven't." Even if he had, he wouldn't admit it now, not with his children's eager faces staring up at him and

Bridget's encouraging smile warming his heart. "Let me put away these ledgers and we'll go."

"Lovely."

"I know the perfect place for our picnic," he said as soon as they were heading down the hallway toward the back door.

"Then we'll let you lead the way."

Once outside, Will directed their small party toward a shade tree near the riverbank. Olivia skipped alongside him, her dolly clutched tightly against her. She chattered away, her words tumbling over one another so quickly she wasn't making much sense. Will wasn't sure it mattered.

Caleb carried his boat in one hand while he threw a stick for Digger to chase after with the other. A languid breeze rustled through the trees. Birds chirped, frogs croaked, the mill's wheel churned in the water. It was a beautiful, mild summer day. Perfect for a family picnic.

At their destination, Will retrieved the blanket from under Bridget's arm and laid it carefully on the ground. As soon as he'd smoothed away the wrinkles, Olivia plopped down and proceeded to recite a nursery rhyme to her doll.

"No, Caleb," Bridget called out. "Don't go down by the water on your own."

The little boy threw her a scowl. "But how am I to sail my boat?"

"Your da will help you after we eat." She turned to Will. "Isn't that right?"

"Absolutely. I can't think of a better way to spend the afternoon." His words were directed at Caleb, but they carried far more meaning than he'd intended.

Still scowling, the little boy muttered something under his breath but obediently trudged over to the blanket and set down his boat near Olivia. She shoved it aside with a careless flick of her wrist.

"Don't hurt it!" he yelled in outrage.

She lifted her tiny shoulders. "Don't put it in my way."

"*You're* in the way." He puffed out his chest in angry, childish frustration.

"No, you are."

"You are."

Just as Will stepped forward to intervene, Bridget moved in between the twins and picked up the boat herself. "Why don't I just put this over here, next to the picnic basket where it'll be safe?"

"Excellent idea," Will said, aligning himself next to her, shoulder to shoulder.

Looking from one to the other, Caleb opened his mouth to argue, thought better of it, shook his head roughly, then sighed in defeat. "I guess that'll be all right."

Nodding in satisfaction, Bridget set the boat where she'd indicated. She wiped her palms together in a gesture that said the matter was settled. "Now, Caleb. Please chase down that naughty dog and bring him back over here."

"Digger." Caleb ran toward the animal. "*Digger,* no. Naughty boy. Naughty. You stop that right now."

The dog, Will noted with a suppressed grin, was proving true to his name. He was digging frantically in a bed of wild-flowers on the other side of the tree. Tiny stars of color flew in every direction. Caleb continued to scold the animal.

In that instant, if anyone had asked him, Will would have said there was nowhere else he would rather be than right here, with his children and Bridget and that crazy hound. The thought brought a moment of peace, followed by a sudden wave of regret.

For his entire life he'd been a man of action, committed to seeing matters through to the end. When he'd needed some-one to care for his children he'd done the logical thing. He'd drawn up a list of specific criteria and then designed a plan to find a woman who would meet his requirements.

A little more than a week ago he'd been willing to marry a stranger and have her care for the twins. At the time his reasoning had made sense. With her erratic behavior Fanny had put them through years of instability. Her inconsistent schedule and ultimate abandonment had left Olivia and Caleb unnaturally reserved. They'd wound up trapped in abnormally good behavior.

Considering all that had transpired, Will had believed his children needed permanency above all else. Now he knew better. They didn't need consistency as much as they needed unconditional love, the kind that Bridget had shown them.

Today, as he sat on the blanket and watched Bridget unpack the picnic basket, he realized his lack of foresight. And, of course, faith.

Bridget Murphy was an extraordinary woman. Her heart was so pure, her compassion so strong, she gave all of herself. She deserved a man who could give her the same level of devotion she would provide him in return. She deserved a man who would give her his entire heart, and hold nothing back.

Will was not that man.

If he made an offer of marriage to her again, and she accepted, he feared he would let her down eventually. As he had Fanny, and Bridget Collins.

No. He couldn't risk hurting her.

But how could he allow any other man to have her?

His heart lodged in his throat, and a portion of his previous joy left him.

Then Olivia crawled into his lap and rested her tiny head against his chest. Overwhelmed with love, he pulled his daughter close and dropped a kiss on the top of her head. He was thinking too hard. This was supposed to be an easy, carefree day. "Having fun, darling?"

"Oh, yes." She let out a happy sigh. "Quite a lot, actually."

Will's stomach twisted. His daughter had sounded just like Bridget, all the way down to the sweet Irish accent.

Olivia turned her face to his. "Are you having fun, too?"

He caught Bridget's eye before answering. She gave him a quick, almost imperceptible wink. The intimate gesture sent his pulse beating in a fury.

Bewildered at his reaction, he shifted his gaze to a spot just over Bridget's shoulder. "Yes, my darling." He kissed Olivia's head again. "I'm having a lot of fun."

"Oh, good," she said, then jumped up as Caleb and the dog returned.

Will endured the rest of their picnic with a smile on his face and a stoic resolve in his heart. No matter how hard he tried to enjoy the afternoon, his mind kept rounding back to one very important question, the one Flynn had posed last night.

What were Will's intentions toward Bridget Murphy?

As Bridget helped prepare the children for bed later that evening, she was acutely aware of the man working silently beside her. Something had altered in their relationship this afternoon, but she wasn't precisely sure she knew what. Will seemed especially careful with her tonight, and overly cautious, as if he didn't want to do or say the wrong thing.

But that made no sense. Will was not a man to tiptoe around a difficult situation. What had changed? Had she said something this afternoon? Had she crossed some sort of invisible line?

The wink. It must have been the wink. He probably thought the gesture had been too bold for a woman in his employ.

Swallowing in dismay, she focused on pulling Olivia's arms gently through the sleeves of her nightgown. The child smiled up at her and Bridget responded in kind, her heart wrenching at the sight of all that innocence staring back at her.

This nightly custom was always the best and worst part of her job, a bittersweet time when she felt the closest to all four of the Blacks yet not quite a part of their family. Sadly the sensation was magnified tonight.

Will hadn't looked at her once. Come to think of it, he hadn't looked at her since arriving home tonight, not even during the evening meal.

With this strange new tension between them, she was grateful it was Will's turn to read tonight. Bridget wasn't sure she could speak without her voice cracking.

She only hoped she gathered her emotions into some semblance of control before it was time to kneel beside the twins for their bedtime prayers.

Will's soothing baritone eventually filled the room and Bridget found herself relaxing, despite her nerves. The man had a lovely voice. She could listen to him read for hours. But all too quickly the story came to an end and he set the book down on the floor at his feet.

Without having to be told Olivia and Caleb knelt beside their individual beds, folded their hands together then rested their elbows on the mattresses in front of them.

Bridget joined them. Will came to her side, brushed his fingers across her sleeve before lowering to his knees, as well.

Heart pounding, afraid to see what was in his gaze, she squeezed her eyes tightly shut.

"Dear God," Caleb began. "Please feed the hungry, clothe the poor and—" he paused "—and, oh, yes. Please, if You have time, can You make Digger come when I call him?"

As if hearing his name, the dog raced down the hallway, his toenails striking the floor with a *click, click, click.*

Thankful for the interruption, Bridget quickly rose and

caught the bundle of fur before he charged into the room. She held him in place while the children continued praying.

"My turn now," Olivia said without looking up, her forehead resting heavily on her clasped hands. "Dear God, please give us rain for the garden and sunshine for the plants. Please bless Nene and Papa and Caleb."

"And Miss Bridget, too," Caleb reminded her.

Olivia opened her eyes and shot him a scowl. "And of course Miss Bridget, too. And, God, please, oh, please—" she lifted her face to the heavens "—*please* make Miss Bridget our new mommy."

Bridget's hand flew to her throat. Her heart pounded hard against her ribs, so hard she was sure everyone could hear the rapid staccato. She couldn't breathe, couldn't think.

Her gaze shot to Will. He rose and joined her in the doorway, his eyes dark and full of emotion. It wasn't shock she saw looking back at her, but an apology. Did he think he had to apologize for Olivia's prayer?

Bridget wanted to assure him that she understood how children thought. If not with words, with a touch or a look, but she couldn't force herself to move. God save her, she wanted the same thing Olivia did. She wanted to be the children's mother. She wanted to be Will's wife.

Holding back a sob, her lips moved in a soundless whisper.

Gaze softening, Will touched her arm. Overwhelmed with emotion, she quickly looked away and caught Caleb and Olivia staring at them.

"Those were lovely prayers," she said, hoping her voice didn't register her nervousness.

"Yes, they were," Will agreed, dropping his hand. "Now hop in bed, both of you."

"Can Digger sleep with us tonight?" Caleb asked.

"Yes." Will nodded. "That'll be fine."

What? Bridget blinked at him in surprise. He must have been taken off guard by Olivia's prayer, more than he was letting on. Yes, he'd given in and allowed the dog inside the house, but he'd never allowed the animal to sleep in the children's room before.

Throat tight, Bridget watched Digger crawl atop Caleb's bed, circle three times, then settle in. She took great care settling the covers around Olivia's shoulders. When she leaned down to kiss the child's cheek, Olivia whispered in her ear, "I meant what I said. I want you to be my mommy."

Bridget shut her eyes and squeezed back the tears. "Me, too," she whispered back, knowing how inappropriate it was to promise such a thing, yet unable to censure herself.

She shouldn't get this child's hopes up, or her own. But maybe, *maybe* there was a way to make Olivia's prayer come true.

Bridget couldn't marry Will, not given his current restrictions. But she could stay on in the role of the children's nanny for as long as possible, indefinitely if necessary.

What if Will asks you to leave? What if he finds another woman to marry, one who meets his stringent requirements?

Well, if that travesty occurred…

No, it simply would not happen. Bridget wouldn't let it.

Chapter Eighteen

Bridget didn't remember walking out of the children's room. Nor did she recall saying good-night to Caleb, although she was confident that she had. She probably even gave him a bedtime kiss on the forehead as always.

Yet, now, only moments after entering the kitchen behind Will all her mind could focus on was him and the fact that his deep blue eyes were full of piercing intensity.

Bridget pressed her lips together, determined not to break the silence between them this time.

Olivia might have prayed for her to become her mommy, and Will might have failed to tell the little girl that her request was impossible, but he hadn't encouraged her, either. In truth, as Bridget reviewed the past few minutes in the children's room, she realized Will had ignored the situation entirely.

Would he continue to do so now that they were alone?

She had her answer the moment he opened his mouth. "I brought home some special chocolate I want you to try."

Turning his back on her, he moved toward the counter directly behind him. "My chocolatiers are working on a new recipe." He picked up a package wrapped in plain white paper and then pivoted back around. "I want you to tell me what you think."

"It's…grayish-brown."

He laughed, them pinched off a bite-size piece and handed it to her. "Taste it."

She stared at his hand. "You want me to eat that? By itself? Won't it be bitter?"

"Not if we got the formula correct."

"Oh." She gave him an exaggerated smile as she took the piece of chocolate. Rolling it around in her fingers, she realized the texture was much softer than the large cakes he'd left at the house yesterday. The color was lighter, too.

Prepared to hate the taste, she closed her eyes and popped the confection in her mouth. The chocolate melted on her tongue, the sweet flavor both a shock and a pleasant delight. "It's…quite good."

Her answer didn't appear to satisfy him. "But not great."

Bridget thought for a moment, remembered the full, rich flavor of Nora's famous chocolate cake. "No," she admitted honestly. "Not great. Not as good as some of the sweets Nora makes. Although the piece you gave me was far better than I expected, something is—"

"Missing?" he finished for her.

"Yes," she agreed, surprised he could read her mind so well. "Something is missing."

"Can you think what?" He seemed genuinely interested in her opinion.

Honored, and touched by his trust in her, Bridget closed her eyes and thought for a moment. She could think of nothing. Not one thing. Of course she was a bit out of her depth here. "Unfortunately, no, but my sister could. Nora's a baking genius."

"Why, yes she is." A booming voice sounded from behind them. "I can vouch for that myself."

Surprised to hear the familiar gravelly voice in Will's

home, Bridget turned quickly. Her gaze landed on Deputy MacDuff standing in the doorway grinning at her.

"Your sister is a cooking marvel," he said, winking at her with his wide grin still firmly planted on his face. "Hiring Nora was the best decision that boy Cameron has made in years." He patted his belly with satisfaction. "Maybe ever."

Confused, Bridget blinked at the older man. What was Ben doing here at this hour?

As though he were equally confused, Will's eyebrows pulled together. "What are you doing here, Ben? Is there a problem I don't know about?"

Perhaps Ben was here because of Bridget. Had something happened to Nora? Or baby Grace?

"Now don't you two start worrying, there's no problem." Esther maneuvered past the deputy and entered the kitchen with a smile. "Ben is here visiting me."

"You," Bridget and Will said simultaneously.

"We're having coffee and scones."

Will stared at his mother, blinked down at Bridget, then turned back to stare at Esther again. "You're having scones and coffee, at night?"

"Oh, honestly, Will. Don't look at me like that." Esther made a frustrated sound in her throat. "Ben is an old friend of your father's, and mine. We haven't talked in a good long while. It's time we did some catching up."

Will continued blinking at her, as did Bridget, their mutual silence an indication of their common surprise. An image from the day before filled Bridget's mind. She remembered Ben and Esther at church, heads bent together, whispering softly to one another. Was there something more happening between the two, something sweet and possibly—romantic?

Lips pursed, Esther took Will's shoulder in a firm grip. The bold gesture spoke of her continued healing.

"William, *son,* I think it's long past time you escorted

Bridget home for the night." With a flick of her wrist she turned him around to face the back door, then motioned to Bridget. "Now run along, both of you."

Before either could utter a word they were unceremoniously shoved onto the back stoop and enveloped in twilight. The door shut behind them with a firm bang.

A moment of shocked silence fell over them.

Then to her horror, a laugh bubbled out of Bridget's mouth. Esther had certainly made her intentions clear, quite boldly in fact. She slid a covert glance in Will's direction. Was he pleased by this unexpected turn of events?

"Think my mother wanted to be alone with Ben?" he asked, amusement in his voice.

Another giggle slipped out. "That would be my guess."

Joining in the laughter, he took her arm and steered her toward his carriage. "I'm glad. She deserves some masculine attention after all her years of loneliness."

"Your mother was positively glowing."

"That she was." There was genuine pleasure in his tone.

They walked side by side, smiling at one another, the tension gone between them. The moment was light and happy and yet surprisingly intimate.

Bridget glanced to the sky, a ribbon of pink mixed with orange rode along the horizon. The moon had begun its initial ascent in the sky, a fat, glowing crescent that hadn't fully taken shape. Croaking frogs sounded their nocturnal presence. A soft breeze swept over them.

Several feet away from the carriage Will abruptly stopped walking. Nearly losing her balance, Bridget was forced to do so, as well. When he pulled slightly away from her, she looked up at him and waited for—well, she didn't know what she was waiting for him to do.

As he turned to face her, his strong warm fingers took hold of her hand. There was no more amusement in his eyes, only serious attentiveness. He was staring at her with such purpose her blood ran molten in her veins. Yet she shivered.

"Will?"

He continued staring down at her, saying nothing, his gaze filled with gleaming, silvery-eyed intent.

That look. It made her knees go weak. She should pull away, move apart from him, but she took a step forward instead, closing the distance between them to mere inches.

The wind kicked her hair around her face, obscuring her view for a moment.

Hand reaching out, he pushed the tangles away from her forehead. "Bridget, my beautiful, beautiful girl."

The words sent another shiver whipping down her spine. Beautiful? He thought she was beautiful?

He raised her hand tenderly to his lips, pressing a soft kiss to her knuckles before cradling it against his chest. His heat seemed to echo through her, to the very core of her heart.

She closed her eyes and simply breathed in the moment.

"Bridget," he whispered her name again, this time in a low, rough voice that was no longer steady. "What am I going to do about you?"

She shivered a third time, looking down as she flushed.

"Oh, Will."

A second passed, and then another. He placed his fingertip under her chin and then lifted her head with gentle pressure.

The kiss shouldn't have surprised her. She saw it coming, saw the intent in Will's eyes before he lowered his head to meet hers. Yet it still made her heart pound and her head swim. She sighed into the kiss, marveling at the rightness of the moment, and the contentment flowing through her.

This was where she belonged. With this man.

All too quickly he pulled his head away.

Her hand reached to her mouth of its own accord. *"Oh, my."*

"My thoughts precisely." He brushed a fingertip down her arm, the gesture both casual and intimate. His smile was so tender she nearly lost her footing again. Surely, with that look in his gaze, he was about to say something important to her, something that would change her life forever. Indeed, the yearning look on his face seemed to confirm it. But his expression was so uncertain. Surely he didn't doubt her feelings for him.

He touched her cheek. "Let's get you home."

What? That was it? The man had just kissed her oh-so-tenderly, had looked at her as though she was the most important thing in his life, and all he could say was *let's get you home?*

Wasn't this the moment when he was supposed to make a declaration or a promise or—something?

Eyes blinking rapidly, Bridget waited for him to begin again and make the moment special. Instead he said nothing. He took her arm with solicitous care—she'd give him credit for his impeccable manners—and then helped her into the carriage.

And *still* he said nothing.

When Daniel had kissed her he'd given her flowery words and endless promises. He'd meant none of them.

What was worse? she wondered. Words that had no meaning? Or no words at all?

Fighting back an onslaught of tears, Bridget waited in stunned silence as Will walked around to his side of the carriage. Had she done something wrong?

She desperately wanted to ask. But she couldn't find it in her to look at him just yet, not directly. Staring straight ahead, feeling hollow and bleak, her vision blurred as the truth hit her at last.

Even without the words, even without the promises, Bridget realized she was in love William Black, desperately, unequivocally in love with the man. If his current dreadful silence was any indication, he didn't feel the same way about her.

Lord, what have I gotten myself into?

Will gripped the horse's reins tightly in his hands, his knuckles turning white from the effort. He knew he was handling the situation badly, knew he needed to tell Bridget he loved her, wanted to make her his wife. In short, he needed to tell her the truth.

Yet the words wouldn't come. Not even when she looked at him with that lost, confused expression.

Lord, what have I done?

Without thinking about the consequences, without caring about the possible repercussions, he'd given in to temptation and had kissed Bridget soundly on the mouth.

One moment he was thinking happily about his mother huddled over coffee with Ben, the next Will was letting his emotions take over without any of the logic or careful consideration that usually guarded his decisions.

He should have left her alone, should have stepped back before he'd given in and kissed her. Hadn't he decided she deserved better than him?

He'd been incapable of resisting. Because right or wrong, good or bad, he'd wanted to show Bridget how he felt. The kiss had seemed the most natural step.

Now he needed to explain himself.

He wasn't sure where to start.

Hoping for an idea—any would do—he cast a glance in her direction. She looked sad and confused and so completely adorable he wanted to grab her and never let her go. He refrained. Her brother-in-law had made a valid point last night, one that had haunted Will all day, even during their picnic.

He had been committed to marrying another woman for

very specific reasons, reasons that were still important to him. How could he know for sure he wasn't replacing Bridget Collins with the first suitable prospect that came along?

The thought made his stomach roil. The woman sitting by his side was so much more to him than a substitute for a bride he'd never met. Bridget, this Bridget, *his* Bridget had brought music and laughter back into his home. She'd brought joy back into his heart and had won over the children within moments of meeting them.

How could he not want her for his bride? How could any man not want her?

A disturbing memory came to mind, one that had him reaching out and closing his hand over hers. "Tell me about your fiancé and the day of your wedding," he said. "Tell me what happened."

Her shocked gasp and swift yank on her hand out from under his warned Will he'd hit on a highly sensitive subject. Flynn had told him only the basics.

She was devastated.

Right, *now* he remembered that very important part of the story. A minute too late. He shouldn't have blurted out the question.

"You…you know about Daniel? You…" Her voice hitched on a sob. "How?"

"Your brother-in-law told me last night."

A lone tear escaped from her eye and trailed down her cheek. "He shouldn't have said anything. It wasn't his place."

"Probably not." Will reached up and caught the next rogue tear with his thumb. "If it makes you feel any better I forced the issue. And he didn't give any details."

She looked away, put a trembling hand to her mouth and sighed. "Well, I suppose that's something."

"If you tell me where the man lives I'll hunt him down and beat him to a pulp."

Instead of making her smile, the statement unleashed an onslaught of sobs. Tears rolled unchecked down her cheeks.

Excellent, Will, now you've made her really cry.

Hurting for her, he pulled the carriage to a halt.

"Bridget." He spoke her name on a whisper. "I didn't mean to upset you."

"I know." She looked to the heavens, waved her hand in a fanning motion by her face to no avail. The tears kept coming.

Will couldn't stand it. He simply couldn't stand seeing her in such misery. He tugged her into his arms and held her close. "I'm sorry he hurt you."

"He said he loved me. But he didn't, not really. Not enough to follow through with his promise to marry me." The words tumbled out of her mouth in a choked, hiccupping rush of air. "He claimed he loved me…" She let out another sob. "But he didn't…even…understand me."

Unsure what to say, or how to say it, Will stroked his hand along her spine in a soothing up-and-down motion.

Slowly, stroke by stroke, she relaxed into his arms. "We'd known each other all our lives. He'd seen how I was with our neighbors, helping whenever I could, doing whatever was needed. Yet, in the end, he said I gave too much of myself to everyone else. He feared I wouldn't have anything left for him, so he decided to marry Amy Doyle, a woman he claimed would put him first."

Will's hand stilled. What a selfish clod.

"How could Daniel think I didn't love him enough?" she said into his shirt. "The capacity to love isn't finite. It's a growing, expanding gift from God that only grows larger and fuller with use."

Not always. But in Bridget's case, that was true.

There was a certain fierceness to her capacity to love that went beyond what others had within them. She would never withhold an ounce of her devotion, not from her husband or from any living creature on this earth. Will had a mangy, very spoiled dog sleeping in his children's room to prove that particular point.

The man Bridget eventually vowed to love till death do them part wouldn't get a portion of her, he'd get the very best of her.

"The scoundrel didn't deserve you," he said through a tight jaw.

She held silent a moment, then turned her face up to his. "You really believe that?"

Lost in her watery gaze, he nodded slowly. "I do."

"Do you know what hurt the most?"

He shook his head.

"My life with Daniel had been nothing but a lie. He'd allowed me to believe he loved me and that my future was with him. Then he broke his word at the very last moment."

She clutched at Will's arms, as though hanging on for dear life. But then her eyes took on a distant gleam. "How could he have done that? How could he have lied so completely? To me, a woman he'd known all his life?"

"I don't know," Will said, his gut churning with rage. How could her fiancé have done something so heinous? A man was nothing without his word. *Let your yes be yes and your no be no,* that had been the Biblical principle Will had lived by all his life.

"Will?" Bridget said his name very softly. "Do you think I give too much of myself?"

"No, I don't."

Her fingers dug into his sleeves. "Truly?"

"Bridget, my darling." He drew in a breath. "The Bible teaches us everything we need to know about love. Above all, it's supposed to be selfless. When we truly love someone we should want to serve that other person. It's not about what we get from them in return. It's about what we give."

"Is that how you love?" She reached up and cupped his cheek, her eyes full of tenderness. "Are you a man who gives rather than receives?"

Wanting to answer her truthfully, he closed his eyes and concentrated on her question. As a parent his answer was an unequivocal yes. He would give anything for his children, even his life. But as a man, one who'd been served the ultimate betrayal by a woman he'd vowed to spend the rest of life with, he wasn't sure anymore.

And until he knew the answer he couldn't make any promises to Bridget. She'd been lied to before. The result had broken her heart. Will would not subject her to that pain again.

He opened his eyes and stared into her beautiful, trusting face. Even after what her fiancé had done to her she was still willing to give of herself. She was the most incredible woman he'd ever met.

Afraid he might lean down and kiss her again, he pulled slightly back. "I'm a man who wants the very best for you." He set her out of reach and took hold of the reins. "At the moment that means getting you home before the sky turns completely dark."

Chapter Nineteen

An eerie stillness hung over the road as Will steered his carriage down the lane leading to Bridget's house. They hadn't spoken since he'd set the carriage in motion. Bridget couldn't help but think the silence between them was excruciating, painful even.

No one would ever know they'd recently shared a sweet, tender kiss that had changed her life forever. Or that Bridget had revealed her darkest secret only moments before and Will had responded by saying just the right words to help her release the shame from her heart at last.

Sighing, she dropped her gaze to his hands holding the reins. He had strong, sure hands, capable of such tenderness, the kind that made a woman feel protected and adored at the same time.

Head still down, Bridget cast a covert glance back to his face. Will kept his gaze fixed straight ahead but she could see that his eyes bore signs of quiet distress.

There would be no declarations from him tonight, no renewal of his marriage proposal. After what she'd revealed about her past, she should be thankful he didn't attempt to give her empty words or false promises. After all, he knew exactly how much Daniel's rejection had hurt her.

Will's steadiness of character ought to be awe-inspiring. By not saying anything, he was showing her the greatest sign of respect.

But right now, at this very moment, Bridget wanted to hear Will say he cared. For her, only her. He didn't have to say he loved her, nothing so earth-shattering, just that he cared what happened to her, that their kiss had meant something to him.

She'd thought the Lord had brought her to this man and his family for a purpose. Had she been wrong? Was more grief in her future?

Before that terrible thought could creep into her heart and settle, her new home came into view. Although the repairs the men had begun yesterday weren't nearly enough to make the structure attractive, the soft glow of twilight cast the building in a more flattering manner than ever before. Bridget felt the weight of her troubles lift ever-so-slightly.

Nora met them on the stoop. She was alone and smiling, a clear indication she'd had a good day. *At least someone had,* Bridget thought.

"Hello, Bridget." Without waiting for a reply she directed her gaze to Will. "Mr. Black, won't you come inside a moment? I have something I'd like to show you." Her voice was filled with satisfaction.

Seconds ticked by before he responded. For a shocking moment Bridget thought he would refuse Nora's request and thus leave her to explain his rude behavior. Instead he allowed a small smile to spread across his lips and let out a dry chuckle. "That sounds ominous."

"Not at all." Nora took his arm and led him into the house ahead of Bridget. "I've been working on a cake recipe with the chocolate you left yesterday. Since you're the expert I want to get your opinion on the mix of flavors."

Following behind at a slower pace Bridget didn't catch all of his reply, but she was pretty sure she heard him mention his chocolatiers attempt to formulate a soft candy and ask if Nora would be interested in helping them.

Despite knowing Will was simply being a smart businessman, Bridget felt her chin tremble. Why was he so easy with Nora, so comfortable, when only moments before he'd been distant and silent with her?

She wasn't jealous of her sister, not precisely—well, maybe, but that wasn't the point. *The point,* Bridget realized as she knuckled an errant curl out of her eyes, was that she loved Will—it scared her how much—and from all outward appearances he did not return her feelings, at least not on the same level.

She never expected falling in love would feel like a physical blow. She'd always prayed the Lord would gift her a capacity to love that would overflow abundantly and increase daily. To Bridget's way of thinking, a person could never love too much or too hard.

But this new type of love with its very real pain in the vicinity of her heart, was nearly too much to bear.

"Bridget," Nora called from the kitchen. "Get in here. Will and I want your opinion, too."

Guard your heart, Bridget.

The silent warning came entirely too late.

The following Saturday morning, Bridget woke with a dark sense of foreboding. Although she'd been feeling off-kilter ever since Will had kissed her, the sensation was stronger today. Perhaps avoiding him all week had been a mistake.

Or perhaps not.

Bridget had needed the time apart to understand this all-consuming love she felt for the man. The strong emotion was still so new, both frightening and thrilling at the same time, but mostly frightening. Mainly because she had no idea how he felt in return.

Her solution to the problem was to avoid thinking about Will altogether. And their kiss. And the way he'd held her tenderly in his arms and let her cry into his shirt over Daniel's betrayal. He'd helped her heal, when she hadn't known she still needed to do so.

Will is your employer, she reminded herself. *And you're his children's nanny.* That kiss had been…it had been…

Glorious.

No. No, no, no. She was not thinking about that particular event this morning. Today she and Nora were welcoming their first official guests to their new home. Mrs. Fitzwilliam and the McCorkle brothers were due to arrive sometime before noon.

Thankfully Gavin had ridden over to the jailhouse two days prior, and alerted Nora of the impending visit. Apparently he'd stayed much longer than necessary, plying Cameron with questions about possible job openings in the Sheriff's Office.

The young man clearly knew what he wanted.

Bridget did, too. She wanted a family of her own, with Will as her husband and the twins as the first of their many children. Surely he wanted the same things. She'd caught him watching her with considerable longing in his eyes.

So what was stopping him from declaring himself?

She knew he cared for her. After all, he'd been very gracious when she'd asked for the morning off to prepare for Mrs. Fitzwilliam's visit. When Bridget had impulsively asked him to come, too, and meet her friends, he'd readily agreed, smiling into her gaze in the way she treasured. He'd promised to bring Olivia and Caleb along, as well. Perhaps even Esther.

The sound of a hammer banging on the roof interrupted her musings. Bridget lifted her head toward the sound and smiled. Cameron must have decided to work on the house today.

Despite the sense of unease she felt, Bridget wanted today to be a happy one full of blessings. With that in mind, she finished tying the laces on her boots and lifted up a prayer. *Oh, Lord, may today bring only joy.*

Shrugging off the last of her somber mood, she hurried down to the kitchen. Nora was already busy rolling dough.

"I'm here to help," Bridget said, spreading her arms wide. "What do you want me to do first?"

"The pies." Nora handed over the rolling pin.

Bridget got straight to work.

Several hours later with most of the preparations complete and the pies baking, she took Grace outside so Nora could have a break. Setting the baby on a blanket under a large shade tree, Bridget knelt down beside her.

She positioned herself so she had an unobstructed view of the lane. It wasn't long before she was rewarded with the sight of Will's open-top carriage coming around the bend. He looked as relaxed as she'd ever seen him, holding the reins in a loose-fingered grip. Two giggling children and one large dog rode alongside him.

Her family. And yet, not.

Swallowing back a pang of yearning, Bridget lifted her hand and waved. Will returned the gesture, a smile sliding into place. Her heart gave a little skip and she quickly broke eye contact. Would she ever get tired of looking into that handsome face?

Would she ever stop hoping the man was hers?

Sighing, she tickled the baby's belly. Grace responded with a merry kick of her legs. Laughing, Bridget bent at the waist and kissed the flawless cheek. "You're a good girl, aren't you?"

One day, she silently prayed. *Oh, Lord, one day may You bless me with a child of my own.*

As Will watched Bridget leaning over the baby something in him released, unwound. For weeks he'd been fighting the inevitable. Now he accepted the truth. He loved Bridget Murphy. He didn't know when she'd taken up residence in his heart. Long before he'd kissed her, that much he knew for certain.

The beautiful Irish lass with the sweet smile and unruly hair was everything he wanted in a wife. Ever since Fanny's tragic death he'd been afraid to love again.

But then Bridget had shown up and changed everything. Will had to tell her how he felt about her. How she'd changed him, and taught him to open his heart. He had to tell her today. But not now. When they were alone. When there wouldn't be anything to distract either of them.

As if to solidify his point, Digger leaped out of the carriage before Will pulled the horse to a complete stop.

"Digger, no." Caleb attempted to follow the animal, leap and all, but Will grabbed the boy by his shirt.

"Wait until we've stopped."

Practically bouncing in place, Caleb obeyed. The second Will swung open the door the boy jumped to the ground and ran after the dog. The ridiculous animal had stopped midstride and was now chasing his tail, literally. Caleb joined in the game.

Olivia departed the carriage in a more regal manner. But just like her brother, the moment her feet hit the ground she launched herself forward, this time in Bridget's direction. Sinking to her knees near the baby, she began an onslaught of questions. Bridget responded with her characteristic patience.

"Hey, Will," Cam called down from the rooftop and then

rubbed the sweat out of his eyes with his sleeve. "You gonna cool your heels all day or get up here and help with the man work?"

Will turned to Bridget and lifted an eyebrow.

Reading his silent query correctly, she laughed and waved him off. "Go on. I have things under control here."

"Be right there," he shouted up to Cam.

Three steps later a stately carriage pulled by two perfectly matched white horses rolled to a smooth stop. Digger and Caleb froze in the midst of their game. The dog moved in front of the boy as if to shield him from an unknown threat. The animal didn't growl, but he dropped to his haunches, appearing ready for a sudden attack.

In that moment Digger became Digger Black in Will's mind, a permanent member of their family. Just in case the animal decided to pounce on Bridget's friends, he crossed over to stand next to dog and boy.

A tall, imperious-looking woman exited the carriage first. Dressed in a fashionable emerald silk dress, with a perfectly coordinated hat on her auburn head, she looked completely out of place in the country. Nose in the air, seemingly oblivious to the heat, she took a slow, methodical turn, surveying the area with what Will thought was a highly critical eye.

"Needs considerable work," she declared.

"Mrs. Fitzwilliam." Bridget rose to her feet in a quick, fluid movement. "I'm so pleased you could make it."

The older woman hesitated then smiled. The gesture softened her otherwise hard features. "Well, Bridget Murphy, you are looking very well. Very well, indeed. But this house…" She waved her hand in the general direction of the front stoop. "It's ghastly."

"It's coming along," Bridget said defensively, her shoulders flinching. "We'll have it in shape before winter."

The older woman sniffed indelicately. "I should hope so."

Nose back in the air, she shuffled over to the blanket, caught sight of the baby and smiled broader than before. "My, my. That child has grown."

"Several pounds, at least." Bridget picked up Grace, introduced Olivia, and then the three proceeded to fuss over the baby.

Will started over, more intent on protecting Bridget from further censure than meeting the widow, when a movement from the carriage caught his eye.

He turned and watched as three boys jumped to the ground in rapid succession and headed toward Bridget. The first two were considerably smaller than the third, but they all had the same eager smiles, red hair and pleasant, honest faces. These had to be the McCorkle brothers Bridget had told him about.

Deciding he liked the look of the boys, Digger rose to his feet and barked a happy greeting. The younger two immediately changed directions.

"A dog," one of them declared, nearly tripping over his own feet in his haste to greet the animal.

"A *big* dog," the other one announced, moving at a more lumbering pace.

Chest out, chin high, Caleb beamed at the approaching boys. "His name is Digger. And I'm Caleb. Want to play with us?"

That was all the encouragement the McCorkle brothers needed. They introduced themselves as Sean and Emmett. Will wasn't sure which was which. Before he could sort it out the three boys were wrestling on the ground with the dog.

Laughing at their antics the older brother crossed to Will. "I'm Gavin. Gavin McCorkle."

Will shook the outstretched hand. "William Black."

Recognition lit in Gavin's eyes. "You're Miss Bridget's employer."

"That would be me."

"Pleased to meet you, sir." He started to say more but then his gaze landed on Cam's horse. "Sheriff Long is here?"

"Up there, working on the roof." Will angled his head to where Cam was engrossed in fixing shingles. "I was just headed up there myself."

"I'll come along."

"Suit yourself."

Before heading out, Will approached Bridget and introduced himself to Mrs. Fitzwilliam.

Eyes narrowed, the widow looked him up and down and back again. Knowing this woman meant a lot to Bridget, Will remained unmoving under the rude appraisal.

She continued to take his measure, as if she were determined to find him wanting. Holding steady, he shot a quick glance at Bridget. A wordless message passed between them, one that was filled with apology on her side and amusement on his. His mouth curved into a slow, easy smile and Bridget blushed.

Catching their silent interaction, Mrs. Fitzwilliam's gaze widened. She looked from Will to Bridget and back again. After a tense moment she gave one firm nod. "You'll do, Mr. Black. Yes, you'll do quite well." With a toss of her head she dismissed him. "You may go now."

His amusement increased. Apparently he'd passed the test. He gave the widow a slight bow, touched his daughter's head with the tips of his fingers and then strode off.

With a stab of surprise Will realized he was whistling. Prior to Bridget's arrival in his home, he'd never whistled before in his life.

With so many people in attendance, and the day milder than usual, Nora made the decision to serve lunch outside on the lawn. The men had quickly set up a table to accommodate the adults, while the children sat happily on the ground.

Bridget found herself seated directly next to Will. Instead of feeling scandalized she experienced a warm, happy glow of contentment.

Something had changed this morning. Or rather something in Will had changed. He'd been overly attentive since arriving, whenever they were in the same room, at times visibly affectionate. A slide of his fingers over hers, a hand on her back, a secretive smile just for her, he was making his intentions clear. In front of her family and friends. Despite Nora's occasional scowls, and Flynn's silent warnings, Bridget couldn't have been happier.

The two youngest McCorkles and Caleb finished eating first. After seeking permission, the three boys set off toward the front of the house for a game of hide and seek. Olivia squirmed onto Bridget's lap and promptly fell asleep in her arms.

Bridget smiled at Will over the child's head. With everyone else involved in their own conversations, she decided to ask him a question that had been weighing on her mind since his arrival. "Esther didn't want to come with you today? She was more than welcome."

"She sent her regrets." He leaned in closer. "When the children and I left she was preparing a special lunch for Ben. The deputy had been left all alone to fend for himself at the jailhouse."

Bridget shook her head in mock chagrin. "That poor man."

They shared a laugh.

Will started to say more, but Mrs. Fitzwilliam's booming voice cut him off. "Although this house isn't up to my usual standards and the grounds need considerable work, that pretty, wild sort of garden around the side of the house caught my eye."

"That's Colleen's Garden," James Coulter said, setting his fork down with deliberate slowness. "Laird planted it for the girls' mother. Agnes and I plan to restore it to its original grandeur once my hip is better and she's feeling stronger."

"A fine idea," Mrs. Fitzwilliam said in an approving voice, then swung her gaze around the table as if looking for her next victim or rather the next person to engage in conversation. Her eyes narrowed on Will.

Before the widow could open her mouth—no telling what she would say—Bridget spoke first. "Mrs. Fitzwilliam, how is the search for your stepgranddaughter progressing?"

The older woman blinked, drew in a single, catchy breath then sighed heavily. "Not well, not well at all. Although there is evidence Mary set off for America with that no-good boyfriend of hers, the detective has been unable to determine precisely where the two settled."

"So she is not in the Boston slums as you feared?"

"Apparently not."

Was that good news or bad? Bridget wondered. "Perhaps the girl is in a much better situation than you feared." And wouldn't that be a blessing?

"Perhaps." Mrs. Fitzwilliam took a slow sip of her tea, her gaze growing distant. "Or perhaps my stepgranddaughter is in a far worse predicament."

Nora touched the widow's arm. "We're keeping her in our prayers."

The older woman set her cup on the table, shook her head, then pinned Cameron with a glare. "You." She jabbed her finger in his direction. "Am I to understand you are the sheriff of this town?"

Cam leaned his forearms on the table. "That's me."

"So you're the one putting ideas into my boy's head." She indicated Gavin with a hitch of her chin. "Offering him a chance to be your apprentice when he's already enrolled in school."

Nora gasped in surprise, effectively pulling his attention to her. "You actually did it? You offered Gavin a job?"

He lifted a shoulder. "Yeah, well, he wore me down."

Bridget sensed there was more to the story. Cameron Long was not the type to be worn down by anyone, especially not an eighteen-year-old boy. By the way the man smiled at Nora, with that lopsided grin of his, Bridget suspected pleasing her sister had been the real motivation behind the unusual hire.

When Cam continued smiling at Nora, all but ignoring Mrs. Fitzwilliam's loud huff, the widow swung her angry gaze in the other direction. "Explain yourself, young man."

Gavin cleared his throat. "I've told you, Mrs. F. I don't want to go to school." He threw his shoulders back. "I want to be a lawman."

"Well, I like that." She sounded outraged, but Bridget saw the hurt in her eyes. "After all I've done for you and your brothers."

"You've been very generous." Sincerity filled Gavin's gaze. "But Emmett and Sean need the schooling, not me. Like I said, I'd rather—"

A commotion on the other side of the house silenced him.

"Papa, Papa," Caleb shouted, running straight for the table of adults, Digger and the McCorkle brothers hard on his heels.

The dog barked frantically, spinning in circles. Caleb was breathing hard. The other boys were babbling, something about a horse.

Will jumped up and rushed to Caleb. "Calm down, son." He took the boy's shoulders and then turned his gaze to the older boys. "Tell me what's happened."

The taller of the two gulped in several hard breaths. "We tried, Mr. Black. We really did. But we couldn't stop him."

"Stop who?"

"The boy. The one stealing the sheriff's horse."

Chapter Twenty

To everyone's surprise Gavin McCorkle was the first to run down the horse and rider. He'd raced ahead of Will without breaking stride, passed Cam without much more effort, covering ground in a fleet-footed flash of speed. Will had never seen anyone move that fast.

With shockingly quick reflexes, Gavin reached out and grabbed the horse's reins. It was a gutsy move. No fear. No hesitation. He was going to make a good lawman one day.

Taking charge of the situation, he ordered the thief off the horse.

The boy refused to relinquish the reins. Will couldn't see the kid's face due to the shadows cast by his hat. From the look of his small stature and painfully thin shoulders he was probably fourteen, maybe fifteen, full of youthful defiance and bad attitude.

Will squinted into the glaring sun. There was something odd about the way the kid fought to maintain his seat, hunched over and wobbling, his grip on the reins almost delicate.

"Get down. Now," Gavin ordered.

"No."

An ill-thought-out tug of war ensued, where Gavin proved as stubborn as the boy. "Get off that horse. He's not yours."

A string of high-pitched oaths followed, and Will found himself reassessing the thief's age. Clearly, he was younger than fourteen. His voice hadn't changed yet.

Cam, knowing better than to get too close, watched the fray next to Will with tight-lipped intensity.

Will knew that look. His friend was barely holding on to his anger.

"How long you gonna let this go on?" he asked.

"Not a second more." Cam stepped forward. "Gavin." He lifted his voice above the fray. "Pull back, now, you're spooking Fletch."

The warning came a second too late. The horse snorted, tossed his head back in panic, then reared, his front hooves punching the air with vicious intent.

Screeching in fear, the thief flung himself forward and hung on to the horse's neck for dear life. The sudden motion sent his hat to the ground.

Long, curly hair cascaded down his—*her*—back.

Gasping in shock, Gavin's hand slipped from the reins and he lost his footing. He went down hard.

As one, Cam and Will rushed forward and grabbed him. They tugged him away from the horse, moving as quickly as possible. There was a moment when time stood still. And then...

The horse's hooves slammed to the ground, landing inches from Gavin's face.

In a whirlwind of angry snorts, female screams and flying dust, horse and rider galloped away.

Cam took off after them, yelling something over his shoulder about needing to borrow one of Will's horses to pursue the girl.

Will paid more attention to Gavin, who was still sprawled

on the ground. He was checking for injury when Bridget and Mrs. Fitzwilliam careened around the house. The children and the Coulters tried to follow, but Nora held them all back. "Give them room," she ordered, barring their way with an outstretched hand.

"Gavin." Bridget dropped to her knees. "Talk to me. Are you hurt?"

Will helped the boy to a sitting position. He wobbled a few seconds then collapsed back to the ground, groaning.

Bridget turned her concerned gaze onto Will. "What happened?"

"Gavin took a tumble," he said, but didn't expand. Bridget was already shaking with concern. He would not add to her anxiety.

Besides, the boy was fine. Or he would be, once he gained his bearings. Best not to tell her how close he'd come to disaster. Had Will and Cam been a shade too slow, had the horse swiveled a few inches to his left, Gavin would be dead.

"Praise God you're all right," she said to the boy.

Mrs. Fitzwilliam echoed the sentiment. She'd been studying Gavin with equal parts fear and frustration. "This just makes my point. School is where you belong."

Moaning, Gavin lifted to his elbows, swallowed hard, then collapsed back to the ground a second time. "I'm not talking about that now."

"Fine." The widow relented, for now, but her tense shoulders and pursed lips said the conversation was long from over.

Will predicted Gavin was in for an earful on the ride back to Boston.

Seemingly unconcerned with his fate, Gavin sighed. "Did you see her?" He blinked up to the sky. "That marvelous face, all that gorgeous long curly hair, I've never seen anything, or anyone, so beautiful."

"Long curly hair?" Bridget glanced at Will in confusion.

"The horse thief was a girl," he said.

"A *beautiful* girl," Gavin corrected, wiping the back of his hand across his mouth but making no attempt to sit up a third time.

Moving to her left, Mrs. Fitzwilliam stared off into the distance, as if she could see horse and rider through the dense forest. "My stepgranddaughter had long curly hair." She shook her head almost wistfully. "All that beauty wasted on a ruffian."

Will wasn't sure what the woman's stepgranddaughter had to do with the situation. He dismissed the thought, deciding she was still thinking about the girl because of the earlier discussion at the table. He turned back to Gavin, who was still mooning over the female horse thief. He'd gone into a litany of her fine attributes.

Maybe the boy wouldn't be a good lawman, after all. He seemed entirely too distracted by a pretty face.

"Right." Will shared a look with Bridget. "Let's see if we can get him to stand."

With Bridget's help they had Gavin on his feet a few moments later. He took four full steps before his knees buckled. Will ducked under his right arm. Bridget did the same under his left.

Leaning heavily on them both, Gavin half stumbled, half dragged himself back to the house. Whereby he was surrounded by fussing women and a myriad of questions from the children.

The boy took the whole incident in stride. Now that he'd had a taste of adventure he seemed more committed than ever to begin work as Cam's apprentice.

Less than fifteen minutes later Cam returned with both horses in tow and no thief.

"I found Fletch, unharmed, grazing in a patch of grass

halfway down the lane." His lips tightened along the edges, the only outward sign of his true reaction to the incident. "I wanted to return your horse before I continued searching for the girl."

"I'm coming with you." Gavin rose to his feet, winced, but then righted himself.

Cam eyed him a moment, then nodded. "Not a bad idea. Might as well get you started as my apprentice."

"You're still going to hire me, even after I let the girl get away?"

"We all lose a few." Cam clapped him on the back. "From what I saw you have the instincts and speed necessary for the job, but we're going to have to work on your discipline. You're far too impulsive for your own good."

Gavin let out a whoop. "I'm going to be a sheriff one day."

Mrs. Fitzwilliam had a few things to say about that. "Not so fast, young man. I haven't given my approval."

A litany of reasons for the job—these from Gavin— and just as many against the job—these from the widow— ensued.

Moments into the argument Will had no doubt Gavin would win, eventually.

Wanting to focus on his own unfinished business, he went in search of Bridget. He found her with the twins, sitting on the ground in the backyard. Digger was spread out beside her, his head lulling in her lap. As Will drew closer he had to set his jaw against a quiver of emotion.

The children were listening intently to whatever tale she was spinning for them.

Will was enthralled himself by the tranquil picture his family made. By the way the sunlight spread fingers of burnished fire through Bridget's hair. By the gut-wrenching desire to join them on that blanket and get lost in the moment.

He felt a lot of other things, as well—hope, longing and a fierce need to ask Bridget to become a permanent part of his life.

Bridget's mouth went dry. Will was approaching her and the children with his gaze full of intense emotion. He was a sight to behold. She felt time slow to a crawl, and then certainty took hold. This was the man for her, the one the Lord had brought into her life at this perfect time.

"Hello," she said, proud of the fact that she kept her voice even. Somehow, she managed a smile.

He did not smile back. In fact, his eyes were very serious. Was he about to say the words she'd been waiting to hear? Was he going to declare his feelings for her now? In front of the children?

"Bridget," he said, his voice giving nothing away. "Would you come home with me?" He looked down at the children, "I mean, us. Would you come home with *us* today?"

That wasn't what she'd expected him to say. "But the day is already half over."

"The children are tired, they need their naps and I'd like you to come with us." He crouched in front of her, took her hand and kissed her knuckles. Right there in front of his children.

"I have something I want to say to you," he continued, "and I'd like us to be alone when I do. I'll get you home before dark, if that's what concerns you."

Oh. Oh, my. He was going to propose again, and this time for all the right reasons, she saw the truth in his eyes.

How could she possibly say no, when she loved him so much and wanted nothing more than to be his wife? "Yes, of course I'll come home with you. I just need to let Nora know where I'm going and when I'll be back. I—"

"But, Papa." Caleb jutted out his bottom lip. "Do we have to go now?"

Will's eyes never left hers as he rose and stretched out his hand. "Yes, son, we have to go home now. It's time."

Why did she sense his words had a double meaning?

"But I want to play with Emmett and Sean some more."

"They'll be leaving soon, too." He helped Bridget stand, and didn't let go of her hand once she was firmly on her feet.

Mesmerized by what she saw in Will's eyes, she couldn't look away. "Don't worry, Caleb," she said without looking at him. "You'll see the boys again."

"Promise?"

She smiled. "Promise."

"Papa?" Olivia pulled on his pant leg. "How come you're holding Miss Bridget's hand?"

"Because I like her."

"I like her, too."

He chuckled. "Then take her other hand."

Olivia did as her father suggested. Hand in hand in hand, they walked back toward the house. Caleb and Digger meandered behind them in a crisscross pattern.

The next half hour passed in a blur. Bridget barely remembered saying goodbye to Mrs. Fitzwilliam and the two youngest McCorkle brothers, or the many promises she'd uttered to see them all again before too long. The parting was very anticlimactic after the dramatic events of the previous hour.

A moment before Will helped her into his carriage Bridget flatly denied Nora's request to speak with her a moment, *alone.* She refused to allow anything to dampen the rest of her afternoon, especially not a well-meaning lecture from her overprotective big sister.

The ride back to town was filled with effortless camaraderie. It was as if the children sensed something exciting was about to happen. Will seemed remarkably relaxed.

How could anyone think him severe? He was one of the most calm, tender, compassionate men she knew. It would be a joy to spend the rest of her life by his side.

A thread of doubt tried to braid through her excitement and a renewed sense of foreboding took hold of her heart.

Where was this reservation coming from? Will cared about her, Bridget saw it in his eyes and in the way he reached out to touch her hand.

When they turned onto the road leading to his house, Will's hand closed over hers again. His thumb moved in a gentle sweep across her knuckles. The touch caused her to take in a quick, disjointed breath.

"We're nearly home," he said.

Home. With Will and the twins. Her pulse went wild, thrumming hard against her ribs. Bridget lowered her head and clutched Will's hand tighter. She'd journeyed to America with hope bursting in her heart. At every turn she'd clung to the Lord, knowing He was leading her to a new life and a new home. She never dreamed her destiny would include this incredible man and his adorable children.

God's plan for her life had been larger, grander and far richer than anything Bridget could have imagined for herself.

She sighed. They were a few hundred yards away from Will's home when she noticed Ben coming toward them on his horse. His face was scrunched in a grave expression, his eyes filled with urgency.

Bridget had never seen Ben look so grim. He must have heard about the horse thief and was on his way to meet the sheriff. But then he came to a stop alongside their carriage.

Will let go of Bridget's hand and pulled his horse to a halt, as well. Apparently recognizing the older man's unusual shift in mood, he leaned forward, his gaze sharp. "Ben? Has something happened?"

The deputy whipped off his hat and wasted no time with pleasantries. "Your mother sent me to find you."

Motionless, Will glanced briefly at Bridget. She saw the barely concealed panic in his eyes. Hoping to calm his worries, she closed her hand over his arm and asked the question they both feared most. "Is Esther unwell?"

"No, nothing like that, it's…" He shot Bridget an apologetic grimace then made a specific point of speaking directly to Will. "You have a visitor."

"A visitor?" Will echoed, sounding as confused as Bridget felt.

"That's right. It's a—" Ben glanced at Bridget again "—a woman."

Why was the man looking at her like that, as though he pitied her? Apprehension dug deep, all the way to the depths of her soul.

Ben placed his hat back on his head and heaved a sigh. "You'll understand once you get to the house."

He rode off toward the center of town without another word.

Esther met them at the door, her hands wringing over one another, her gaze darting over her shoulder every few seconds.

Digger raced for the kitchen, probably in search of his water bowl. In their attempt to tell their grandmother about their day, the twins started talking over one another.

"…and then Papa talked Miss Bridget into coming home with us today. They've been holding hands the *whole way,*" Caleb announced, proving nothing got past his little-boy eyes.

"Oh, Bridget, my dear girl." Unease rang in Esther's voice while her hand wringing increased. "I didn't realize you were coming home with Will and the children this afternoon. This makes everything all the more awkward."

It wasn't the actual words the older woman spoke but the

quiver in her voice that sent panic shuffling through Bridget. Her hands coiled and flexed.

"Mother, what's going on? Ben mentioned something about a visitor." Will lifted a dark eyebrow. "Perhaps you would care to explain."

Esther looked pointedly at the children, who were staring up at her, mouths gaping open. She cleared her expression and smiled down at them. "Olivia, Caleb, I made you a very special treat while you were gone. Run along into the kitchen and wait for me there. I'll be right behind you."

Her voice was low and strained but the children didn't seem to notice. They rushed to the kitchen as quickly as Digger had, loudly speculating over what their treat might be.

"William, son, I..." She drew in a tight breath. "I put your visitor in your study."

Will straightened his waistcoat with a hard snap, a sure sign of his agitation. "Who is this visitor? Why the secrecy?"

"Her name is Bridget." Esther glanced at him with cha- grin. "Bridget Collins."

"Collins?" He sputtered out the name. "No. Impossible."

"It can't be true," Bridget whispered, her mouth dry with the tinny taste of fear. "It just can't be."

Yet deep down in the part of her filling with despair, she knew Esther spoke the truth. Bridget Collins was alive.

And she was here, in Will's home.

Bridget glanced at him, her heart beating as though it would leap out of her chest. But he wasn't looking at her. He was staring at his mother in stunned silence.

"I'm sorry, son." Esther touched his arm, then turned to Bridget. "I'm sorry for you both."

"No, Mother." Will wrenched his arm free of her grip. "Bridget Collins is dead. Flynn Gallagher verified it himself."

"I'm afraid the doctor was mistaken." A thin, dark-haired

girl wearing a shabby dress and a tortured expression ambled down the hallway. She kept her hand flat against the wall, looking as though she would fall without the added support. "I am very much alive."

Will swung around to face the newcomer. "*Who* are you?"

The girl stumbled under his angry glare. Cloaked in shadow, she looked frail, defeated even, and Bridget's heart went out to her. Clearly something horrible had happened to her in recent days.

"I asked you a question."

A shudder was her only response.

Couldn't Will see he was scaring the poor girl? Bridget touched his arm, hoping to calm his anger. After a few tight breaths, he visibly relaxed.

"Who are you?" he asked again, this time in a softer tone.

"My—my friends call me Birdie. But my real name is Bridget." She lifted a shaky hand to her forehead, brushed the hair away to reveal a stricken expression. "Bridget Collins."

"You cannot be her." Will's voice was full of shocked grief, the same emotion Bridget felt herself.

"Oh, but…but I am Bridget Collins. And I—" she raised her trembling chin a fraction higher "—I can prove it."

Chapter Twenty-One

Will escorted Bridget Collins—Birdie—into his study and shut the door behind them. Closing his eyes, he rested his forehead against the warm wood and desperately tried to gather his thoughts. The last image of Bridget, *his* Bridget, played in his mind. Her eyes had been filled with grief, mortification and sheer unhappiness. The same painful mix of emotions he struggled with now.

He'd planned to tell her he loved her this afternoon.

How could he declare himself now—when he was, apparently, still engaged to be married to another woman?

Perhaps there was still a way to fix this debacle. He and Bridget were meant to be together. With love and the Lord on their side no problem would be too big for them to conquer.

But if this young woman was truly Bridget Collins, they weren't facing a problem. They were facing a quandary. There were no solutions to quandaries, only strategies to manage the worst of the consequences. Until he knew what he was dealing with, there was no reason to despair.

Determined to uncover the truth, Will shoved away from the door and turned to face Bridget, *Birdie.* She would never be Bridget to him. "Show me your proof."

His words came out hard and unforgiving. Without the

calming influence of the woman he loved by his side, without her comforting touch, he was unable to temper his emotions. He regretted that, regretted that he couldn't try harder to listen without judgment. This girl was both ragged and miserable, that much was clear. Wherever she'd been in the weeks since departing the *Annie McGee,* she'd not had an easy time of it.

He tried to remember that as he spoke again. "Birdie." He kept his voice soft. "You said you have proof of your identity."

Dropping her gaze, the young woman nodded. "I—I have all the letters you sent me."

"Show me."

She reached into a tattered reticule, pulled out a handful of papers and set them on his desk.

He recognized his own handwriting, but didn't reach for the letters. "You could have stolen those."

"I may have done terrible things of late, unforgivable things—" her lips quivered "—but I am *not* a thief."

Will said nothing. He'd sent her considerable funds to make the journey to America, yet she hadn't fulfilled her end of the bargain. What was that sort of behavior, if not stealing?

As though reading his mind, Birdie looked away. Bottom lip stuck between her teeth, her gaze darted around the room, then locked onto the battered suitcase the ship's authorities had given him, proof of the dead girl's identity. Or so they'd all thought.

"That's my luggage." She turned to face him. "I can describe its contents."

"Perhaps you better." He retrieved the case, set it on his desk and then opened the lid, making sure she couldn't see inside. "Proceed."

In a halting voice she gave an accurate accounting of every item, all the way down to a pair of scuffed slippers.

Will lowered the lid and secured the latch, closing off his emotions as firmly as he shut the case. She might look remorseful, but looks could be deceiving.

"All right, Miss Collins. You have convinced me. But the question still remains. Where have you been these past two weeks?"

"I…met a man aboard the *Annie McGee.*" A tiny, almost imperceptible shudder revealed far more than her words had.

Just like Fanny, this girl had turned to another man instead of trusting Will to understand her plight.

Pride warred with a growing sense of pity. This woman, the one he'd mourned with equal parts guilt and sadness, had *met a man.* By the looks of her now Will already knew how the story ended. Nevertheless, he said, "Go on."

As though the floodgates had been opened Birdie's story tumbled out of her mouth. "Cyrus was so handsome. He said he loved me. He made promises." She wiped her eyes with a quick swipe of her wrist. "I believed him."

No matter what lies the man had told her, Will had a hard time feeling sorry for Birdie. She'd made her choice, before ever having met him. "So you ran off with Cyrus once the ship docked."

"He said he would marry me." Will saw the humiliation in her gaze, and the pain. The same look Fanny had in her eyes the day her lover had sent her packing.

"I'd planned to tell you once we docked," she claimed. "I figured you'd understand."

Thinking about the man he'd been back then, just over three weeks ago, before Bridget had come into his life, Will wasn't sure he would have understood. But he wouldn't have tried to change Birdie's mind either, not after Fanny.

"I had it all figured out. I knew exactly what I would say.

But then that girl fell from the forecastle and…" She sighed. "I knew her, you know."

How would he know that?

"She had the bed next to mine," she explained. "She was a timid girl named Bethany, or Brittany or something like that. I'm ashamed to say I never learned her name. I was too caught up with…Cyrus."

Was Birdie as contrite as she sounded? With so much at stake, Will reserved judgment. "I'm still unclear how you managed to switch identities with the girl."

She clasped her hands together. "When the authorities came asking if anyone knew her, I told them she was Bridget Collins. I gave them my luggage and said it was hers. They didn't question me any further. So with that simple exchange, the girl became me. And I became her."

Will shoved a hand through his hair. Her story made a sad sort of sense, except for one very important detail. Why had Birdie been in a bunk in the first place?

"Miss Collins, I sent you enough money to purchase a stateroom."

"Yes, well, I…" She broke eye contact and brushed her palms down her skirt. "That is, my family needed the money more than I needed a stateroom."

Frustration filled him. Will would have sent her more money had she asked. But that wasn't the important point here. "What happened with…Cyrus?"

Her face went dead-white. "He found a better prospect."

Of course he had. His kind always did.

"All those promises meant nothing to him." She wiped her nose on her sleeve and sniffed. "*I* meant nothing to him."

"And so you came back to me."

"I have nowhere else to go." She ran to him and clutched his sleeve, her hands curling into fists. "I have no money, no job. If…if you don't take me back…I…I don't know what 'll do." She gulped in huge gasps of air and tears welled in her eyes. "I… Please, Mr. Black. Have mercy. Don't turn me away."

Will had seen that same desperate look in another woman's gaze. Fanny had been similarly distraught, her threat almost identical in nature, uttered mere hours before she'd thrown herself off a cliff.

His gut wrenched as memories came flooding back. The agony on Fanny's face. Him reaching her moments too late.

How could he toss Birdie out of his home, knowing the possible consequences of doing so? He'd made a promise to her. And as hard as it was to think about what he would lose if he followed through, he was responsible for this woman. He was the reason she was in this country. He couldn't turn his back on her.

But what she'd done, switching identities with a stranger and then running off with another man when she'd promised to marry Will, those were grievous acts. Had Birdie's actions been driven by a temporary error in judgment, a youthful indiscretion? Or were they signs of her true character?

Only time would tell.

Fingers still clutching his sleeve, Birdie choked out a strangled sob. "I made a mistake. Please, Mr. Black, give me a chance to fix this terrible wrong."

How could he refuse her request when he'd made his share of mistakes? As the Bible said, *for all have sinned and fall short of the glory of God.* No matter what she'd done, or why, he would not send her away and risk another tragic ending.

"All right, Birdie." He spoke without inflection. "You may have a second chance."

Even as he said the words he wondered how he could ever marry Birdie, especially with her character still in question. She could just as easily run off again. How could Will put his children through that pain a second time, the pain of wondering where their mother was, wondering if they were loved as completely as they deserved?

And more important, what sort of lessons would a woman like Birdie teach them? Nothing but sadness. His children deserved to know happiness and joy. Olivia and Caleb—and maybe even Will, himself—deserved a woman like Bridge in their lives.

Wincing at the repercussions of his actions, Will shoved a hand through his hair. This current disaster was of his making. Out of desperation he'd trusted in his own power to solve his problems instead of waiting on the Lord.

Now he had a woman in his home he didn't completely trust.

Unaware of his internal battle, Birdie let go of his sleeve. "So I am to stay here, in this home, with you and your family?"

"Yes." *For now.*

"Thank you." She collapsed to the ground with a sob, as if all the fight had left her. Sitting there, staring up at him with those large round eyes she looked very, very young. And extremely pitiful.

Sighing, Will lifted her in his arms and set her in one of the leather, wing-backed chairs.

Her stomach growled.

"When was the last time you ate?"

She brought a shaky hand to her throat. "I don't remember."

"Right." He found a blanket folded neatly on the settee and wrapped it around her shoulders. "I'll have my mother bring in some food."

He headed for the door.

"Will...will you be coming back?" she asked in a panicked voice.

"Eventually. I have something I must do first." He didn't

expand. The fact that he was about to break the heart of the woman he loved wasn't any of this girl's concern, no matter what role she eventually played in his life. Or in this home.

As if understanding finally dawned, Birdie's eyes widened. "That woman in the hallway with you earlier, who is she?"

"My children's nanny." Again, he didn't expand.

"You won't need her anymore, now that I'm here."

Sorrow slammed in his chest. "I know."

He left the room without uttering another word.

Bridget heard Will's approach before she actually saw him enter the kitchen. His dark hair stood in disarray around his handsome face, as if he'd been running his fingers through it over and over again.

His gaze found hers. Oh, the grief she saw in those clear blue eyes. Her heart lurched with unspeakable pain for him. She wanted to run to him, to throw her arms around him and tell him everything would work out. That God was in control.

She didn't have that right. He wasn't hers anymore. He'd never been hers. And that was the saddest part of all.

He reached out to her, casually, as if it was the most natural thing to do. Her heart took an extra hard thump but she didn't go to him.

Lowering his hand, he looked around the room. "Where's my mother?"

"She took the children and the dog for a walk."

Bridget moved closer to him, unable to help herself, and touched her fingertips to his face. She would never forget this man. "Is that girl in your study, is she...your intended?"

He leaned into her open palm. "She is, indeed, Bridget Collins."

"And you're going to honor your promise to her."

Sorrow drained out of him and slammed into her. "I can't send her away."

Of course he couldn't, Bridget thought. Nevertheless, her insides turned cold and she dropped her hand to her side.

"I'm sorry," he said.

She wanted to tell him he had nothing to apologize for. After all, he wouldn't be the man she loved if he sent Birdie away. But she couldn't make the words come.

"I'll take you home now."

Even through the thick haze of her regret she couldn't let him do that. "I think it will be best if I have Ben escort me."

"Please, I have things I need to say to you."

Her common sense fought a hard battle with her desire to spend a few more moments in his company. "No, Will, it wouldn't be wise."

The haunted way he looked at her reminded her of the man she'd first met on the docks in Boston. He'd come so far, her handsome, serious-minded Will had learned to laugh. And even whistle for no good reason.

She wanted to weep in frustration at all they'd lost in a single afternoon. "We both know how the conversation will go. You'll tell me you care about me but—"

"I can't walk away from Birdie right now." His mouth became a grim slash.

Hearing him speak the words aloud was like a solid punch to her heart. "I know that," she said very softly. "You would never break your word."

And she loved him all the more for it.

Will rubbed the bridge of his nose between his thumb and forefinger. "What you don't know is *why* I can't walk away."

"But I do." She pulled his hand away from his face. "It's because you are a man of integrity."

"There's more to it than that, another reason why I can't throw her out of my home. My wife, Fanny, she hated life in

Faith Glen, hated being married to me and despised being a mother." He swallowed. "After the twins were weaned, she found solace in another man's arms."

Bridget could see how hard this was for him. She laid a hand on his shoulder in a show of comfort. "You don't have to tell me this."

"Yes, Bridget, I do." He covered her hand with his, squeezed, then moved away to lean against the doorjamb. "The short version is that when the man decided he'd had enough and tossed her aside, something in Fanny snapped. She ended her misery by jumping off a cliff. I was there, but I'd arrived too late to save her."

"Oh, Will." The horror he must have felt, the helplessness, the guilt.

"Now do you understand? Fanny chose death over life. She didn't want me or the children." His eyes went dark and turbulent. "Maybe if I'd tried harder to make her happy, she would still be alive."

"You can't know that."

"I let her down in the worst possible way. She's dead because of me."

"No, Will, your wife made her own choices. She could have turned to the Lord for comfort, or she could have sought godly counsel. She could have done any number of things. Instead she turned to another man who was not her husband to ease her unhappiness. And when that didn't work she chose to jump off that cliff."

"If I had only been there sooner…"

"Your presence might have made a difference, or it might not. Listen to me, Will, you have to forgive yourself."

Head down, he didn't answer her for a very long time. Then he looked up and glanced directly into her eyes. What she saw in his gaze made her heart twist. "Thank you, Bridget."

Although he didn't say the words, she knew, in that moment, she *knew* he was on the road toward forgiveness, for Fanny, and maybe even for himself.

"I won't make the same mistakes with Birdie." The weary resignation in his voice told its own story. "She's suffered a similar rejection as Fanny."

How...horrible for them all.

Bridget took one long breath and accepted the truth at last. The man she loved was promised to another woman. "I need to say goodbye to the children."

Nodding, he reached inside his coat and pulled out a leather wallet with a grim twist of his lips. When he tried to hand her a wad of bills, she simply stared at him, appalled.

He might as well have slapped her. "I don't want your money."

"These are the wages I owe you, for services rendered as the children's nanny." His voice was so businesslike, so distant.

Humiliation sliced through the fabric of her control. For one black moment Bridget was tempted to tell him what he could do with his *wages* in a very unladylike manner. "It's too much."

"Consider it my thank-you, for...everything."

"Your words are enough."

His jaw clenched so tightly a muscle jumped in his neck. "Bridget, you and your sister need the money for repairs to your house."

"We'll make do."

He tried to stuff the money into her hand. She reared back, hands splayed in the air. "Stop it, Will."

He cast her a quick, pained look. "Then let me offer you a job at the mill. I'm still responsible for you."

Therein lay the problem. She didn't want him to feel responsible for her. She wanted him to love her. "Will, I am not alone in this world, nor am I destitute. I have a home now, and a garden that will supply food, eventually. I also have family." *Just not your family.*

"Bridget, please, allow me this honor. Let me help you."

"I won't take money from you." She threw her shoulders back. "I won't."

A thousand unspoken words passed between them. Then he shook his head sadly. "You might understand how to give of yourself, but you have no idea how to receive."

"It's better to give than receive," she shot back, hurt by the censure she heard in his voice. "You said so yourself."

"Yes. But how can you truly understand God's grace if you can't accept earthly help from someone who cares about you, someone who has no ulterior motive?" He crumpled the money in his hand. "How can you understand the depth of the Lord's sacrifice if you never admit to your own need for help?"

He had a point. A valid one, but she couldn't accept his charity, no matter what argument he used. "Goodbye, Will."

Eyes fixed on the doorway, Bridget walked past him. At the last possible moment she reached out and touched his arm gently with her fingertips.

Surprisingly she managed to hold her emotions in check when she found the children playing in the front yard. She stayed in control as she told them goodbye and promised to see them at church the next morning. For fear of breaking, she avoided Esther's gaze altogether.

The older woman didn't press the issue.

With Ben filling her in on the missing portions of Birdie's story, Bridget remained stoic and brave throughout the ride back to her home. She even managed to hold it together during Nora's rapid-fire questioning over why she'd left with Will earlier in the day, putting off her sister by saying that she was tired, but would tell her everything after resting.

It wasn't until she was in her room, with the door firmly shut behind her that she finally gave in to her grief. Alone at last, Bridget folded her arms around her middle and wept. She wept for all that could never be, for the family that had almost been hers but now belonged to Bridget Collins.

Oh, Lord, she whispered into the darkened room, *how will I ever survive without Will and the children in my life?*

Bridget woke to find Nora sitting on her bed, her warm gaze staring down at her with unveiled concern.

"Nora?" She rubbed her eyes, then noticed the sky was still a cold, gloomy gray. "What time is it?"

"Early," she said. "Not yet six in the morning."

"Oh." She rolled onto her side and cradled her head with her hands. "Why are you here?"

"I heard you crying."

Those four simple words brought back all the misery of the day before. Breathing in slowly, carefully, she squeezed her eyes shut and told Nora the worst of it. "Bridget Collins is alive."

"What?"

Bridget struggled to sit up, but the effort was too great and she collapsed back on her pillow.

"I don't know all the particulars, but she apparently switched identities with that dead girl we thought was her."

"Why would she do something like that?"

"So she could run off with another man." Bridget spoke each word with deliberate slowness so as not to start crying again. "Now the other man doesn't want her and she's back to claim her position as Will's bride."

Nora processed the tale in silence. Then her face scrunched into a frown. "What an awful, selfish girl."

Bridget wasn't so sure. "Oh, Nora, I wish I could dislike her, too. But the girl I met yesterday was so utterly defeated.

I just can't find it in me to hate her. And besides, it's her right to claim what was promised to her."

At that, Nora had a few choice things to say, but Bridget couldn't make out the words through the blood rushing in her ears. Her throat closed on a miserable sob.

Muddled thoughts coursed through her mind. She couldn't face Will and the children at church today, not if Birdie was sitting between them. She'd never experienced jealousy before. Now it ate at her.

She wanted to cry out in agony but then she heard Nora turn her anger onto Will. "How dare he hurt you like this?"

"No, Nora, you don't understand. Will made a promise to the girl long before he met me. He has to follow through. He's a man of his word. That's one of the things I love about him. And yet…"

She promptly burst into tears.

"Oh, Bridget." Nora smoothed her hair off her face. "No matter what you say to defend the man, he carries some of the blame."

Bridget's entire body stiffened. "He has reasons for honoring his promise, reasons that go beyond his inherent integrity, reasons I can't tell you."

Nora remained unmoved. "Is that so?"

"He's trying to make things right, for Bridget Collins and for me, in the only way he knows how." Why hadn't she seen that sooner, why had she been so insulted by his kind gesture? "He offered me money and then a job at the mill."

"And you refused both."

Something in Nora's voice, something that sounded far too much like censure, had Bridget gaping at her. "Why are you so sure I refused Will's assistance?"

"You never accept help, not even from family."

"I…" She frowned. "Never? Surely that can't be right."

"Sadly, it is." Nora slid down on the bed next to Bridget

and stared up at the ceiling. "Your refusal to lean on your loved ones in times of crisis is your most frustrating quality, dear sister."

Bridget twisted the edge of the blanket between her fingers and stared up at the ceiling. "Will said something similar. He said that I knew how to give but not how to receive."

Nora snorted in agreement. "He knows you very well."

The echo of a smile trembled on her lips. "Yes, he does."

After a moment Nora rose and helped Bridget up, as well. "What are you going to do now that Will is determined to honor his promise to that awful, awful girl?"

Bridget cringed at Nora's hard tone. "Don't, Nora. Don't judge her so harshly. She's had a hard go of it."

"So have we all. But sometimes we don't always get what we want."

"I know. Oh, Nora, I know."

Nora pulled her into her arms and gave her a tight, sisterly hug. "You deserve happiness, Bridget. And so does Will."

"I thought you didn't like him."

"I thought so, too." She stepped back and shook her head. "But he has goodness in him. I was so busy looking for flaws I missed that at first. It wasn't until I saw the way he was with you and the children yesterday that I changed my mind. He adores you, Bridget. He would have made you happy."

Futile disappointment tinged her vision. "It doesn't matter anymore. All I can do is step aside and try to build my life without him and the children."

"The twins. Oh, Bridget." Nora's hand flew to her mouth. "What are you going to do about Olivia and Caleb? You can't walk away from them, not after all they've been through."

A cold, thin pain slid through her heart. "No, I can't."

Bridget would not abandon the twins like their mother had. She had to stay in their lives and, if necessary, when the time came, she would slowly ease away. But *only* if necessary.

Surely Will would understand her need to stay in the children's lives.

For their sake, he had to.

Chapter Twenty-Two

Less than a week with Birdie in residence and Will's home had lost much of the joy Bridget had so effortlessly restored. It wasn't that Birdie was a terrible person. She was simply miserable. And no matter how hard she tried she couldn't seem to snap out of her melancholy.

At least she put on a brave face around the children. The three of them got along well enough, but there was no real connection. Impromptu picnics were a thing of the past. There was no more spontaneous laughter at meals, no more musical performances or rousing games of tag. In four short days, Olivia and Caleb had reverted back to the overly polite, well-behaved children they'd been before Bridget had come into their lives.

The only time the twins showed any signs of enthusiasm was when Ben came by and took them on a ride in Cam's rickety wagon. Because they were usually gone all afternoon Will suspected Ben took them to see Bridget.

He would have to thank that old coot one day.

And Bridget, as well. Even when he'd pushed her out of all their lives, she hadn't abandoned the children.

Sitting behind his desk in his study at home, Will leaned back in his chair. The sun was finally setting, marking the end of another disastrous day. A kaleidoscope of moving shadows flickered across the floor, creating an eerie picture—a perfect accompaniment to his grave mood.

He couldn't marry Birdie. That much he was ready to admit to himself. He could never subject his children to a lifetime with a woman even more unhappy than their mother had been.

Nevertheless she was his responsibility.

Lord, what am I to do?

The obvious answer was to set her up in her own home and provide her a job, either at the mill or somewhere else. There were other options as well, including sending her back to Ireland. The problem he faced was that he had no idea what Birdie wanted. All he knew was that she was wretchedly unhappy in his home.

A tentative knock jolted him out of his reverie. Will called out, "Come in."

The door creaked open and his mother's head of silver-white hair poked through the opening. He motioned her forward.

As she stepped deeper into the room a burning throb knotted in his throat. The purple smudges were back under her eyes. A clear indication Will had made a mess of all their lives.

His future bride was supposed to have taken the burden off his mother, but Birdie was too caught up in her own pain to provide much help. Bottom line, she was no Bridget.

Bridget. His beautiful, wild-haired, Irish lass with the tender heart and...

No, Will. Bridget Murphy is not yours, not anymore.

He closed his eyes and offered up a silent prayer for discernment. Hope for the future drifted just out of reach.

"We need to talk," his mother said in a firm voice that belied the look of exhaustion in her eyes. "About Birdie."

He nodded, reconciled with the inevitability of the impending conversation.

"I understand why you brought the girl into this house, but you must realize how unhappy she is. She doesn't want to be here."

No, she didn't.

He forced himself to rise from his chair and make his way around the desk. "As much as I value your opinion, this is my misstep to unravel."

"But you *will* unravel it, son. Promise me."

"Yes, mother." He took her by the shoulders and pulled her into a gentle hug. "I promise."

She slumped against him in relief. "You'll do so soon?"

"No, not soon." He flattened his lips into a determined line. "Now. This very minute."

He released her and started for the door.

His mother stopped him with a hand on his arm. "I know that look in your eyes. You've come to a decision, haven't you?"

"I have." Or at least he was close to doing so. There were a few points he needed clarified first.

"What are you planning to do?"

Several options came to mind, long-term solutions. But before he made any move he had to discover where Birdie stood on several matters, including their supposed marriage. "I'll know more once I speak with the girl."

"No need to seek me out, Mr. Black." The door creaked on its hinges and Birdie pushed into the room. "I'm right here."

Not taking his eyes off the girl, he said, "Mother, will you please excuse us."

Esther gave a heavy sigh but made her way out of the room without argument.

Will held his tongue until he was certain he and Birdie

were completely alone. "I think you will agree that our current arrangement is not working out."

"No." Her lower lip trembled. "It is not."

"I have several possible solutions. But first I want to ask you a question." He took her hand and guided her to a nearby chair. "Do you wish to marry me?"

Her gaze widened at his blunt question, making her look very young, more child than woman. "No, Mr. Black. I do not."

He forced himself to speak calmly. "You are sure?"

"Yes. I *never* wanted to marry you." She clasped her hand over her mouth as though shocked the truth had slipped out.

"It's all right, Birdie. You may speak plainly with me. There will be no penalty for speaking your mind."

She lowered her hand, swallowed hard. "Our marriage was a way to make money for my family. They didn't want me to do it—" a sob wrenched past her lips "—but I told them I wanted to help. Money was so scarce…"

What a terrible situation for them all. And Will had played his part. He'd made the offer, had sent the money. He winced at his own shortsightedness.

Forgive me, Lord.

Now that he knew the truth, Will would do his part to rectify the situation. He would give Birdie the second chance she needed. And he would do so generously.

"You are sure, Birdie?" He asked the question very slowly, very carefully, giving her one last chance to state her wishes as truthfully as possible. "You are absolutely sure you do not want to marry me?"

"I—I want to go home." Two fat tears fell from her eyes. "Please, Mr. Black, send me back to Ireland."

Bridget tried to move on with her life as best she could, but the brave face she presented to the world was a lie. Every day without Will became harder to bear than the one before, and with each new dawn came a renewed internal struggle. Should she yank the blanket back over her head and remain there all day? Or should she buck up and pull herself together?

As Nora liked to remind her, Murphy women never gave in to defeat.

And so, like all five mornings prior to this one, Bridget forced herself to climb out of bed and dress for the day.

Her fingers were clumsy, her eyes gritty from lack of sleep. There was no denying she missed Will desperately. She actually longed for him as though a part of her very soul had been ripped out. Even her afternoons with the children were bittersweet because he wasn't there to share them.

It had been Esther's idea to send Olivia and Caleb to Bridget for a few hours every afternoon, a way to help ease the transition for them all. Ben had been kind enough to offer to transport them out to the house every day.

Bridget wondered what Will thought of the arrangement. Surely he knew. Ben and Esther would never go behind his back. Would they?

Mind working through the question, wondering why she sensed he'd been kept in the dark, she stepped into the kitchen and poured herself a cup of tea. Perhaps she should seek him out this next week and tell him. It would give her a chance to see him, to—

No. That would only make matters worse.

Sighing, she looked up. The incessant banging indicated Cameron was already hard at work on the roof. He seemed determined to spend every free moment he had helping them prepare the house for the coming winter. Was he acting out of simple kindness, or something more? Something to do with Nora?

Smiling for the first time in days, Bridget glanced out the

window to where Nora and Agnes were weeding together in the garden. Well, Nora was weeding. Agnes was perched on a bench, chattering away, baby Grace in her arms. The older woman looked happy, so did Nora, except when she glanced toward the roof. Then she looked uncertain, nervous even, uncharacteristically so.

Bridget's smile widened, just as a movement off to the left captured her attention.

Doing his part, James shuffled back and forth between the house and garden, clearing away the piles of weeds when Nora's stack grew too large.

Watching the Coulters and Nora get along so well, Bridget thought about how far she and her sisters had come in less than two months. The journey across the ocean had started out with little hope and a lot of prayer. All the fear and uncertainty had been worth it in the end. They'd found a home and life in a new country.

Meeting Will and his beautiful children, getting to know and love them, had been an added blessing. The Lord's plan for her life wasn't entirely clear in her mind anymore, but Bridget had no regrets.

Not…one…single…regret.

Then why the wrenching gasps of agony? Why the burning throb in her throat? Giving in to her misery, she buried her face in her hands and let the sobs come.

And then she heard someone say her name.

Will. Will was here. "Please, go away. I can't speak with you right now. I—"

Strong arms gathered her close.

"Bridget, my love, don't cry." His deep voice washed over her, soothing her.

The simple pleasure of being wrapped in his arms made her feel so much worse. The sobs came harder, faster, louder. She tried to push him away, humiliated, but his hold tightened and he began murmuring words of comfort, the meaning of which she couldn't seem to make out.

For several seconds he stroked his hand down her hair, then brushed his lips against her forehead. "There's no need to cry."

She quivered, caught between yearning and lost hope.

Will's hand worked small circles along her back, up and down, round and round. All the tension drained out of her and she relaxed into him. She just wanted a moment with the man she loved, just one, but then sanity returned and she pushed him away with a hard shove.

The air between them pulsed with tension.

Bridget studied his face, surprised to see the stubble shading his strong jaw and the tangled hair on his head. Will never left the house disheveled. What had happened?

What did it matter?

She wiped the tears off her cheek and closed off her heart. "You can't hold me like that ever again. You're to marry another woman. Being here, with me, like this." She waved her hand between them. "It's wrong."

"Felt right to me." The flare of love that flashed in his eyes sent her pulse rioting out of control.

I love you, too, her heart whispered. Longing filled with hope reared, lingered, but she fought the painful emotion back. A torrent of words came rushing forward, none of which made it past her lips.

Eyes softening, Will wordlessly reached for her again. She leaned forward a little then caught herself and took a pointed step back.

A deep frown etched his forehead. "You're making it hard to tell you how I feel."

"I don't have the right to hear it." It would hurt too much. "And you don't have the right to tell me."

"I'm botching this." He rubbed his face with both hands.

And for the first time since he'd arrived Bridget realized he wasn't simply disheveled but fatigued, as well.

"Will?"

"I put Bridget Collins on a ship back to Ireland early this morning, before dawn."

Bridget's heart stumbled. "You—you what? Why?"

"She wanted to go home."

"She—she didn't want to marry you?"

He gave her a wry smile. "Not in the least. Praise the Lord, she'd never wanted to marry me. The arrangement had been a way for her to make money for her family."

Bridget nodded in comprehension. After the potato famine many families had resorted to all sorts of creative means to survive. But for Will to have to hear from his bride's own mouth that she didn't want to marry him, that must have been painful. Bridget had lived that humiliation herself.

Except Will didn't look sad or embarrassed or hurt. In fact, he was grinning at her.

"You're not upset Birdie didn't want to marry you?"

He roped her body against his and bent his head so that his mouth landed just shy of hers. "Not in the least."

He pressed his lips to her forehead, then her cheek, then her mouth, where he stayed put for a while.

"You've ruined me for other women, Bridget Murphy."

She liked the sound of that, very much.

He kissed her nose. "You brought music and joy into my home again. You are a mixture of grace and strength, a woman who gives all of herself and holds nothing back. You taught me to enjoy life again and to love with all that I am."

Her heart stopped altogether and then started beating faster, harder, leaving her happily dizzy. "Oh, Will, the capacity to love has always been in you. You've never held back with Olivia and Caleb."

"But I did with everyone else. I shut off any desire to love again. You broke down my defenses, with your sweetness and giving nature." He nipped tenderly at her ear. "I love you, Bridget Murphy. I think I have from the moment I first saw you on the docks."

"I love you, too," she whispered in return. "And I *know* it was from the very moment I first saw you on the docks."

He chuckled. "Marry me. Be my wife and the mother of my children. We'll let God direct our path. And I promise, I'll no longer try to control every outcome on my own."

This wonderful man declaring his love for her was full of surprises. Her hand stole up the side of his face. "And I'll no longer refuse your gifts, tangible or otherwise. I want you to take care of me, Will, in the same way I'll take care of you. I want to receive all that you have to give to me, as well as give all that I am to you."

"Is that a yes?"

"Yes." She kissed him on the mouth. "Yes, yes, yes. I'll marry you."

"As soon as possible?" he asked.

"As soon as possible."

Setting her out of his arms, his manner seemed easy and relaxed but his eyes were full of emotion. "Come, Bridget." He reached out his hand to her. "Come greet the rest of our family."

He guided her outside. Waiting in his carriage were two very excited children and one rambunctious dog.

Her sorrow instantly vanished. Yes, Bridget thought with happy tears welling in her eyes, this was her family now.

Epilogue

Years after the blessed event, Bridget knew she would remember her wedding as a happy affair shared with family, friends and many of Will's employees. The event had come together seamlessly, thanks to the welcome assistance of her sisters and future mother-in-law.

Now she was standing in front of the preacher, with Will by her side reciting his vows as she'd done herself moments before.

Smiling into his eyes, Bridget fingered the light blue silk of her dress. Maeve had supplied the lovely handmade creation as a wedding gift, with the help of Ardeen Nolan and her aunt Mrs. Kennedy's skillful assistance. Not to be outdone, Nora had created a special cake—a chocolate one, of course—for the celebration after the ceremony.

Will squeezed her hand as he finished his vows. "…until death do us part."

The preacher nodded, then took a moment to impart a bit of sage advice. "Wise couples recognize that they're going to see things differently, and this will cause them conflict. The solution will be loving compromise."

Bridget shared a meaningful look with Will. The day after asking her to marry him he'd hired a work crew to rebuild the stairwell in her house. She'd not only accepted his gift, but had sent him a thank-you note that was so full of gratitude he deemed it the sweetest love letter he'd ever received.

Oh, how she adored this man. He looked especially handsome in his black frock coat, matching trousers and crisp white shirt. A shiver of anticipation traveled up her spine. The ceremony was almost complete. She was moments away from becoming Will's wife.

As her groom slid a beautiful diamond ring onto her finger, Bridget cast a glance at the children standing at the front of the church with them. Olivia and Caleb were behaving beautifully.

Of course the very moment she had the thought, Caleb began fidgeting.

Bridget couldn't really blame the little boy. The ceremony must seem impossibly long to a child his age. Despite several whispered orders from his grandmother to stand still, it was clear Caleb had had enough of minding his manners.

Eyes dancing with mischief, he reached out and pinched his twin sister. Olivia pinched him back.

Instead of stopping the misconduct, Bridget shared a secretive smile with Will. Their children were back to normal, at last.

As soon as Bridget slid the gold band onto Will's finger, Caleb swiveled his head toward the back of the church and let out a war whoop. Before either parent could grab him, he tore down the aisle. Olivia was one step behind.

Neither had been given their cue.

Squealing in delight, the twins dodged outstretched hands and all other attempts to slow them down. They were met at the end of the aisle by a very handsome, well-groomed dog that had somehow broken free of his restraint.

The preacher's eyes widened at the mayhem erupting right in front of him. "I—I now pronounce you husband and wife."

Seemingly undaunted by the uproar brewing at the opposite end of the church, Will pulled Bridget into his arms and kissed her soundly on the mouth. "I love you."

She smiled into his blue, blue eyes, lifted on her toes and kissed him right back. "I love you more."

"Not possible." His arms slid around her and he went for another kiss.

The preacher cleared his throat and they laughingly broke apart. Arm in arm, they began their walk back down the aisle, heading straight for their children.

Bridget's gaze landed on so many dear faces. Mrs. Fitzwilliam and the McCorkle brothers. Ardeen Nolan and her aunt. Ben MacDuff. Esther. Standing in the front row, Maeve winked at Bridget. She returned the gesture then smiled at her sister's handsome husband. Flynn smiled back. Although the Gallaghers had been married less than a month, they were no longer the reigning newlyweds in the family. As of today, that honor belonged to Bridget and Will.

Three sisters, but only two happy endings.

A burst of unease shot through Bridget and her steps faltered. Nora was alone now, left to build her life in America without her sisters. She had Grace, but for how long? The baby's family could claim her at any moment. Surely Nora deserved her share of happiness, too. She'd guided their family through lean years after their mother's death, and had held them together when all seemed lost.

What would become of Nora now that Bridget and Maeve were married?

As if to drive home the point, Bridget caught Nora's eye at the very moment a tear slid down her older sister's cheek.

Bridget's steps faltered. But then Cameron Long moved into view and whispered something into Nora's ear.

Nora laughed in response, the gesture transforming her face.

Bridget sighed. This time the sound was full of hope. Perhaps her sister would be all right after all.

Will continued guiding Bridget down the aisle. Each step pulled her away from her past and closer toward her future, the one she would share with her husband. *Her husband.*

She turned her face to his.

He planted a tender kiss on her nose.

At the end of the aisle he turned and looked out over the crowd. "Please, everyone, follow us back to our home and celebrate our new family with us."

Smiling at Bridget in a way that nearly made her swoon, he escorted their entire family into the carriage waiting for them outside the church.

Once everyone was settled, Will kissed Bridget again, on her lips, longer and with more enthusiasm than he had in the church.

When he finally pulled away, his eyes were full of promises. Promises she knew he would fulfill down to the letter.

"Ready to go home, Mrs. Black?"

"Oh, yes, Mr. Black." She reached out and pulled both children close. "Oh, my, *yes.*"

To Bridget's way of thinking, the journey across town was more than an exciting adventure. It was the perfect beginning to her new life as Mrs. William Black.

* * * * *

Dear Reader,

Thank you for choosing *Mistaken Bride*. I so enjoyed creating this story about an Irish immigrant and her journey to America, where she found true love with an honorable man and his adorable little children.

This book was especially fun for me to write because I had the chance to include young siblings who also happen to be twins. As a twin myself, I relished this opportunity to tap into memories from my childhood. According to my mother, my sister and I were very pleasant children, until we joined forces. Together, we personified the term "double trouble." Robin and I were especially proficient at escaping closed-in spaces. This included our crib. My sister, the more adventurous of us, would climb to the top of the railing and then help me over the edge with a hard shove. Once I landed on the floor (thank you so much, Robin) I would then help her down onto the floor with an equally enthusiastic pull (take that, sister dear). Free at last, we would proceed to empty shelves, explore cabinets, release the dog and generally wreak havoc. The only off-limits area was our brothers' baby-alligator tank. Even the dynamic diaper duo knew better than to mess with those toothy reptiles.

Although Olivia and Caleb are far better behaved for most of their story, I made sure they overcame their shyness by the end of the book. I predict their parents have a lot of "joy" ahead of them in the coming years. Praise God for little children, especially twins!

I always love hearing from readers. Please feel free to contact me at my website, www.reneeryan.com.

In the meantime, happy reading!
Renee

Questions for Discussion

1. What led Bridget and her sisters to America in the first place? What makes this journey especially risky for them? Why do you think they took this chance, even knowing the risks? What will they do if their new home doesn't pan out? Would you have taken such a chance? Why or why not?

2. When Bridget first meets Will he mistakes her for his mail-order bride. Why did he make this mistake? What is motivating him to find a bride as soon as possible? Have you ever been in a situation that left you desperate to find an immediate solution, even if it's not the best solution? What did you do and what was the result?

3. What happened to Will's mail-order bride? Why does he only want a bride instead of a nanny for his twins? What eventually changes his mind?

4. Why does Bridget take the job as the twins' nanny? What is the stipulation she gives Will? Do you think this is a good idea or a bad one? Why or why not?

5. What does Will discover when he arrives home early on Bridget's first day of work? Why did he react that way? What immediate changes does he see in his children? How do those changes affect him?

6. How does Nora react when Bridget arrives home after her first day of work? What does she warn her sister about? Do you think she's overreacting? Why or why not? Have you ever had someone in your life, a family

member or friend, who warned you in a similar fashion? Did you take their advice? Why or why not, and what was the result?

7. How does Will react when he sees Bridget and the children bathing the stray dog? Have you ever adopted a stray pet? What was the result? Do you think Digger was a good addition to the family? Why or why not?

8. When Bridget and Nora move into their new home, Will offers to help. What does he discover about the Murphy women that day? Even knowing how important this house is to Bridget, why does he ask her to move into his home? Do you think he overstepped his bounds? Why or why not?

9. What does Flynn tell Will about Bridget's life back in Ireland? How does Will react to the news of her heartbreak? Have you ever received startling information about a person that instantly changed your view of them? How did you react?

10. Why do you think Will is fighting his attraction to Bridget? Why do you think she is fighting her attraction to him? Do you think their reasons are valid? Why or why not? Have you ever held back a part of yourself because of something that happened to you in the past? What was the result?

11. How does Bridget react when Olivia asks God to make Bridget her new mommy? Do you think she should have agreed with Olivia, even if it was only between the two of them? Why or why not? Have you ever been in a situ-

ation that required you to be careful not to get someone's hopes up? What did you do and why?

12. When Will and Bridget finally decide to declare their love for one another, who shows up at his house? Why is her presence such a disaster? What does Will decide to do about her? Do you think this is a good decision on his part? Why or why not?

13. How does Bridget react to Birdie's sudden appearance? Do you think Bridget should have stepped aside like she did? Why or why not? Have you ever had to make a sacrifice for a loved one that meant unhappiness for yourself? What happened?

14. When Will offers to pay Bridget her wages, how does she react? Why does Will find her refusal of his money so frustrating?

15. What happened once Birdie joined Will's household? What did Will decide to do for the girl? Was this a good solution? Why or why not?

INSPIRATIONAL

Love Inspired.
HISTORICAL

celebrating
15
YEARS

COMING NEXT MONTH
AVAILABLE JUNE 12, 2012

A BABY BETWEEN THEM
Irish Brides
Winnie Griggs

THE BARON'S GOVERNESS BRIDE
Glass Slipper Brides
Deborah Hale

A PROPER COMPANION
Ladies in Waiting
Louise M. Gouge

WINNING THE WIDOW'S HEART
Sherri Shackelford

REQUEST YOUR FREE BOOKS!

2 FREE INSPIRATIONAL NOVELS
PLUS 2
FREE
MYSTERY GIFTS

Love Inspired.
HISTORICAL
INSPIRATIONAL HISTORICAL ROMANCE

YES! Please send me 2 FREE Love Inspired® Historical novels and my 2 FREE mystery gifts (gifts are worth about $10). After receiving them, if I don't wish to receive any more books, I can return the shipping statement marked "cancel." If I don't cancel, I will receive 4 brand-new novels every month and be billed just $4.49 per book in the U.S. or $4.99 per book in Canada. That's a saving of at least 22% off the cover price. It's quite a bargain! Shipping and handling is just 50¢ per book in the U.S. and 75¢ per book in Canada.* I understand that accepting the 2 free books and gifts places me under no obligation to buy anything. I can always return a shipment and cancel at any time. Even if I never buy another book, the two free books and gifts are mine to keep forever.

102/302 IDN FEHF

Name _____ (PLEASE PRINT)

Address _____ Apt. #

City _____ State/Prov. _____ Zip/Postal Code

Signature (if under 18, a parent or guardian must sign)

Mail to the **Reader Service:**
IN U.S.A.: P.O. Box 1867, Buffalo, NY 14240-1867
IN CANADA: P.O. Box 609, Fort Erie, Ontario L2A 5X3

Not valid for current subscribers to Love Inspired Historical books.

Want to try two free books from another series?
Call 1-800-873-8635 or visit www.ReaderService.com.

* Terms and prices subject to change without notice. Prices do not include applicable taxes. Sales tax applicable in N.Y. Canadian residents will be charged applicable taxes. Offer not valid in Quebec. This offer is limited to one order per household. All orders subject to credit approval. Credit or debit balances in a customer's account(s) may be offset by any other outstanding balance owed by or to the customer. Please allow 4 to 6 weeks for delivery. Offer available while quantities last.

Your Privacy—The Reader Service is committed to protecting your privacy. Our Privacy Policy is available online at www.ReaderService.com or upon request from the Reader Service.

We make a portion of our mailing list available to reputable third parties that offer products we believe may interest you. If you prefer that we not exchange your name with third parties, or if you wish to clarify or modify your communication preferences, please visit us at www.ReaderService.com/consumerschoice or write to us at Reader Service Preference Service, P.O. Box 9062, Buffalo, NY 14269. Include your complete name and address.

LIHI1B

Get swept away with author

Carolyne Aarsen

Saving lives is what E.R. nurse Shannon Deacon excels at. It also distracts her from painful romantic memories and the fact that her ex-fiancé's brother, Dr. Ben Brouwer, just moved in next door. She doesn't want anything to do with him, but Ben is also hurting from a failed marriage…and two determined matchmakers think Ben and Shannon can help each other heal. Will they take a second chance at love?

Healing the Doctor's Heart

Home to
Hartley Creek

Available June 2012 wherever books are sold.

LI87747